PROLOGUE

He had not been prepared for this. Definitely not prepared for the sheer viciousness of the attack. Now he had to bear witness to something he was partly responsible for in full and painful knowledge that if he intervened it would cost him his own life.

He could see that, fear and brutality having taken away any capacity to stand alone, the man's legs had given way and he was held upright by two of his associates and practically dragged to stand in front of their boss. Their boss held a gun and it was clear that there was only one way this was going to turn out.

He had always known that this day would come, when something would happen and he would have to get away and get away fast, and he realised that moment was now. There was absolutely nothing he could do to prevent the inevitable, but he knew that it was only a matter of time before their attention turned to him. He and Gray had been friends, the suspicion that had fallen on Graham Stevens would soon turn on him. And the worst of it was, Gray was innocent, completely ignorant of the offences he was now going to be paying for.

And there was absolutely nothing he could do.

The focus of attention was on the man in charge and the bloody, beaten figure dragged before him. No one was taking any notice of him, standing quietly as he was at the rear of the warehouse, arms folded and a look of studied nonchalance plastered across his face. If he didn't take his chance now it would be gone. Quietly he stepped back a few paces, watching carefully in case the movement attracted attention, but the half dozen men standing around the warehouse space had only one thing on their minds.

His back to the door, he pushed it open and slipped through, walked swiftly down the corridor, horrified at how loud his footsteps sounded, past what had once been offices, and headed for the rear exit. He hoped the door would still be unlocked but felt for the key in his pocket, just in case. He'd managed to purloin a spare and then got his own cut weeks before and was relieved now at the foresight. In the usual run of things someone would have been stationed at the exits, but they'd all been summoned to the main space tonight, to witness the execution, and he was in no doubt that it would be an execution. An object lesson in obedience and loyalty.

The key turned in the lock, it was stiff and opened with a crack that seemed to echo all around him. He did not wait to see if anyone had heard. He ran, not daring to risk going around to the front of the building to collect his car. He lost himself in the industrial estate, between high buildings and single-storey units and eventually the little bit of scrubby woodland beyond, and only then did he dare stop and look back. He dialled, making an anonymous call to the police saying he was sure he'd heard shots, giving the address of the warehouse and knowing that was all he could do. He could almost imagine that he had heard the shot, and in his mind it had sounded loud and final. He could see no movement between the buildings, but he knew it was only a matter of time before they noticed he had gone, and put two and two together. He listened for the siren that might announce the arrival of the police but, apart from the sound of traffic on the main road, the night was quiet and calm.

He turned and ran again, through the wood, down the little alleyway that led onto the housing estate and then paused to catch his breath, checking the street was clear. At two in the morning there was no one around as he walked on, hands thrust in his pockets, head down until he reached the run of shops on the main road. He walked quickly past the shops, the little convenience store, the off-licence, the betting shop, and then clambered over a gate into the yard at the back of the Triangles pub. The security light blinked on but he knew the landlord's flat overlooked the road at the front and it was unlikely anyone would see. Once there he crouched between the bins, his chest tight and his whole body shaking. The security light blinked out again and he was left in darkness and a quietness that felt profound. The lights were out in the shops and in the pub and the only sounds were the cars going by on the road, a cat yowling, a baby crying in one of the houses. No sound of thundering feet or shouts of pursuit.

He had got this far, and that was more than he felt he deserved, but he could do no more on his own. Taking his phone from his pocket he dialled a number he had memorised six months before. "I need help," he said. "I need it now."

Two days later the body of Graham Stevens was fished out of the canal and DS Terry Pritchard was on a train, his debrief ended and the full force of relief and guilt finally hitting him. Terry stared resolutely out of the window, wilfully blocking out the stares and looks of concern from his fellow passengers, tears streaming down his face.

CHAPTER 1

Five days before Bridie Duggan married Reggie Fitch, Detective Inspector Sebastian MacGregor was summoned to the office of the chief constable. Such meetings were so vanishingly rare that Mac could not help but feel slightly anxious as to what this might be about. He arrived at the designated time, took a seat in reception and waited. The seats in the waiting area were low and grey and both seat and back angled in such a way that the occupant was obliged to lean back and stare at the ceiling. It was not comfortable. Mac stared up at the section of ceiling above his head. The acoustic tiles were stained and in need of a dust, the tiny holes like blackheads against the pale grey surface. Abstractedly, he set to counting them, multiplying the number of holes by the number of tiles, all the while trying to avoid getting a crick in his neck.

Fifteen minutes went by.

Mac fidgeted in his seat. He tipped himself forward and perched on the edge of the chair, still uncomfortable but at least feeling less like an astronaut preparing for take-off. The secretary at the reception desk paused and glanced his way and then resumed her typing, but he was certain he'd seen her hide a smile. She must be used to the acrobatic fidgeting of those in reception, forced to await the summons of her boss.

Who designed furniture like this, he wanted to ask. Then thought that maybe they should use chairs like this in the interview rooms. The legal eagles might not like it, but it would most likely speed the throughput of confessions. He remembered reading something about old-time, pre-PACE — so before the first iteration of the Police and Criminal Evidence Act changed policing forever — police interrogators, sitting suspects on chairs with one shortened leg so the effort to get comfortable and keep balance threw the criminal's focus. It was a thought that led him to his own office chair, the one with the failing gas ram that tended to drop the seat, and him with it, at unexpected moments. He'd put in a request for a replacement but was fast concluding that he'd be better off just buying his own.

The door to the main private office opened and the chief constable, Bradley Cotton looked out.

"Ah, there you are," he said as though he'd been the one kept waiting and Mac had been tardy.

Mac followed him through and took a seat as directed in front of a large wooden desk. His Big Boss returned to a very comfortable looking leather chair behind. He was not alone, Mac realised, glancing at a slim, thirtyish, dark-haired man installed by the coffee table at the end of the room. Mac, as the secretary had done, hid the smile when he noticed that whoever this stranger was, he too was struggling with an impossible chair. He had a notepad balanced on his lap and was perched as awkwardly as Mac had been. Mac was waiting for an introduction, wondering if he should introduce himself when his boss spoke.

"So," the chief constable said. "You're going to the Duggan wedding."

Mac was startled. He'd speculated on all kinds of possibilities for the sudden summons but that had not been among them. "To Bridie Duggan's wedding, yes," he replied trying hard not to frown at the other man's dismissive and disapproving tone.

"A strange thing for a serving officer to be doing, don't you think?"

Mac considered. So that was it, he thought. Bridie's first husband had definitely been on the other side of the law, but things had changed since then. "It would be odd if I didn't turn up," he said. "I'm going to be the best man."

That earned him a raised eyebrow and, from the sound of it, a scribbled note from the man by the coffee table.

"The Duggan family are known criminals, Inspector."

"Duggan senior certainly was," Mac agreed. "But Bridie Duggan's business is clean. I happen to know that a forensic audit was carried out not eighteen months ago and came up with nothing. Since her first husband was killed, she's gone out of her way to disentangle herself from anything dubious." He kept his voice steady but in truth he was quite disturbed by this line of questioning.

What exactly was this all about? Yes, if you looked at things objectively, as an outsider, then maybe his friendship with Bridie, her fiancé Fitch, and her daughter Joy, seemed a little off-kilter, but they had been thrown together by events that had led to the death of Bridie's husband Jimmy Duggan, his son Patrick and the kidnap of young Joy. Mac had been instrumental in bringing the perpetrators to justice and since then Bridie, with the help of eldest son, Brian, had continued the process her husband had already begun to legitimise what she could of his previous dealings and abandoning those that could not be fixed. It was not, Mac knew, out of any real sense of guilt on Bridie's part; more it was about keeping what was left of her family safe from harm and ensuring they had a secure financial future.

Mac had also called upon her on several occasions when he'd needed help and Bridie had always, *always*, stepped up.

"If she's so legitimate and yes—" the chief constable held up a hand to silence any possible objection on Mac's part — "I know all appearances suggest she is, then why invite the Donovans and the Carlisles to this little shindig?"

Ah, Mac thought, so that was it. "You're forgetting the Brewsters and the Caprisi," he said and earned himself a raised eyebrow. "There'll be around a hundred people there for the ceremony and the reception. I understand a few will be staying on overnight and yes, most of the families that Duggan associated with are sending representatives. There are some people you don't *not* invite. Some people you definitely don't want to offend."

The chief regarded him thoughtfully for a moment and Mac noted the flick of his gaze towards the man in the corner and heard more scribbling on the notepad. Mac would have given a great deal to know who he was, but, as his boss had so pointedly *not* introduced them, certainly wasn't going to give either man the satisfaction of asking.

"And how do you think they'll react to you?" his boss asked.

"Bridie Duggan has made no secret of our friendship," Mac said. "Any more than I have. And Miriam, my partner, will also be attending along with various other mutual friends including of course Joy Duggan and her fiancé. Most of us will be travelling to the wedding together."

He gleaned a small degree of satisfaction from the look of surprise he intercepted between the chief constable and coffee table man.

"Quite a contingent."

You don't know the half of it, Mac thought. Joy was to be maid of honour and their young friend, Ursula, a bridesmaid, so they needed to get there early enough for — another — final fitting. The two young women would be driving up the day before the rest of the guests. They were travelling in Joy's car, that being more reliable than the archaic Fiat Panda Ursula somehow managed to keep on the road.

Mac, his partner Miriam Hastings, Rina Martin and the Montmorency twins and Peters sisters, George Parker — Ursula's boyfriend and long-term friend of the rest of the party — and Tim, Joy's fiancé were all travelling up by minibus. Yes, it was quite a contingent, but they were all people who had come to care deeply for Bridie Duggan and her intended and wild horses would not have kept any of them away.

His boss nodded as though Mac had confirmed something important though Mac could not begin to guess what — though he had the feeling he wasn't going to like what was coming.

He didn't.

"So," the chief constable said, "I'm sure we can rely on you to keep your eyes and ears open and report back accordingly."

"Report back?" Mac questioned, unable to keep the note of annoyance from his tone.

"A police officer is always on duty," he was reprimanded.

"And what am I supposed to be reporting on?" Mac asked. "This is a social event; it's considered neutral ground by all parties . . ." He knew as soon as he said it that this was the crux of the matter. "All right," he conceded, "so what's going on?"

"Rumours," the chief constable told him. "Of a merger. Or a reorganisation of territories if you like. Of the possibility of a turf war."

So which is it, Mac wondered. A reorganisation of business interests? Not as uncommon as it had once been, one organised crime group trading with another where it suited the interest of both. Or something far messier? He waited for the answer. None came. Coffee table man got up from his uncomfortable perch — Mac imagined he could hear his spine realigning — and crossed to the desk. He laid an old-style manila folder in front of Mac and then retreated, though Mac noted that this time he chose to perch on the coffee table, rather than the inclined chair.

"What's this?" Mac asked.

"Just some background information for your consideration," he was told. The chief constable got to his feet and Mac realised that the interview was at an end. The door was opened for him and he picked up the folder and left, feeling somewhat bemused.

"So, who do you think coffee table man was?" Miriam asked him later as he glanced through the folder. It consisted of photographs, accompanied by identification and brief biographies, some of which Mac was already familiar with.

"My guess is he's someone from Serious and Organised Crime," he said. "Though a messenger boy rather than anyone high up. As I reminded the boss man, I've never made any secret of my friendship with Joy and Bridie Duggan or Fitch. That would be impossible even if I wanted to, especially as we must see Joy and Tim at least once a week, so I suppose it was inevitable something like this would happen sooner or later."

"So, what will you do about it?"

Mac laughed. "Well we're all going up the day before the wedding, so I'll get Bridie to spare me a few minutes and show her the file. If anyone knows more about what's going on, it will be Bridie or Fitch. She might not be involved in anything nefarious these days, but she finds it behoves her to keep a finger on the pulse of her husband's previous associates. Those that are still alive, anyway."

"And what do you think it's all about?" Miriam asked.

Mac tapped one of the photos. "Malcolm Brewster, died about four months back. Natural causes, he'd smoked since his teens and cancer got him in the end. Had three children. The eldest, Ruari, left for the wide blue yonder straight out of school and is a film director or something like that. The other two, the son, Charlie, and the daughter, Mia, hate one another's shadows and now Daddy's no longer there to promote what passed for family harmony there are rumours of a split and that other organised crime groups are manoeuvring in support of one side or another."

"Hence the possible merger, possible turf war scenario or all-out civil war," Miriam said.

Mac nodded. "Either way someone will lose out and the fight is likely to be a messy one," he said. "Let's just hope they hold off the opening volleys until after Bridie and Fitch's wedding."

* * *

"We should have briefed him properly," DS Terry Pritchard, Mike's 'coffee table man', said later, when he reported the meeting to his own boss. "He shouldn't be walking into this blind."

"He's going to a wedding. He's not headed under-cover." The superintendent's voice was calm. Gentle even. Unconcerned. "Terry, are you sure you're ready to come back full time? Everyone would understand if—"

"I'm fine. I just don't think it's fair to just tell the bloke half the story. It could turn bad. You know that as well as I do."

Superintendent Evelyn Mackie shook her head. "As I've said, he's going to a wedding. Nothing's likely to happen but he might just come up with something useful. That's really all there is to it." She paused. "Terry, don't you think you're overreacting, just a little? His boss seems perfectly satisfied with the situation. We're not asking the man to spy, just to keep his eyes open."

"DI MacGregor's boss doesn't know how volatile the situation has become, does he? You think he's still going to be happy when he finds out?"

The superintendent sighed. "We'll be monitoring the situation," she said. "Now go home and get some rest . . . and do try to stop worrying."

"Worrying? A man died. He died because I wanted to save my own skin."

"And they'd have killed him anyway, you know that as well as I do. Look, remorse is all well and good but you had no other option. Better one dead than two and better one of theirs than one of our own."

He stared at her, knowing she was just saying out loud what everyone else thought but it still felt like . . . what *did* it feel like? It felt cold, that's what. A killing kind of cold that chilled him to the core and did nothing to make him feel better. Would he ever feel better? The shrink had told him that guilt was a difficult thing to work through but that given time, it would become easier. That the pain would become manageable.

Manageable. Did he really want to live with manageable?

"Go home," his boss told him and, reluctantly, Terry headed for the door. Home, that was another joke. An empty flat filled with stuff that must have meant something to him once upon a time but that now felt as though it belonged to someone else and he was just camping out. Flat sitting until the rightful owner returned.

But he knew he was right. When he'd met DI MacGregor in the office of the chief constable earlier that day, he'd felt it — that heightened instinct for trouble that had kept him alive all those months. That meant he'd escaped by the skin of his teeth. For now. But they'd be looking for him, wouldn't they, Terry was certain of that. Even though the warehouse where Gray had died was miles away, and now, with his close-cropped hair and neat beard and absence of the contact lenses that turned his blue eyes brown, he barely even recognised himself. They would not let this go.

CHAPTER 2

Mac had only a vague idea of where they were going and had resigned himself to trusting the satnav and heading north. The wedding venue was a large house that had once been owned by a ceramics magnate, a rival of the likes of Wedgwood. It had been built on a sizeable island in the middle of a large artificial lake — Capability Brown style, Mac had thought when he had seen the brochure, and wondered about rising damp. The house had been erected in the eighteenth century, but apparently there were considerable nineteenth century additions, formal gardens and perhaps, more surprisingly, what had been a small monastic community in the grounds, together with several smaller cottages housing the workers servicing the estate and the walled gardens. The whole was now a conference centre and wedding venue, the cottages were holiday lets and from the pictures Mac had seen, it was all rather impressive. Though he would have expected no less considering whose wedding it was.

Mac crossed the two bridges, one across the canal and the second across a fast-flowing river, the height of which reminded Mac that they'd had a solid week of rain up here in Staffordshire. He then manoeuvred the minibus along the tightly curving drive. He could not see the house, hidden by trees and the sweep of the driveway and it was only when it opened out into an impressively wide turning circle that they saw Milbourn House in all its glory.

"Is that the ferry?" Eliza Peters asked. "Ooh, this is so exciting."

"I would have expected a bridge or a causeway," Stephen Montmorency observed. "With all the money it must have taken to build a place like that, you'd expect them to have built a bridge. Imagine the inconvenience of having to row everything across in the old days."

Mac was inclined to agree. He pressed the button that opened the minibus door, it released with a fierce, reluctant sounding hiss. Out of the bus he stretched, feeling the kinks in his back release just as reluctantly as the doors — though with more cracks and clicks than hisses.

"Uncomfortable seat?" Miriam asked, standing beside him and taking his hand. "I'll spell the driving on the way back."

"If you can stay awake." He smiled at her. Miriam had slept for most of the journey having just come off a shift before they set out. Miriam, a CSI, wasn't entirely happy about the new rotating shift patterns introduced earlier that year. Mac hoped that once she'd finished her PhD she'd be able to apply for jobs with more regular hours.

"It's a good-looking place," Miriam commented as they waited for the others to emerge from the bus.

Mac nodded. The house had a massive central doorway and two equally massive bay windows, practically floor to ceiling on either side. It was oddly square and very symmetrical and appeared, Mac thought, self-satisfied and content, looking out over its gardens and woodland and circular lawn on which a marquee had already been erected.

"Impressive," Miriam added. "And look, that must be the old abbey or monastery or whatever it is, it's literally sitting next to the house. To be honest I expected it to be ruined, but it looks as though it's still in use."

"I read the brochure and then took a look online. It's now part of the conference centre and has been restored and apparently has a rather fine library, whatever that means. The website said that it was built in the middle of the nineteenth century after the act of Catholic emancipation in 1829. It was in use until the 1980s, then the community left and gradually, like the house, it became very run-down until it was taken over by the people who own the venue now."

He glanced around enjoying the gleam of sunshine sparkling on water and the absurdly blue and utterly cloudless sky. Tall trees blocked the view of the road but allowed glimpses of the fields beyond. The day was warm, the air still, the birds singing, and all seemed incredibly peaceful. The ferry, flat-bottomed and with an engine in the back, and a little cabin at the front, looked capable of taking the entire party and their luggage over in one go, despite the Peters sisters having packed the equivalent of steamer trunks. It was all pretty much perfect.

So what could possibly go wrong, Mac asked himself suddenly aware that the meeting with his boss and the folder now packed in his suitcase troubled him far more than he had allowed. He didn't want anything to upset Bridie's wedding.

According to the information Bridie had sent them a couple of weeks before, some guests would be staying in the house, some in the guest house attached to the monastic buildings. He was rather pleased that he and Miriam were staying in the big house.

"Well, this is quite something," Rina said, trundling her modest wheely suitcase behind her. "That's rather a wonderful view. Apparently, there were coal mines around here years ago and until about five years ago, a blooming great power station complete with cooling towers, just the way." She pointed to where he could make out the line of a canal and, now his attention had been drawn to it, something large and redbrick and concrete which was obviously in the process of being demolished.

"Part of our great industrial past," he said wryly. "Though I suppose that's true of this whole estate. Wasn't the original owner an industrialist?"

"Ceramics," Rina said. "But I don't think it was the pretty stuff, at least not to start with. Vitrified drainpipes and then bathroom fittings, I believe, before his son branched out into fancy tiles."

Behind him he could hear the Peters sisters twittering happily and the Montmorency twins organising the removal of luggage. Rina led the way onto the ferry, the others in her eccentric little household following in her wake, like a school crocodile. Rina was an actress, playing the lead in the highly successful *Lydia Marchant Investigates*, a show that had run for fifteen series before being cancelled. It had recently been revived and was showing every sign of becoming as popular as the first time round. The Peters sisters and the ersatz twins, the Montmorencys, were older than Rina and all long-time friends. They had also been performers, though more vaudeville than television. All four had long since retired and they had settled in the safe harbour of Rina's Peverill Lodge back in Frantham. Mac had become attached to them.

Mac stood in the stern of the boat, watching the land recede. In truth they were, he thought, only perhaps the length of three or four swimming pools from shore. Proper, Olympic-sized pools, that was. But Mac reckoned he would be able to swim that distance at a push, even though it was years since he'd donned a pair of swimming trunks. Was the water deep, he wondered? He peered over the side but the wake of the boat made it hard to judge. Mac frowned.

"Planning your escape route?"

Mac laughed. "Maybe," he admitted, knowing that George would understand the impulse.

Years of running, trying to escape a violent father, never settling anywhere for long until his family had fetched up in Frantham had left its mark on George. Mac knew he still never settled in any space without checking out the exits.

"Got to admit, I'm not that keen on being stuck on an island," George admitted. "But then, I've got history on the escaping front. What's your excuse?"

George was grinning but Mac knew that this was a serious question. He was saved the trouble of thinking up an appropriate response. The ferryman had cut the engine and was tying up at the long wooden jetty, the twin of the one across the lake.

"Rowing boats," George said, indicating three small vessels tied up on the other side of the jetty. "So now we've got our escape plan worked out maybe we can both relax."

"But can you row?" Mac asked.

* * *

Two young men emerged from the house with trolleys onto which they loaded the luggage. And then Bridie's voice.

"Oh, you're all here, now I know everything is going to be fine."

Mac turned, smiling and was immediately engulfed in a warm hug. Rina was next and when the whole party had been welcomed, they followed Bridie into the enormous square reception, the cubic space and black-and-white tiled floor reminiscent of a masonic lodge. Mac's father had been a Freemason; Mac had never quite understood the attraction, though as a young man he'd helped out with charity events and open days. A wide flight of stairs led upwards to a mezzanine almost as big as the reception area, set out with comfortable chairs and little tables and then on to two flights of stairs leading, from the look of it, into two separate wings. Below the mezzanine a wide corridor disappeared, and Mac could glimpse other doors leading off. The house obviously went back further than he had originally thought.

The sound of rapid footsteps drew his attention upward and as he looked up at the left-hand staircase two young women appeared, rushing down to meet them. Redhaired Joy, Bridie's daughter and, a few years younger, eighteen-year-old Ursula, her fair hair whipping around her face as she hurtled down the final flight of stairs and wrapped her arms around George Parker. Mac smiled. George and Ursula had met at the children's home, Hill House, where they had both found themselves in their early teens. Ursula had lost her parents as had George, though in his case the circumstances had perhaps been more dramatic. Mac still found it hard to come to terms with the fact that George's mother had killed herself in what had then been Mac's rented flat.

"Hello everyone," Joy said, reclaiming Tim, her fiancé, with an equally enthusiastic hug. "Come up and see your rooms, this is a fab place."

Mac hung back for a moment and managed a word with Bridie. "I need a chat later, if you've got the time."

She raised a beautifully plucked eyebrow. "Trouble?" she asked.

"Hopefully not, but I need to give you and Fitch a bit of a heads up."

"Ah," she said. "Let me guess. Someone much, much higher up the food chain than you has got wind that you'll be here, surrounded by the criminal classes, and thinks you should be doing your policemanlike duty?"

Mac laughed. There was never any fooling Bridie. "Something like that," he said.

Bridie just grinned at him. "Fitch and I half expected it. Just don't let it spoil your fun."

Mac promised that he certainly wouldn't allow that to happen and turned to follow the others upstairs. It was all going to be fine, he told himself — so what was the little nag of anxiety doing at the back of his mind, that little irritation that told him things were not going to be that simple?

* * *

Miles away and from separate directions, two men were also making their way towards the island but with no intention of joining the celebrations. One was Regis Crick, once Mal Brewster's right-hand man, an individual that DS Terry Pritchard would have known as the man who had killed Graham Stevens, and the second Terry would have recognised from his presence at Mal Brewster's funeral. He had seen the man only briefly, his face reddened by anger as he argued with Mia Brewster. Terry had gathered the argument was about a will, presumably Mal Brewster's, as rumour had it that it seemed to have been written with the intent to cause the most conflict possible. From what little he had overheard, Terry had gathered that this slightly older man was the half brother, Ruari, and that maybe he'd not separated himself from Mal Brewster's business quite as completely as everyone had reckoned.

One thing was for certain, as Ruari drove up the motorway, his anger in check, his focus on keeping just above the speed limit, but not so far above as to attract attention, he was not a man content with his lot, and he didn't much care who might have to suffer so long as he improved it.

Ruari spared a brief thought for his half siblings, but it was not a thought filled with affection or even interest. They were simply in his way and the circumstances of Bridie Duggan's wedding would afford him the perfect opportunity for dealing with them both. He spared another even briefer thought for the man with whom he was so inconveniently allied. Regis Crick. As Mal's second-in-command he'd had expectations of his own, expectations that had not been fulfilled in Mal Brewster's will. He was now as intent on getting what he thought was his due like Ruari. And that was all they had in common. But even that wasn't going to last. Crick was his means to an end and once he'd achieved that end it would be goodbye Regis Crick. The sort of terminal goodbye that the big man, who Ruari regarded as little more than a hired thug, would not be coming back from.

CHAPTER 3

"How did you find this place?" Rina asked as she and Bridie took a turn around the gardens later that afternoon.

Bridie slipped her arm through Rina's. "I've known about it for a long time. I came here a couple of times when I was a schoolkid and never forgot it. The house was pretty run-down then, more like a big scruffy youth hostel than a grand house, all shared bathrooms and dormitories and everyone pitching in with the cooking and washing up. They held these long weekend events for inner city kids here and, like I say, I came on a couple of them."

"What did you do here?" Rina enquired.

"Swam, messed around in boats, made dens in the woods, you know all the stuff they thought you couldn't do in a terraced street."

Rina smiled. She'd grown up in a very similar area to Bridie, though several decades before. "I remember we went swimming at the local lido," she said, "and we made dens on the building site where they'd demolished a factory after it had been bomb-damaged in the war. It was the late seventies before they cleared the land and built on it. I've got pictures of me and my friends taken on my dad's box brownie and you could substitute pictures from the 1930s and not tell the difference. They've all gone now, of course, all those little streets where we grew up. They called it slum clearance, can you believe that?"

"Cheeky beggars," Bridie agreed. "Anyway, I came here because my friends were coming. It wasn't really my thing, or that's what I thought. But it's surprising, isn't it, what you'll do when you're away that you'd not get caught dead doing back at home. Anyway, it meant getting a day or two off school because we stayed over the long weekend and to be honest, I'd do a lot just to bunk off lessons. If I hadn't come, well, I'd have been on my own at lunchtimes and that was . . . well, that wasn't going to happen."

Rina squeezed her friend's arm, suddenly aware of a sadness in Bridie's tone. "I hated lunchtimes," she said. "Lesson times were bearable, I suppose, but I found it hard to make friends when I was a kid, so . . ."

"Really?" Bridie looked surprised. "I always assumed you must have had loads of friends. Been a real queen bee."

Rina shook her head. "I'd have thought the same about you. But no, I was really shy. I know that's hard to imagine now, but back then I just didn't seem to know how to talk to other girls and being at an all-girls school, I certainly didn't know how to talk to boys!"

The truth was she'd only really started to gain confidence once she'd learned she had a talent for being someone else.

"There was a teacher," Rina said, "really into amateur dramatics and she wanted to start an after-school drama club and put on plays as fundraisers for the school. I got involved behind the scenes and then got a tiny part and then realised I'd got the bug."

Bridie nodded. "Funny how great big things can start with really tiny stuff," she said. "Me, I came here just so I wouldn't be left behind and I ended up really enjoying it. The place was run by this Christian trust that had taken over the monastery but none of what we did was really about religion. It was about food and dancing and meeting new people and having fun in the lake and talking about all these philosophical questions I'd never even thought about. I mean, no one would ever think about me discussing that sort of stuff, would they?"

"Oh, I don't know," Rina said. "From what I've seen there's not much you're not interested in. So, there was a more serious side to the trips?"

"Yeah, we also had seminars and workshops, I discovered I liked singing, had my first crush, told ghost stories in the tunnels under the house."

"There are tunnels under the house?"

"Oh, I thought you'd like the sound of that! The entrance is in the sunken garden and the tunnels used to go right under the house. I think some of them have been filled in because they were threatening the foundations and I guess the lower sections might even go below the level of the water. They were certainly damp and chilly with water running down the walls even back then, but the first section's been restored, and we'll be taking a trip later on." She giggled suddenly, reminding Rina of Joy. "Hopefully not a literal trip. I remember the first time we went in there. About a dozen of us students, one teacher, one torch. It's a wonder no one broke their necks."

"I don't think health and safety was a thing back then," Rina agreed. "And I doubt anyone had even heard of a risk assessment. What were the tunnels for?"

"I don't think they were for anything. The story is that there was some problem with the mines, put a lot of the miners out of work and so the owner of the big house, one of the Milbourn bigwigs paid them to dig the sunken gardens, and then the tunnels, to keep them going until things got back to normal. Like the rest of the house, it all fell into disrepair. I suppose it got too expensive to maintain. I certainly wouldn't want the bills for a place like this. It was in such a sad state the last time I saw it that I half expected it to have fallen down."

"And then you came across it when you were looking for a wedding venue?"

"No, actually, that was Fitch. I must have told him about coming here and he remembered and anyway *I* was looking, *he* was looking and he came across an advert for this place and realised it must have been the house I'd told him about."

Rina smiled. She could just imagine how pleased Fitch must have been. When she'd first met him she'd marked him down as nothing more than a paid thug. Then, after the Peters sisters and Montmorencys had plied him and his then boss with a rather fine meal followed by chocolate dessert, revised that to a polite thug. Later she had come to realise that Fitch — no one called him by his first name — was far more than that. Loyal and fiercely protective and, Rina thought, essentially a good man . . . with a not so good past. He adored Bridie and loved Joy as though she was his own daughter and Rina was now very happy to think of him as her friend.

"Where is he, anyway?" she asked.

"Picking up the flowers and other bits and pieces. The caterers arranged for the floral displays in the house and the marquee but the flowers for me and the girls, well, I've sorted those out and I'd rather Fitch collected them today than risk a last-minute hitch tomorrow. There's a big cold pantry at the back of the kitchen, they'll stay nice and fresh in there."

"I'm looking forward to seeing the dresses," Rina hinted.

"Ah, Rina, even you will have to wait until tomorrow," Bridie told her and Rina could see that her friend was fizzing with excitement. "We are going to look magnificent."

Rina had no doubt of that.

Bridie glanced back towards the ferry as they heard the sound of a car coming up the drive.

"More guests?" Rina asked.

"Shouldn't be. A few people are arriving this evening, but most will be coming in the morning. There'll be a buffet lunch and drinks and then the wedding at three o'clock, then photographs and so on and then the wedding breakfast at five . . . It should be wedding afternoon tea really, shouldn't it? Then dancing and more food and we'll be leaving at about nine and heading to the airport. We expect everyone else to keep on dancing, of course."

It sounded like a long, busy day, Rina thought. She wondered how long she'd actually be able to stay on her feet and how much this had all cost.

They had turned back towards the house on hearing the car and now rounded the side of the building and looked across the water.

"A few people will be staying the night and leaving the following morning," Bridie went on, "and a few of you will be staying on for another day. Oh, Rina, I hope you all enjoy it. I'm so glad you could all come."

"Wouldn't have missed it for anything," Rina told her. She glanced curiously at Bridie who had paused and was now looking at the man who had got out of a black four-by-four, grabbed a suit bag and overnight case from the back seat and was now walking swiftly towards the boat.

"Who's that?" she asked.

"An early guest," Bridie said. She didn't sound too pleased. Rina watched as her friend fixed the smile back on her face and headed towards the jetty. They waited as the man was brought over, jumping impatiently from the boat before the boatman had cut the engine.

"Charlie, we didn't expect you until this evening. How are you?"

"I'm fine, thank you. Looking forward to you finally tying the knot. Bridie, I know I've turned up before you expected me, if it's a problem I can go away again."

"No problem," Bridie reassured him. "Your room's ready anyway, you're over in the monastery guest house. I'll show you. And this is my friend, Rina. Rina, this is Charlie Brewster."

He shook her hand, studying her face, Rina felt, as intently as she was examining his. He was a handsome young man, olive skin, dark hair, very dark brown eyes, approaching six feet, she thought, but Mac would have the advantage of him by several inches. Well-cut suit, expensive nails and soft hands that had, as Rina's father would have said, never done a day's work. Her father's classification of work being only that which constituted manual labour.

"I've put your sister in the main house," Bridie commented, trying for casual, Rina thought but not quite making it. The young man laughed and Rina heard the relief in the sound. "Well, thank you for that," he said. "I promise I'll be on my best behaviour. I really can't speak for her."

Interesting, Rina thought. Sibling rivalry writ large. Now who the devil was he and why was Bridie being so careful with him?

She excused herself and went back into the house. Glancing back, she saw Bridie and Charlie Brewster heading towards the monastery. She really must go and have a poke around in there, Rina told herself. After she'd finished exploring the house and gardens and not before she'd asked Mac who the young guest was and why he disliked his sister. Instinct told Rina that this was a shadow from Bridie's days with her first husband. One of the criminal fraternities that Jimmy Duggan had been embroiled with before events had killed him and his son, and nearly taken Joy.

* * *

Crick had watched from the shelter of the woods as the two women walked by, unconcerned and unknowing. He had shifted his position when they had headed back towards the house, their attention attracted by the little ferryboat crossing noisily with its single passenger. Watched as Bridie Duggan had greeted Charlie Brewster and the other woman had left them to return to the house. He didn't know who this older woman was, but she was clearly a good friend of the bride-to-be. Unlike Charlie Brewster; even at this distance he could sense that Bridie Duggan was handling Charlie with kid gloves.

But then she would, wouldn't she. Bridie had been around long enough to know the score and now Brewster senior was dead everything was in flux. The old man had left a vacuum that the siblings had as yet failed to fill. And that was something a great many people would come to regret.

CHAPTER 4

Dinner had been excellent, Rina thought. Good food, very good company and she had even allowed herself a couple of glasses of wine. Bridie had suggested an evening adventure to the sunken gardens which Rina, George and Ursula had decided sounded fun. Mac and Miriam had gone for a walk by the lake to watch the sunset and the Peters sisters, Eliza and Bethany, and Matthew and Steven Montmorency, had joined the older couple who had been sitting at their table for coffee in one of the smaller sitting rooms off the main reception.

Rina had been slightly surprised to find other guests already present but it turned out that the older couple, the Chapels, had been neighbours of her grandparents when Bridie had been a child and the Myers had worked for Jimmy Duggan's grandparents in the corner shop and then the little chemist's shop which had also doubled as an informal café and community meeting place. Bridie's grandmother had also worked there part-time which was how Bridie had come to meet her first husband. Bridie, Rina knew, held very tightly to her childhood. She had adored her grandparents, who had pretty much raised her, Bridie's mother having moved back home with them when her father had walked out. The Formica-topped table that had once stood in the shop and around which thousands of cups of tea and coffee had been drunk over the years still had pride of place in her very modern kitchen. Rina asked the Chapels if they would be staying on after the wedding but was told they would not be. The Chapels planned to spend a few days touring the area before returning home.

After dinner Rina had gone upstairs to change her shoes, when she came back down it was to find George and Ursula in conversation with Charlie Brewster. Charlie had sat at Bridie's table at dinner, with Fitch and the Chapels, the Myers on the next table along with the Peters sisters and their corner of the room had been particularly lively. Not that the Frantham contingent had been exactly quiet, Rina thought.

When Rina came back down the stairs she saw that George, Ursula and Charlie were sitting on the mezzanine landing and seemed to be getting on famously. George was telling Charlie Brewster about his apprenticeship in the boatyard. He'd worked there casually for the past year and would be starting full time at the end of September. Ursula would be at university a week or so after that.

"I'm learning to sail," Charlie was telling them. "I'm not very good yet, but I love it."

"I'd love to give it a go," George told him. "But it's far too expensive to even think about. We're looking for a place to live closer to the boatyard," he added. "And then any spare cash we've got has to go into me learning to drive. Ursula passed her test a while ago so she can at least drive to uni, but I've got to be closer to work."

"Can your parents not help out?" Charlie asked.

Rina saw George and Ursula exchange a glance. "We don't really have family," she said. "Or at least not actual relatives. I've got an aunt I see occasionally but George and I have been in care since we were thirteen. We're in local authority accommodation at the moment, we've both got these little bedsits they call studio flats and that's all fine, but we'd like to get somewhere together when we can."

Rina could see Charlie appraising the two young people with interest and, she thought, a certain respect. Footsteps on the stairs drew his attention away and the party turned to see Bridie and Tim and Joy making their way down.

"So, here we all are," Bridie said. "The intrepid few ready to adventure."

She was still wearing her heels, Rina noticed, but come to think of it, she'd never really seen Bridie in flats and wondered if she even owned a pair.

Bridie led the way, George and Ursula falling in behind and Tim and Joy following on. Rina found herself walking beside Charlie Brewster. "You're on the television," Charlie said. "You play that detective. Lydia somebody."

"Lydia Marchant," Rina told him. "Yes, I do."

"Didn't it get cancelled and then revived? My dad loved it, used to watch the reruns on one of the cable channels. He lived long enough to see the first new series and was very relieved to see they'd not 'mucked about with it' as he put it."

"I was relieved about that too," Rina told him. "Often these things get new and improved and it's rarely an improvement. Did you lose him recently?"

"Almost four months ago. It was a funny thing, he'd got no time at all for police drama or thrillers or anything like that, but he really liked your show."

"I'm glad to hear it. And what do you do, Mr Brewster, apart from learn to sail."

He laughed. "At the moment I'm negotiating with my sister, or rather our lawyers are negotiating with each other on our behalf, as to how our father's business interests are divided."

"Did he not leave a will?"

"He left a will but let's say it was open to interpretation," Charlie said. "He never did anything the easy way. You might say he left instructions and suggestions and left the rest for us to work out."

He sounded decidedly bitter, Rina thought. "Family disagreements are always painful," Rina said. "I think we might be here."

Bridie had halted and waited for everyone to gather around. She held a powerful torch in her hand even though it was not yet fully dark. Rina supposed they would need this for the promised tunnels and was glad she'd thought to tuck her own penlight into her pocket.

"Be careful on your way down," Bridie warned. "The steps are quite steep and narrow and it's a bit of a drop if you should happen to slip."

Charlie raised an amused eyebrow. "After you, Rina," he said.

Bridie hadn't been joking about steep and narrow, Rina thought. There was a handrail on the open side of the steps, supported every few feet by a series of metal poles but Rina felt wary of trusting it. She kept one hand on the wall as they descended, making a mental note that she should come back for a proper look in daylight. The earth wall had been faced with stone and the steps constructed of more dressed stone — here and there infilled with concrete in what Rina regarded as a not very sympathetic attempt at restoration. She was relieved when they arrived on the terra firma of the sunken garden.

Large flagstones marked the paths around raised beds, low walls built in the same grey gritstone, filled with lavender and rosemary and other fragrant herbs. It was surprisingly dry down here, Rina thought, though if you got bad weather would it flood? She could see that the garden designer had taken this problem on board. Spaces had been left at the base of the retaining walls, from which loose gravel spilled onto the paths to keep the beds free for drainage.

"It's still going to flood in winter," Charlie said, "however well the beds drain."

Rina looked at him in surprise. "You like gardening?" she asked.

"Not something I've got time for, but I like gardens. I take it you do?"

"I take great pleasure in making things grow," she told him. "I suppose for you it's all business?"

"I suppose it is. Especially since my father died. There's a lot to work out. Things he let slide when he was ill that now have to be put right." He smiled tightly. "I'm afraid I can't abide a mess."

"I always think that depends on the context," Rina said cheerfully. "I do like a clean workspace, I prefer to be organised, but where the garden's concerned for example, I like a bit of disorder."

They had reached a small iron gate set into the wall of the garden and Bridie undid the padlock holding it shut. "Here we go," she said. "Everyone got their torch?"

Rina took hers from her pocket and Charlie produced his mobile phone and switched on the torch app. Tim did the same. Joy had a proper torch, as did Ursula. Of course she did, Rina thought, Ursula was always prepared.

The passage they entered was narrow and low enough that Tim had to duck his head. Bridie led the way, Tim and Joy next in line followed by Ursula and George. Then Rina, Charlie bringing up the rear. It occurred to her suddenly that she'd much rather he was ahead. It was like being followed by an irritating tailgating driver; always a relief when they overtook and zoomed away. Rina analysed the feeling. Charlie had been pleasant enough, had done or said nothing that made her feel wary of him, but all the same she found she was on full alert when he was around. Was it just Bridie's reaction to his early arrival? That sense of barely concealed anxiety Bridie had exhibited. Or was it also that Rina had always been very good at recognising a predator?

The tunnel was narrowing now, close and claustrophobic and in places brushing both of Rina's arms.

"Almost there," Bridie reassured them and a moment later the space opened out into a rough circle with stone benches cut along the walls. Above them the ceiling arched and here and there Rina could make out rough carvings; faces and swirls and leaves. While in the tunnels the air had felt close and damp and every sound — breathing, footsteps, murmured conversations had been both amplified and

29

dampened — here the sounds seemed to echo to an extent that seemed at odds with the quite small space.

Rina estimated that about a dozen people could be seated comfortably around the walls and recalled what Bridie had told her about the first time she had been in the tunnels.

"Was this where you told the ghost stories?" she asked.

"It was, yes. There's another space like this a bit further along." She turned her torch to a point over Rina's shoulder and revealed another exit, this one angled so that at first glance it looked narrower than the one they had taken. Rina stepped over to examine the space and realised that it turned back on itself almost immediately, shooting off somewhere behind this open room.

"How far back does it go?" Tim asked.

"That passage goes on for, I don't know, maybe thirty feet and then there's another of these spaces and then two tunnels that go down. They're off limits now and I think the ones under the house have been filled in. There's a gate blocking them off, but we did go down there when we were kids and it was cold and damp and there was water running down the walls. I suppose where it went under the house it was interfering with the foundations as well."

"Can we go and see?" Tim asked and Rina could hear the excitement in his voice.

"If you don't mind, I'd really like to go, please," a small voice said and Rina turned with concern, shining her torch on Ursula. In the torchlight she looked very pale and Rina could make out a sheen of sweat on her forehead. George was holding tightly onto her hand.

"Oh, my dear, you don't look well. Look, I'll come back with you both. Better to have some extra light."

"We'll all go back," Bridie said decisively. "I'd no idea you were claustrophobic, lovely."

Ursula managed a weak laugh. "Neither did I," she said. "I'm really sorry."

"Nonsense," Rina said stoutly as Joy put an arm around Ursula's shoulder. She caught sight of Charlie Brewster's expression as she turned towards the exit, caught the look of contempt in his eyes and felt a sudden chill.

* * *

Mac and Miriam had returned from their walk and Mac had gone in search of Fitch. He found him sitting on a garden bench beside one of the bay windows, nursing a drink and looking very thoughtful.

"I was waiting for you to come back," Fitch told Mac. "Bridie told me what you said, about the Brewsters, so I thought it might be a good time to exchange a bit of information, before Mia Brewster gets here tomorrow. You should have some idea of what you're dealing with."

Mac had rarely seen Fitch look so serious. He sat down beside him. Fitch reached for the bottle of whisky and spare glass that had been set on the floor beside the bench. He pulled Mac a good measure of Dalwhinnie and handed it to him.

"That serious, is it?" Mac said holding up the glass and examining the generous measure.

"What do you know about the Brewster family?"

"I have a broad sense of the history. Brewster senior started out in race-fixing. He was a runner to start with and learned the business from the ground up. Took over from Percy Gandy when the old man died. Gandy's two sons had predeceased him and I know there were rumours about Brewster being the cause of that but nothing seemed to have been proved . . . or provable. That was almost forty years ago when Brewster was still in his twenties."

"So far so right," Fitch said. "Both sons met with unfortunate accidents, you might say. One got drunk and fell into a river, the other was stabbed in a bar fight. The man accused of doing the stabbing was spirited away in the confusion and found dead a few streets from the pub the following morning. There were rumours, of course, but there are always rumours. Most of the smart money was on Brewster and mine would have been too. He had the means, the opportunity and by that time he knew old man Gandy's business inside out. He dealt with the wife by paying her a lump sum and sending her off to Spain. What she thought about the situation God alone knows but she lived out there for the next ten years, dropped dead one day of I don't know what. She apparently had a weak heart but . . . So far as anyone who knew her was concerned, it was a surprise that she even had one. She and Brewster were one-of-a-kind."

"And yet surely a mother would not stand by while her sons were disposed of?"

"They were his sons, not hers. From a first marriage. The first wife left him, I don't know what happened to her but presumably they got divorced. Second Mrs Gandy moved in about five years or so after the first left, usual story, younger model, suicide blonde in this case, big tits, liked her jewellery and her cars and he liked having her around. But she was purely decorative, and it strikes me she was probably happy just to get out in one piece."

Mac nodded. "So that was thirty odd years ago?" he confirmed.

"Around that time yes. Brewster carried on what had been Gandy's business and then added concerns of his own. Usual thing, fingers in every pie, nightclubs, drugs, prostitution and more recently there was talk about him being involved in people trafficking. He was almost certainly involved in the sex trade and trafficking women to feed that, but if his interest in illegal migrants was more general, well, I wouldn't like to comment on that one. There are always rumours."

"So, he had the children a bit later," Mac observed. "Charlie is what, mid-twenties?"

"Charlie is twenty-seven, Mia is twenty-five and as you've probably heard they don't like one another very much. Their dad played them off one another. Pretty much from the moment they were able to walk, they were competing for his attention. Charlie was in favour one day, Mia the next. It's no wonder they've grown up the way they are."

"And the mother? From what I read, she disappeared when they were very young."

"Mia would have been two or three, I suppose. No one seems to know what happened to her which probably means it isn't good. Brewster put it out that she'd gone off with another man, but I mean, Mac, you know the score, a wife of someone like Brewster does not leave to go off with another man. Not if either of them end up alive to tell the tale."

Mac nodded. "Everything I've read about Brewster implies that he was a violent man."

"No implication required," Fitch said. "You know what kind of man I am, you know what kind of man Jimmy Duggan was. Guilty as hell, both of us, but Brewster made Jimmy look like the Angel Gabriel. Jimmy Duggan came up rough, fought his way to the top, was an all-round street fighter. I make no excuses for him or for me. Bridie is different, solid, honest background she came from, but you don't get to choose who you fall in love with, and she went into the marriage eyes wide open. Bridie's no fool and over time she steered Jimmy away from the worst stuff. Jimmy was looking for a way out long before Patrick was killed, you know that. He wanted a better future for his kids than he had had and the only way he could see that happening was to clear out the dead wood and go legit. But there are those who knew Jimmy in his younger days that haven't been so happy about that. Time goes on and most have come around and Bridie has been wise enough not to shut them out of her life. She's acknowledged friendships and debts and she's managed to walk along the knife edge."

"And representatives of those families are all coming to the wedding," Mac said.

"On the understanding that they make no trouble. You know how it is, Mac, weddings, funerals, the odd christening, they're neutral territory. Anyone makes a scene they'll have everyone else on their backs. At least, that's the way it's been with the older generation who were around with Jimmy Duggan and Malcolm Brewster. Percy Donovan loves a wedding. Gets his sentimental side going. He might drink the place dry but he'll always behave. Same with Ben Caprisi and his lads. Up to their necks in anything worth happening south of the river, London born and bred for the past three generations, even made the Krays think twice about expanding their territory back in the day, but make trouble at a wedding? At Bridie Duggan's wedding?"

"Soon to be Bridie Fitch," Mac reminded him.

"No, she's not. That's the thing. Mac, we all had a long talk last time Joy came up to visit. Me and Bridie and Joy and her brother Brian."

Brian had largely taken over his father's business when he had been killed, Mac knew. Bridie and Fitch were still involved, on the board, as it were, but the day-to-day administration was in Brian's hands. Bridie, the figurehead as the late Jimmy Duggan's wife, signed off on all the major decisions and Fitch's long experience on both sides of lawful business must, he figured, be invaluable. Brian had continued his father's moves to legitimise everything, under his mother's watchful eye.

"A talk about what?"

"Sometimes," Fitch said, "it's the signs and symbols that matter most. As you know, Brian's going to walk his mother down the aisle tomorrow, show the world he's on board with her getting married again and with her getting hitched to me. You'll be there as best man. My best man."

Mac raised an eyebrow. "So I'm symbolic of you all going straight." He laughed, a little uncertain how he felt about that.

"And because I trust you with my life, with Joy's, and with Bridie's; and frankly, Mac, there's very few I could say that about. So yes, you're part of the signs and symbols, as Bridie calls it, but you're my best man because I wanted you to be and you were good enough to say yes."

Mac thought about it, then nodded. "I'm proud to be," he said, realising that was absolutely true. "And I'm really glad we're all here. But you were saying about Bridie not being Mrs Fitch?"

"Brian and Joy reckoned we needed to send a bit more of a message, see? Jimmy started cleaning up his act before he got himself murdered and we all know Pat didn't want anything to do with criminality. Before that bastard shot him, Pat was fixing to finish his degree and then marry his girl. Lovely girl, she is, we keep in touch, Bridie invited her to the wedding but none of us were surprised when she said she couldn't come. And Joy, Joy's happy as Larry with Tim and going back to college and everything. Knowing how much she hated school, no one expected her to do that but she's proved us all wrong. So the danger is, the opposition starts to see us as a soft touch, starts muscling in because they figure we're too weak to stand up to the pressures now Jimmy Duggan's dead and gone. You can end up as the victim in this game, Mac, and that's a bad thing."

Mac could see where he was coming from but the small nagging worry he had carried since speaking with his boss now flared. "So, what are you doing about it?"

"Signs and symbols again, Mac. So, we got together and we talked about it and Joy reckoned that instead of Bridie becoming Mrs Fitch, Fitch being the subordinate, the employee, as you well know, that I should become Mr Duggan."

Mac sipped his drink, savouring the heat on his tongue and the roundness of the flavour, uncertain what to say. His first reaction had been to laugh — though more because of the way Fitch had delivered the news than because it was inherently funny. He was aware of Fitch watching him closely so he nodded, "I can see that would send a signal," he said. "That the Duggans are still in full charge and definitely not pushovers. How do you feel about it?"

Fitch shrugged. "Like Joy says, it's the modern thing to do. Lots of married women keep their family names and a fair few men take their woman's or they double-barrel them. We thought about that, but everyone reckoned Fitch-Duggan sounded like a firm of dodgy solicitors, so we decided just to go with Duggan."

Mac was relieved to be saved from having to respond to that one. Voices told them that Bridie and her party of adventurers were returning.

"Ah, hello you two." Bridie beamed at them as she came into view. "I'm off to get a nightcap and then some beauty sleep." She kissed Fitch and patted Mac on the arm. "Don't be late to bed, love," she said to her fiancé, "it'll be a long day tomorrow."

The others followed Bridie into the house, though Mac was aware of Rina's meaningful glance back at him as she walked beside Charlie Brewster into the house. He'd no doubt be getting a visit from her later.

"So," he said, allowing Fitch to top up his glass in preparation for resuming their conversation. "Do you have grounds for worrying or is this all precautionary?"

"It's good to be prepared," Fitch said. "Brian's heard gossip, not so much about us but about some people not being happy with the way things are divvied up these days. You've got some powerful families, Mac, not being run by powerful heads anymore. It used to be the older generation trained the new, prepared them for taking over, you know? Like in any business. But things move fast now. Technology shifted the balance and now it's the new generation that grew up with it who knows how it all works and the older generation don't always want to hand over the reins despite the fact they've been left behind. Take old Ben Caprisi for instance, a few years back he had to take computer classes just so he could learn to send an email. Not that old Ben's been head of anything except in name for the last twenty years. Gianni took over years ago and it's his kids that are calling the shots now. And it's all new tricks. Insider trading, identity theft, online scams."

Mac raised an eyebrow. "Anything I should be reporting?"

"Probably, but you'll not get anything useful from me. Not my circus, not my monkeys. And Bri reckons they regard the Duggans as a spent force, one that's worth reckoning with only out of courtesy to Bridie and now to me. By the time Brian takes over properly in a few years' time, he'll be better placed to understand what needs doing than either me or his mam. He's a bright one, is Brian, so's his wife, Lynnie. Got a good head on her shoulders."

"And the Brewsters might also be out to cause trouble," Mac guessed. "I spoke to Rina just before dinner and she said that Bridie seemed oddly upset by Charlie Brewster turning up early." He paused, remembering something from the background info he had read. "Wasn't there a third sibling? He left and went to the USA?"

"Ruari, yes. He was a by-blow from some affair Brewster had. Lived with his mother until he was about ten, then Brewster took charge. She was an alcoholic. His dad sent him to boarding school, paid for his education and all that but he was never really part of the family. He's older than the other two, though I think he and Charlie rubbed along well enough. Mia don't get on with anyone. After university Brewster invited Ruari to join the family business, or take a settlement and go far, far away. Ruari chose that option and who can blame him?"

"And he's now a filmmaker or something?"

"Something of the sort. Documentaries, I think. Charlie mentions him from time to time, but I'm not close to Charlie or his sister and I barely knew Ruari."

Mac nodded. "And the two younger kids. There's now a power struggle. I know they don't get on." They hate one another's shadows was how Mac had expressed it to the chief constable. That's what he'd been led to believe on the odd times that his investigations had crossed into Brewster territory.

"Hate one another's guts," Fitch confirmed. "And frankly, who can blame them. Their dad played one off against the other and now he's left a will that means they've got to compete for a controlling share in the business. Or so

I've heard. I don't know details. But one thing I will say, Mac. Charlie Brewster might come over as all charm and light but he's a bastard, same as his sister. He just hides it better."

"Is Bridie worried about them being here?"

"Put it this way, she doesn't want anyone to be caught in the crossfire and will be mightily relieved when they're gone."

Mac nodded. "Did Charlie say why he'd come early?"

"Not so far as I'm aware."

But Mac had the odd feeling there was more he could be saying but that he was still figuring out what he should tell his policeman friend. Despite their genuine liking for one another, there would always be divided loyalties.

Fitch got to his feet. "I'm going to watch some telly and then get some sleep," he said. "Tomorrow's going to be a big day and nothing's going to spoil it for Bridie."

Mac wished him a good night. He sat for a little longer, savouring the whisky and then, retrieving the bottle that Fitch had left by the side of the bench, he returned to his room and Miriam. He was unsurprised to find Rina already there and the two women chatting over coffee.

"What's that you've got there," Miriam asked eyeing the bottle. "Ooh, nice."

"Courtesy of Fitch or as he will be by tomorrow evening, Mr Reggie Duggan."

"What?" Miriam giggled. She glanced at Rina.

"You knew about this?" Mac said, noting Rina's expression.

"Joy told me but it's a surprise so I was sworn to secrecy. Besides, Fitch wanted to tell you himself, man-to-man was how he put it. What you think means a lot to Fitch, so I hope you responded with full gravity."

"I think I managed that," Mac told her. "Fortunately, I didn't have a mouthful of whisky when he told me or I might have choked. Did Joy explain why?"

"Not in depth, but enough to understand they are trying to safeguard the Duggan name and reputation."

Mac nodded. There were only two easy chairs in the tall ceilinged room and the women were occupying those. Mac settled on the window seat. The curtains were still open and the lights in the room had not been switched on, apart from a bedside lamp. He was able to gaze out across the lawn and towards the lake. Bridie really had given them a most lovely room. He had never stayed in a place like this and guessed it would be out of his usual price range — he generally stayed in chain hotels, liking the fact that he knew what he'd be getting no matter what part of the country he happened to be in. But then, most of his hotel stays had been work related and not for leisure. He and Miriam should go away, he thought, just for a few nights and somewhere special, somewhere like this.

A figure moving across the lawn caught his attention. Recognising it Mac asked, "Rina, what did you make of Charlie Brewster?"

He could almost feel her thinking, considering the question from all angles. "I think he's a very bitter young man," she said.

Mac pulled his attention from the view, and the shadowy figure of Charlie Brewster, and looked at her. That was not the response he'd been expecting. "Fitch thinks he's dangerous," he said. "Charming but treacherous."

"He probably is. But I suspect he was made that way. Not that being made rather than being born changes the outcome. I'd not trust him with any sharp objects. He tries hard to be charming and largely succeeds. I think he genuinely wants, no . . . more like needs to be liked. I also suspect he has created his own persona as a direct reaction to his sister who Bridie described as a complete and utter bitch. Considering Bridie usually has something nice to say about nearly everyone, even if that means she has to dig deep and occasionally stretch the truth, I feel we should take notice of her opinion. I'm looking forward to meeting her."

Mac laughed. "Well if anyone can handle her, it would be you." He glanced back out of the window, noting that the figure had now reached the trees beside the lake and another had joined them. One was certainly Charlie Brewster. The

39

other was most definitely Fitch. Mac stiffened and Rina noticed. She came over to the window, staying back out of sight of anyone glancing up, and gazed out across the lawn.

"Now that is interesting," she said. "And they don't seem to be having a very pleasant conversation, do they?" she added, referencing the posturing and arm-waving that was going on.

"No, they don't," Mac agreed.

"Who are you watching?" Miriam asked.

"Charlie and Fitch having a row," Rina told her.

The bedroom window was open, but the two men were far enough away that they could not be heard, even on the still night air that carried sound. For all the arm-waving and posturing, they were clearly at pains to keep their voices down.

"Fitch told me he was off to watch some television and then go to bed," Mac said.

"Well, he could hardly tell you he was heading off to have a knock down row with Charlie Brewster," Rina pointed out.

"True. So, what's it about?"

"I'm sort of hoping we don't find out," Miriam told them both. "This is supposed to be a joyful occasion, you know. A big fat wedding with lots of food and champagne and dancing and two people we love tying the knot. I don't want to know about other people's gripes and grievances, I just want to have a break from work and a good time."

Rina nodded and turned from the window. "And quite right too," she agreed. "And on that note, I'll bid the pair of you goodnight." She kissed them both on the cheek and gave Miriam an extra hug. "Sleep well, you two," she said.

"Rina," Mac warned. "No sneaking around, please."

"As if I would. No, I'm off to my bed."

Mac sighed heavily as she closed the door. He watched from the window a little longer, much to Miriam's amusement, just to ensure that Rina had kept her word and not crept ninja-style through the shrubbery to spy on the two men. To his relief there was no sign of her and after another five minutes or so, Charlie stormed off along the path by the lake and Fitch made his way back to the house. Crossing the lawn, he glanced up at Mac's window and for an instant their eyes locked, then Fitch walked on and Mac stepped back into the room and closed the curtains.

"I know that look," Miriam said. "It usually spells trouble. Can't we ever just have an ordinary weekend away?"

"Believe me, I hope so," he told her. "There's nothing I'd like more."

* * *

Ruari had been watching as the two men met. Surprised by the fact that Charlie would get into it with Fitch on the eve of the wedding though, he supposed there'd not be much opportunity on the day of the ceremony. What the hell did Charlie expect? That the Duggans would roll over and agree to what he wanted? Surely even Charlie Brewster wasn't that dim?

The two men were clearly angry, Fitch gesticulating and Charlie really getting into his face. Amused, he raised his phone, checking the night setting and took a few shots before shifting to the infrared and firing off a few more.

Charlie glanced his way, Fitch, pausing mid-sentence turning to see what had attracted Charlie's attention. Ruari froze, for a moment wondering if they'd heard him or if it was simply that these two men were possessed of the same heightened awareness of potential threat as he was. Somewhat to his relief, Charlie turned away again as though satisfied that there was, after all, nothing worthy of his attention. Fitch, he noticed, took a little longer to pull his gaze away.

He remained where he was, silent and unmoving until Fitch finally walked away and Charlie, frowning, followed him a moment later, crossing the lawn and then veering off towards the guest house. Watching him, Ruari raised his phone again, firing off a few more shots. Brother Charlie had a target on his back; he just didn't know it yet.

CHAPTER 5

The following morning Rina and Tim had set out to explore before the rest of the guests descended. The island was a rough teardrop shape but with an odd, elongated arm protruding from the narrow end, out into the lake. Along this peninsula sat a row of cottages, now holiday lets, and two larger houses, one of which she was told had belonged to the vicar and one to the land manager responsible for the then extensive estate.

It was easy to forget, Rina thought, that the island had been only a small part of what the owners of Milbourn House had controlled. It hadn't even been their main residence. That had been a much larger house, lost to death duties between the wars when it was cheaper to knock it down than to pay the taxes on it. The land on which it stood had been bought for the power station, now in its turn being demolished, only the last remnants of the cooling towers remained alongside the canal that the Milbourns had financed in order to get their goods to market. The canal continued past the house and on to where the factory had stood, then three miles away but long since razed.

The house manager had told Rina that although the guests in the holiday cottages were not connected to Bridie or her party, Bridie had sent out invitations for the evening festivities as a courtesy. Rina doubted the party would be noisy enough to bother anyone so far from the main house, though the music might drift over, she supposed, but it was a nice gesture on Bridie's part and very typical of the woman she had come to know.

Tim had joined her on the walk. The photographer had arrived very early that morning and Bridie, Joy and Ursula were apparently to be involved in recording a complete account of the day. He was therefore very bored.

"Have you seen the dresses?" she asked Tim.

"Not so much as a thread. And Joy won't tell me anything. She says it'll be a nice surprise. Though I do know the mini bridesmaids will be dressed as fairies, complete with little gauzy wings."

"Mini bridesmaids?"

"Children of cousins and old friends, I think, and Brian's little girl. Four of them, all under five, so that'll be fun." He grinned at Rina. "At least I don't have to do the clown act."

"Just as well." Tim was a professional magician and also a consultant on all things magical to a games designer. In his early days, he had performed at far more children's parties than had been good for his sanity. The ceremonial burning of his orange wig, after the last of these, had been a moment of pure relief for both Tim and Rina.

"What's up with Mac?" Tim asked.

"Up with Mac?"

"He's twitchy. He's acting like there's a bear hiding behind every tree. I'm used to Mac being on the alert, but he's usually a bit more relaxed around Bridie and Fitch."

Briefly, Rina filled him in on the events of the previous evening and on the summons Mac had received for an audience with the chief constable before they had left. "So he's finding it hard to relax," she explained.

"And what's Rina's twitchy nose telling her? You expecting trouble?"

Rina thought about it for a moment and then said, "I rather suspect I am. Hopefully nothing serious, but . . ."

Tim nodded. "Fair enough. Look, there's another jetty over there."

"So there is. I suppose that was originally for the servants to get across, away from the main house. They would not have wanted servants landing outside of the front door."

The jetty was stone-built unlike the recently constructed wooden structures on either shore of the lake, closer to the house. Two rowing boats were tied up alongside and a kayak lay upturned on the jetty itself. A wooden pontoon stood at the far side of the lake with another rowing boat tied up beside it. The water was clear and Rina stood for a moment looking for fish. A man emerged from one of the cottages and shouted a good morning which they returned.

"Are you with the wedding party?" he asked as he came closer. "They've got a lovely day for it."

"We are and they have indeed."

Tim fidgeted restlessly and, Rina taking her cue, walked slowly on. "Fancy having a look at the monastery?" he said, as they reached the furthest point of the jutting arm, beyond the row of cottages and the two larger houses which closer inspection revealed were now holiday flats. Rina found herself wondering what kind of people came to stay here. Adults, she would have thought, pretty much exclusively; there was little here for children to do. No play parks or a swimming pool. She remembered what Bridie had said about swimming in the lake and playing in the woods, but would parents be comfortable with their offspring being that adventurous? The kind of parents that could afford to stay in a place like this would most likely want their kids doing supervised activities with personal trainers — or was she just being classist, Rina wondered. She realised with some surprise that she actually knew very few people with young children and those she did tended to be residents on the local housing estate or living in the less desirable, smaller houses backing onto the promenade. George and Ursula, though she had known them since before they became teenagers, certainly no longer qualified as children.

Frantham still had a primary school but once they turned eleven, kids were bussed into Bridport for their secondary education. Finding a place to live once they'd grown was its own challenge. She'd been lucky, buying Peverill Lodge when she did, it was unlikely she could have afforded anything like that these days and be able to house her friends in comfort as she did now. Rina knew she would have been heartbroken had she been unable to provide safe haven for the Peters sisters or the Montmorencys, lifelong performers with precarious incomes and for whom old age had been fearful. Tim had lived with them for a while and occasionally she had offered sanctuary to others who had needed respite and a safe place to be — even Mac in his early days in Frantham.

"Penny for them," Tim said.

"Thinking we are very lucky," Rina told him.

He took her arm and slipped it through his. "That we are."

They entered the monastery through the chapel door. Inside it was surprisingly large with pretty but, Rina felt, over-sentimental Victorian stained glass, though she did admire the way the blue and yellow light poured down onto the altar. The ceiling was vaulted with wooden planks rather than carved stone and looked like the upturned hull of a boat. The wedding ceremony was to be in the marquee on the lawn rather than in here, the ceremony being civil rather than religious and besides, this place would never have been big enough to accommodate the guests. "I'm guessing it was quite a small community," she said.

Tim had picked up a brochure from the table just inside the door and they followed the helpful map out of the side door and into the main building. A long corridor, this time barrel-vaulted, with doors to small rooms on one side and arched windows looking out onto a small, enclosed garden on the other, led through the building towards what according to the guidebook was the kitchen and dining room, no longer in use. Rina supposed that guests must come over to eat in the main dining room in the big house.

It was oddly quiet, she thought. She wore soft-soled shoes and Tim ordinary trainers but even so their footsteps seemed to echo and she felt as though she was intruding on the building's peace. Tim had no such qualms. He opened one of the doors and exclaimed in delight, "This must have been one of the cells."

Rina looked inside. A small but comfortable room with a single bed, a desk beneath a window and a bookcase. She stepped through the door and examined it with interest. On the back of the door was a notice talking about fire exits and instructions that guests 'on retreat' should be in their rooms by ten. So this religious house was still connected to its original purpose, she thought.

Further on down the corridor was a larger door and according to the map this gave access to the library. Rina tried the handle and was pleased when it opened.

"Oh, this is all right," Tim said eagerly.

Rina smiled at his enthusiasm. "If I leave you here, promise to set an alarm on your phone. If you're late for the wedding Joy will never forgive you."

The ceiling rose to double height with skylights flooding the centre of the room with natural light. The books were shelved on two floors, a mezzanine running around all four sides of the room. Ladders attached to rails could be moved into position to access books on both levels. A few of the books were in closed glass cabinets but most were on open shelves and the guidebook invited guests to read but not to take the volumes from the room. Looking at the titles, mostly theology and philosophy, Rina wondered how many of these studies had been read since the religious community left. Had they left the library behind? Had it been restored since then? She wondered if the little guidebook would enlighten her or if she'd have to do a search online. The library seemed like a friendly place to be, furnished with deep chairs and handy tables, the odd lectern set up for the heavier tomes. She could see herself retreating here on a wet afternoon and settling in for the duration. Though she might have to bring her own book.

But not today. Rina glanced at her watch. "We should get back," she said. "We both have to change and get ready for the buffet lunch or the rest of the family will be sending out search parties."

"I doubt Eliza and Bethany are even conscious yet," Tim said. "And I told Matthew and Stephen last night that we'd be off for an early morning constitutional, so they won't be sounding the alarm just yet. You're right though, time to don the suit, I suppose."

Rina patted his arm. "And admit it, Tim, you're as curious as I am to see who else is coming to this wedding." And particularly Mia Brewster, she thought; that was going to be interesting.

They walked back the way they had come, out through the chapel and into the sunshine, across the path and narrow lawn that separated the monastic complex from the house. The ferry had just docked, disgorging the first of several wedding guests, including two very small girls dressed in pastel fairy costumes, complete with silvery wings.

"How mucky are they going to be by the time the wedding starts," Tim said, clearly amused.

As they passed by, a young woman, clearly the mother of one little fairy, suggested she take the wings off so they wouldn't get in the way. Not a hope, Rina guessed. The girls would probably want to sleep in them.

She watched as the guests were shepherded by the house manager towards the gazebo and told where all the facilities were and invited to help themselves to drinks and snacks. She glanced at her watch again as the ferry pulled away to collect another tranche of guests already waiting on the other bank. The women brightly dressed in summer frocks, the men in a mix of lounge suits and casual jackets. She remembered the wording on the invitations that had instructed guests to wear what they liked and prepare to enjoy the day.

There were now flowers in the foyer, the corners of the big square space filled with tall displays, the dining room had been furnished with drinks and snacks for anyone who wanted to get out of the sun. Hotel staff, and others she guessed were with the outside caterers, padded around with trays of glasses, others with wedding gifts ready to be stacked on a white-draped table in one of the side rooms.

"Well," Tim said, "when Joy and I tie the knot, I think we might just elope."

"Las Vegas," Rina said. "Get yourselves married by Elvis and we'll have a shindig in the village hall when you get back."

"Sounds good to me."

It would probably be fine with Joy and her mother too, Rina thought. She could not help but think that this was all a tad political. A display of power and status and not just the joining of two people who Rina knew loved one another very much. The thought disturbed her.

Turning onto the landing that led to her room Rina was surprised to find Fitch, clearly loitering with intent outside her door. "I saw you coming in," he said. "Wondered if you'd got a minute."

"Of course." She unlocked the door and stepped inside, noting with some amusement that Fitch glanced both ways as though checking they were unobserved before following her in. He flopped down in one of the easy chairs looking more like a man facing execution, she thought, than one about to be wed. "What's wrong, is Bridie all right?"

"Everyone's fine and I wouldn't bother you but I needed to talk to someone and I know I can rely on you to keep schtum."

Rina took the other chair. "Fitch, what's going on here. I saw you last night with Charlie Brewster. It looked as though you were arguing with him."

"Not arguing exactly. Telling him where to get off. Thinks he's entitled, does Charlie. Mia too for that matter. But I told him, Charlie, all that's water under the bridge and Bridie don't owe you nothing. She's legit now, Brian makes sure everything he does is checked and double-checked by a proper lawyer, not one that's in someone's pocket like Charlie's lot. I told him, Jimmy Duggan started his business any which way he could, just like Charlie's dad and yes, for a while they were partners. But that didn't last. Jimmy and Malcolm Brewster parted within a year or two, divvied it all up and each went their own way."

"I didn't know they had an association," Rina said.

"Like I said, it was brief. Even Jimmy couldn't be doing with Malc for long. Unpredictable, he was, manipulative. Treated people like . . . well anyway."

Interesting, Rina thought, especially considering Jimmy Duggan wasn't known for his kid gloves. Except where his family was concerned. Duggan's family was sacred. "And Charlie is now saying that Jimmy Duggan in some way cheated Malcolm Brewster?"

"Something like that. He wants a slice of Bridie's business, says it's owed and he can make trouble if he doesn't get it."

"And he seemed like such a nice young man," Rina said wryly, noting that it took Fitch a moment to recognise the sarcasm. "No Fitch, I felt there was something wrong from the moment he arrived. Bridie was clearly treating him like he was a hand grenade with the pin pulled. And the sister is here today as well, isn't she?"

"Mia, yes. And believe me, Rina, she don't even pretend to play nice."

"So what can I do to help?" Rina asked.

"You can keep the pair of them away from Bridie for me," Fitch said.

Rina regarded him with surprise. She'd not expected that.

"Look, Rina, I just need them off my back for a few hours and kept away from Bridie. I'm going to let nothing spoil today and by nine o clock tonight we'll be off and I can leave the rest for Bri and the solicitors to sort out while we're gone."

"Bridie won't thank you for keeping this from her," Rina warned him.

"And I won't. Once we've got the ceremony over with I can give her a heads up."

And hope she doesn't decide to call them on it, Rina thought.

"Then we can sort it out but Brian and me, we just want this day to be perfect. She deserves that. I just need you to run interference for me for a bit. Just from when the wedding ceremony finishes until we leave. Mia and Charlie'll not want to make a public scene, they just need keeping busy until I can talk to Bridie, warn her what's going on."

"Can't you go and see her now?"

"Rina, she'd have my balls. It's unlucky to see the bride before the ceremony, you know that."

Rina regarded Fitch with a mix of amusement and exasperation. "All right, I'll do my best," she said. "But I can't promise anything."

Fitch's obvious relief troubled her more than the original request.

"Thank you, Rina. I'll get the caterers to shift the seating plans around so you can keep an eye on Charlie."

"And what about Mia? You can't put her on the same table as her brother."

"Oh," Fitch said. "I thought I could let Mac look after her."

So much for a relaxing weekend, Rina thought after Fitch had gone. Did Mac know yet that he'd be babysitting Mia Brewster? She glanced again at her watch, stroked it gently. This gift from her late husband had accompanied her through many trials and tribulations much worse than this. I wish you were here, Fred, Rina thought, though that was something she had wished every single day since she had lost him only five years into their marriage.

Well, she would have to talk to Mac as soon as possible. Everyone would be gathering for lunch in less than an hour and as Bridie would not be present, she could take a chance to hatch a plan with Mac and Miriam and Tim to keep everything sweet during the formal reception later that afternoon. Meanwhile, she'd better hurry up and put her glad rags on.

* * *

From his position in the bell tower Crick had been able to watch the guests arrive and drift in amiable little knots across the lawn. Crick was staying out of sight, camping out in comfort in the house at the far end of the island. By mutual consent he and Ruari were spending as little time in one another's company as was necessary. This was strictly a business agreement beyond which they had little in common.

Most people gathered on the lawn seemed at least acquainted with one another and he recognised the vast majority, either as business associates, hangers-on or minor celebrities who enjoyed the frisson of danger in mixing with the criminal fraternity. It had, he thought, always been this way, thinking about the showbiz personalities who had enjoyed the notoriety of being photographed with the Krays and their ilk.

He spotted the older woman who'd been with Bridie the day before, chatting to two even older women he also did not recognise. And there was Charlie Brewster, filling up his glass.

Had he his rifle, he could have taken Charlie right here and now. Felled him in an instant. He imagined taking aim, drawing a bead on the young man as he crossed the lawn between the laughing groups of nonentities. For so they were. Sheep who didn't have the wit to know when the wolf was at the door.

CHAPTER 6

By the time Rina came down the others in her party were already assembled outside. The lawn had been set out with tables and chairs, with more in the marquee and long buffet tables already groaning with food. We'll all be thoroughly stuffed before the day's out, Rina thought. She was unsurprised to spy George already loading his plate. George had gone without so often in his childhood that he rarely missed out on an opportunity to eat — though he still managed to remain lanky and skinny.

The Peters sisters, Eliza resplendent in lilac silk and her sister in blue, were gossiping with two women Rina didn't recognise, but that was typical of Eliza and Bethany, they would always find someone to chat to, no matter what the occasion. Matthew Montmorency wore a dark grey suit and a pristine white shirt with a scarlet tie, his mane of white hair tied back with a matching ribbon. His ersatz twin Stephen was similarly dressed, though his hair was cropped short as always. Stephen had long since started to go thin on top, a fact no one ever mentioned. Not as tall as Matthew and looking nothing like him, their 'twin' moniker being a hangover from all the years they had been a double act, he had borrowed one of Rina's large collection of silver-topped walking canes and brought it with him. Stephen's knees hurt him when he walked.

"Tim not here yet?" Rina asked.

"He's somewhere about," Matthew told her. "Looking very smart." Tim had wanted to wear the black suit he used for his stage performances but Rina had persuaded him that perhaps it was not quite the thing. "And Mac and Miriam have gone in search of champagne. Or at least Miriam has, I don't think Mac's too keen."

"Mac would probably rather have a beer," Rina agreed. She caught sight of him, standing at the entrance to the marquee and excusing herself from the twins, went over to him.

"You have that look in your eye," Mac said. "What's up?"

"You're not going to like it," she warned him. Quickly she filled him in on what Fitch had told her and the new seating arrangement for the reception. "You'll be keeping an eye on Mia while I deal with Charlie Brewster," she told him.

"Wonderful. I don't actually think she's arrived yet. I've been looking. I've got a photo of her in my famous file and from what I hear she likes to make an entrance."

Miriam appeared carrying three glasses and an entire a bottle of something fizzy. Rina raised an eyebrow.

"Well, someone had left it unattended." Miriam shrugged. "So I thought I'd help out with service. Just for us, you understand."

The sound of the ferry approaching the dock drew Rina outside. A young woman in a red dress stood in the prow close to the tiny cabin, a little apart from the chattering group seated behind her. The boat docked and two more little fairies ran along the jetty, parents in pursuit. Other guests followed at a more leisurely pace, then the young woman, assisted from the boat by a very well-dressed young man.

"I'm guessing that's Mia Brewster," Rina said.

"Looks like it," Mac agreed.

"Oh, the famous sister. Nice dress, shame about the pout," put in Miriam.

Rina had to agree with Miriam that even at this distance Mia looked dissatisfied with the world.

"Well," she said, "you'll be able to view it at close quarters later on." She drifted off, leaving Mac to explain.

She found Tim examining the buffet and, suddenly feeling peckish, Rina grabbed a plate and joined him in his perusal. He did indeed look smart, she thought, in a suit of slate grey linen over a collarless shirt. Tim didn't do ties. Rina spotted Bridie's hand in the choice — it looked too well-cut and too expensive for Tim to have acquired unaided. Not that Tim didn't dress with style but it was a style definitely his own and tended to be a blend of Sixties bohemian and out-and-out gothic.

Tim turned with a smile. "There's almost too much choice," he said. "Is it too greedy to have a bit of everything?"

"Oh, I don't think so. But leave room for the wedding breakfast, lord knows how many courses that's going to have."

"True, but that's ages away."

Rina spotted the sudden change in expression and looked to see what had attracted Tim's attention. "I take it that's the infamous Mia Brewster," he said.

Rina nodded. "Well, she certainly knows how to command attention."

The red, ankle-length dress was bias cut, reminding Rina of something that might have been worn by a Thirties movie star, an observation reinforced by the deep cowl that left her back and most of her shoulders bare. She was dark-haired like her brother and her hair was cut short, the waves carefully pinned in place with narrow silver clips. The young man who had helped her off the boat appeared at her side, champagne flutes in hand. Mia took a sip, made a face, shrugged. The sweep of her gaze took in the buffet table, the crowd gathered in the marquee, the floral displays beside the entrance and seemed to find them all wanting. Then she turned and glided out of the marquee and Rina sensed, as the volume of conversation returned to its pre-Mia level, that the guests had breathed a sigh of relief to be no longer subjected to her scrutiny.

"Quite a display," Tim commented and Rina smiled. Tim did admire a bravura performance.

She asked where he would be sitting during the reception.

"Oh, I'm going to be at the top table," he said. "On show. Bridie said I should sit next to Joy and as she's maid of honour . . ." He shrugged. "Why?"

Briefly she told him about Fitch's request and that she and Mac would be keeping tabs on Charlie and his sister through the evening. "Where is Charlie? I've not seen him."

Neither had Rina. They turned back to the buffet and the serious business of selecting lunchtime comestibles and then went in search of George. He had found an empty table at the back of the marquee and was working his way through the food mountain he had been assembling earlier.

"Thought you'd come and find me," he said. He reached beneath the table and produced yet another bottle of fizz. Was everyone filching the stock, Rina wondered as Tim went to fetch some glasses. "Miriam liberated it for us," George said. "She guessed we'd all end up together. This is some do, isn't it? I've been Googling the guests. How does Bridie know all these people?"

"How have you been doing that?" Rina asked. "You don't know who they are."

"Oh, I went to look at the board over there to look at the seating plan and see who was sitting where, I took a picture on my phone. Then I did a search to see if anyone was famous. I'm just being nosy really, but to be honest, I'm feeling a bit out of my depth. I'm better if I give myself something to do."

Rina nodded her understanding. "Well, I know the elderly man in the powered wheelchair is Ben Caprisi," she said. "And the man standing next to him is one of his sons."

George looked at the seating plan on his phone. "Probably Simon, then. There's also a Gianni, so it could be the other way around, I suppose. The man over to his right in the bright purple tie."

Rina looked and thought he seemed vaguely familiar. He was chatting to a very bosomy blonde in a short, bright green dress.

"He was a financier then he was a politician and now he's a CEO of some big company in the City again. I found his picture on their website, though he was much thinner when he had it taken and about ten years younger."

"I suppose we can all be a little vain," Rina laughed. "And who's the woman he's talking to?"

"That's his wife," George said. "She was on the website too. There were pictures of them both at some big expensive bash, they were all dressed to kill. She's Mrs Norman King — that's actually what they'd called her in the pictures. But her name's Elaine on Bridie's seating plan."

"Obviously her husband's the old-fashioned type," Tim said. "Can you imagine if I got married to Joy and tried to call her Mrs Tim Brandon?"

Not so long ago that was just the way it was, Rina reflected. Her mother had always been Mrs David Martin on official correspondence and her sister-in-law had been Mrs Christopher Martin. It had seemed quite normal back then.

"The dark-haired woman who's just getting her glass refilled is a singer. Jazz, from the look of her website. Her name is Tina Marsden, but professionally she just goes by Christine and the man with her is an actor."

"Harrison Teach." Rina nodded. "Was he in that spy thing a few years back? I heard he was doing something off Broadway. He always reckoned to love the stage more than the small screen."

"You know him?" Tim asked.

"Let's just say I've encountered him," Rina said. "It's a pretty mixed bunch," she added, wondering as George had done how Bridie had got to know them all.

"Hello, Rina, how's things? Hi Tim, George."

Rina looked up with a smile and Brian, Bridie's eldest child, bent to kiss her cheek. He pulled up a chair and stole a sausage roll from Rina's plate. "Lynnie's taking the kids upstairs to get ready," he said. "She's really gone to town on this, our mum, hasn't she?"

Rina nodded. She was aware that Brian was glancing around with more than casual interest, that like Mac he was hypervigilant on a day when he was supposed to be relaxing and enjoying the celebration.

"The Brewster siblings are both here," she said. "Charlie turned up early as I've no doubt your mother told you and Mia arrived about half an hour ago. She must have been on the crossing before you. The Caprisis are all here, of course, but my impression is they just want to have a pleasant time and wish your mother well. I can't speak for Tod Donovan, though as he's brought just his latest wife and not the full entourage, I'm guessing he feels the same."

Brian laughed. "God, you don't change, do you. Always with your investigating head on. But no, we're not really worried about the Caprisis or Tod, for that matter. He's more concerned about consolidating his business and keeping the Brewsters out of his hair. Charlie's known to be eyeing up his nightclub chain and more to the point, all the backroom business going on when the clubbers have gone home."

Rina nodded. "So you're walking your mother down the aisle." No one would ever claim to be giving Bridie Duggan away.

"I am indeed. I'm glad she's got someone and even happier that it's Fitch, someone Dad would have approved of."

"And how's Ursula?" Brian asked, turning to George. "Mum was so pleased she agreed to be a bridesmaid, she'd have understood if Ursula thought it would be too much, after . . ." After a murderer Mac was hunting had come within a whisker of taking Ursula's life, Rina thought.

"She's doing OK," George said. "Still has nightmares, but she's looking forward to starting uni and we're trying to find a place closer to my work. One that we can actually afford."

Brian nodded. "Look," he said, "you know if we can help out, we will. You only have to ask."

George blushed, his freckled face suddenly as red as his hair. "Thanks," he managed. "Kind of you."

Rina drew the attention away from her young friend. "Are you staying overnight?"

"No, the kids will be knackered and besides, Lynnie isn't that keen on the company. We understand why Mum had to invite certain people but it's still awkward. We're all hoping that this is the opportunity to draw a final line under things, you know." He glanced at his watch. "Better go. See you later, all of you."

Rina watched him go.

"I don't like the feel of this," Tim said. "There are so many undercurrents even a shark could drown."

Rina was inclined to agree.

* * *

Regis Crick was not in fact back at the house, now converted to holiday flats that he had been using as a base, but was quietly assessing the lie of the land. He guessed that no one would stray very far from the food and drink and knew that Ruari was now set up in the nice little perch in the church tower that Crick had occupied earlier. Later he'd have business in the house, preparations to make, but they had decided that would be better left until most of the staff and all of the guests were occupied in the dining room.

Crick moved through the trees that fringed the lawn, keeping in the shadows, concealed by the summer overgrowth of old rhododendrons and brambles, marking where the ground had been cleared and there was a line of sight towards the house. He circled around the rear of the house and back towards the chapel and guest house. Here the ground was clearer and there were remnants of landscaped gardens, half-concealed paths and borders overgrown with the feral relatives of cultivars, all weeds to Crick's eyes, though he recognised straggly roses and the scent of a honeysuckle. From here he could see the other side of the lawn, the toing and froing from the marquee and the little tents from which champagne and Pimm's were being served. He could not see Charlie Brewster, but he had no real concern about that. Charlie was here and the meeting he believed he'd be having just with Ruari, later that evening, would bring him safely into Crick's range.

He caught a glimpse of Mia, tall and slender and gorgeous in her red dress and for a moment or two pondered on what might have been, if she'd been a bit more willing to see him as anything more than her dad's very disposable paid hand. Well, she was going to pay for that, nothing was so certain.

CHAPTER 7

Rina's own wedding had been a simple registry office affair with friends as witnesses and a quick lunch before the newlyweds left with their rep company to go on to their next job. She had no regrets. She remembered feeling profoundly happy and utterly content and though she had lost her beloved husband only five years into their marriage, Rina always believed that she'd had more happiness in her life than many people who had experienced much longer relationships.

Fitch, standing before the celebrant and surrounded by formal displays, looked oddly nervous. Mac, his best man, had attracted some comments from the guests, Mac being on the opposite side of the law to most of them. Signs and signals, Rina remembered. Fitch and Bridie were signalling a change of path very loudly and very publicly. Charlie Brewster was sitting a few rows behind her and Mia was also out of her eyeline so, frustratingly, Rina could not judge their reaction.

Music signalled the bride's arrival and the company swivelled as one to look at Bridie. Like her daughter Joy, Bridie had red hair, now streaked with silver that she embraced rather than sought to colour. Today it was dressed with flowers and little pearl pins, and the teal blue dress she wore seemed to accentuate its brightness.

"Lovely dress," Miriam whispered. "Oh, look at the little fairies."

The tiny bridesmaids skipped beside the bride and Rina wondered if that was really where they ought to be, though no one seemed fussed. Joy as maid of honour and Ursula as a bridesmaid followed on behind and Rina could not hold back a gasp. The young women seemed transformed.

"Black and gold!" Bethany whispered. "How shockingly wonderful."

"Do you think they're vintage dresses?" Miriam wondered.

Looking at the quality of the silk and the encrusted gold-work, Rina thought they must be. To have survived from the 1920s in this wonderful condition spoke of couture, surely. The shoes were modern but they matched the style. The roses and white orchids in the posies both girls carried filled the air with fragrance.

Rina glanced at George who was staring with his mouth open.

"Bridie promised us something special," she whispered to Miriam, "and she certainly delivered."

No one minded that the little fairies fidgeted and sang while the bride and groom took their vows. One held tight to Ursula's hand, suddenly shy of all the people watching and another wandered off completely before she was scooped up and sat on someone's lap. Bridie's voice was loud and firm and Fitch seemed to have shed his nerves, though his gaze was so full of admiration for his bride that he seemed unable to tear it away, even when Mac tried to hand him the ring.

"So sweet," Bethany said, dabbing her tears with a lace hanky that Rina imagined dated to the same vintage as the dresses. It felt like only minutes before they all trooped out of the marquee to have photographs taken.

"Well, that was lovely, wasn't it, Eliza?" Bethany declared. "And don't our Joy and our Ursula look splendid?"

Our Joy and our Ursula, Rina thought. She knew exactly what Bethany meant. The two young women and George had become so much part of the family that, together with

Tim, they could not have been more loved if they had been blood relations.

It was good, she thought, to have younger people around. Bethany and Eliza were a good deal older than Rina and had no living family of their own. Their friends were either very elderly or had already been bid a final farewell, it did them all good to take an interest in a younger generation. Rina liked to think the benefits cut both ways.

"Is it my imagination or are weddings over more quickly these days?" Matthew asked. The red ribbon fastening his ponytail was coming loose so Eliza retied it for him.

"I think that's because church services usually had a set form," Rina said. "I can even recall attending one at which the vicar preached a sermon. There have been so many weddings over the years, haven't there." And babies born and grown — and, latterly, too many funerals.

"We have some lovely memories, don't we," Stephen said, taking her arm — a sure sign that his knees and back were giving him pain and he wanted to sit down. They made their way over to a free table and Matthew and Eliza were dispatched in search of Pimm's. In Rina's view, summer wasn't summer without fruit punch and she also held the slightly controversial view that it had far too much fruit in it to be considered truly alcoholic.

"So when do we start our little job for Fitch?" Bethany asked. "Mia is across the lawn and Charlie is by the marquee. I don't think either of them will make trouble while the photographs are being taken, do you?"

Rina glanced across to where Bridie, Fitch, the wedding party, various relatives and friends and two photographers plus a videographer were engaged in some complicated ballet. No doubt the Frantham contingent would be summoned in due course to take their turn around the grassy dance floor. "No," she agreed, "not unless they really want to make a scene."

The danger points would be between the taking of the photographs and the start of the reception, and then the less formal part of the evening between the wedding breakfast and Bridie and Fitch's departure.

George wandered over and Rina asked, "Seeing as you now have an encyclopaedic knowledge of the other guests, who's that Charlie's talking to?" It looked like the young man who had arrived with Mia and he looked distinctly uncomfortable, glancing around surreptitiously as though for an escape route.

She directed George's attention over to where Charlie was deep in conversation with two men. Whatever was being said, none of them seemed particularly happy about it.

"The older one on the left is one of the Caprisi family. I think he's the eldest grandson. He owns restaurants or something, mostly in London. The other is Silas Bannerman. I didn't need to look him up."

"The actor," Bethany said. "Surely you recognise him, Rina. He's been in that awful thing about the royal family. All that scandal and angst."

"He's been in other things too," George said. "He did a lot of action movies when he was younger. Did his own stunts. Broke an ankle in the last one and had to have it pinned."

Rina raised a quizzical eyebrow. "You seem to know a lot about him."

"I like action movies," George said. "All those unreal explosions and people who carry on running and fighting the bad guys even though they've been shot in the head. I used to watch them with Karen. It was so much better than real life."

Rina supposed it was. For quite a long time, George had been reluctant to talk about his absent sister Karen, the subject a painful one. Rina wasn't sure if she was gladdened or troubled by his casual reference to her now. As she watched, Silas Bannerman finally managed to extricate himself from the conversation and walk away. The Caprisi grandson ignored his departure, but Charlie looked annoyed and almost ready to call him back, Rina thought. She guessed that Charlie was not used to people walking away from him without his say so.

Her thoughts were interrupted both by Matthew and Eliza returning with trays of Pimm's and a summons from Bridie. It was their turn to be immortalised in the wedding photographs.

* * *

Two men held Graham Stevens, held him hard, his legs had given way and they dragged him between them, feet scuffling on the concrete. His face was black with bruises, tears streaking the muck and snot and vomit that stained his chin and tie and suit. And he was screaming, sobbing, begging, his protests falling on deaf ears. Terry was pathetically grateful that Gray could not turn around and look him in the face. Terry knew that should that happen he would have completely fallen apart. He could feel the panic rising, the churning in his belly, the tightness in his lungs, the need to look as though none of this mattered, it was none of his concern.

Terry Pritchard jerked into wakefulness, his heart racing and the breath frozen in his chest. For a few moments the rising panic took control of him and the feeling that he couldn't breathe overwhelmed everything else. Making a major effort, he went through the exercises his therapist had taught him, grounding himself, pulling his thoughts back to this moment, what he could see and feel and touch and smell, away from the flashback dream of seeing Graham Stevens die.

Finally, his lungs relaxed and he was able to take a deeper breath; though it still felt as though someone was tightening a broad belt across his chest and choking the air from him. The dizziness caused by the lack of air, the blurring of his vision warned him that if he didn't get control, he'd pass out again, but the more he fought to control his body's reaction the more it seemed to fight him.

Breathe shallow, his therapist had told him. Take little shallow breaths. It will make you feel light-headed at first, like you're hyperventilating, but gradually it will get easier. Just try not to panic and try not to force it.

Easier said than done, Terry thought.

Slowly, as the dream images faded and the room swam back into focus, his breathing eased. Focus on what you can see: the television, some old movie, black and white, volume turned down. The small sofa, brown cord, blue cushions — neither his choice, donated by his sister when she had moved house and he had first moved in here. Bookshelves, stereo, family photographs. His sister and her kids. His sister and her husband on their wedding day. Terry and Sam when they had both been kids themselves. What would she think if she could see him now?

Slowly he got to his feet, went through to the kitchen and ran the cold tap over his wrists. He splashed water on his face, relishing the controlled shock. Managed a deeper breath. He glanced at the kitchen clock and realised that it was still only four in the afternoon. He'd slept for maybe an hour. There was still the rest of the day to get through and then another day tomorrow. Work was bearable; he was able to keep busy and he felt useful and the colleagues he was now working with had not known him before, a transfer to a different location being part of the deal when he'd resumed his duties. The downside of that was that he was still finding his place within the team.

He'd made an effort to be friendly as them but it was difficult to find a niche within an already established group. It felt too much like being back at school. He just focussed on getting his job done, being accommodating, feeling like he was very much on the outside.

Give it time, he told himself as he had done every day. Give it time. It will get better in the end.

CHAPTER 8

Once the photographs had been taken, there was still about an hour before the formal meal was due to begin and the new-lyweds mingled with their guests, accepting compliments and congratulations. While Rina didn't think that either Charlie or Mia would want to make a scene it was still possible for either of them to corner Bridie under cover of wishing her well and make life uncomfortable for her. Rina and the gang went into action, ensuring that they had Mia and Charlie in view at all times.

When Mia appeared to be making a beeline for Bridie, Eliza and Bethany swooped. "Oh what a lovely dress. It looks like a vintage design, my dear, and so beautifully cut. It looks like a Schiaparelli."

Rina smiled at Mia's look of confusion, a confusion that deepened as Bethany called Mrs Myers to join the conversation and Mia found herself surrounded. She could see the young woman desperately looking for an escape route. By the time she had excused herself from the effusive approval of Bethany, Eliza and Mrs Myers, Bridie had moved on. Rina was satisfied to observe the look of confusion on the young woman's face. Eliza and Bethany, in full flow, could have that effect.

"Did you enjoy the ceremony?" Rina asked politely as Mia passed by. "You're Charlie's sister, aren't you?"

Mia scowled at her, then seemed consciously to change her expression. She sighed. "It was . . . nice," she said. "And yes I am. Who are you?"

Others might have been put off both by the scowl and her tone but Rina was not other people. She extended her hand. Mia shook it automatically. "Rina Martin," she said. "A friend of the family."

Mia's eyes narrowed. "You're the actress," she said. "The interfering detective woman in that television series."

Rina laughed. "*Lydia Marchant Investigates*. Yes, I'm afraid I am. Charlie told me that your father used to like it."

Rina was certain that she saw Mia wince. "He did. Sorry, I'm really not a fan."

She was glancing around as though looking for someone. Rina assumed she was trying to find Bridie but was happy to see that Mia's quarry was deep in conversation with Ben Caprisi and Mia was unlikely to disturb that little tête-à-tête. The look of annoyance on Mia's face a moment later told her that her assumption was correct.

"I think your plus one is looking for you," Rina told her, indicating the young man coming towards them with champagne flutes gripped a little too tightly in his fists. She stepped aside with a smile. "Lovely to meet you," she added and went on her way.

"Meeting averted," Eliza said coming to Rina's side.

"For now. I get the impression that she's not trying too hard, as yet."

"Or doesn't want to be seen as trying too hard," Eliza mused. "I don't think she's someone who wants to look desperate."

Rina nodded, realising that Eliza was probably correct. "But desperate about what?" she wondered. "What is so important that it needs to be settled here and now?"

"Whatever it was that Charlie tackled Fitch about, I suppose. Oh Rina, I've suddenly thought, if Fitch isn't Fitch anymore, what on earth do we call him? I couldn't bear to call him Reggie or Reginald, it just doesn't suit."

Rina suppressed a laugh at the sudden change in conversational direction. "I think he'll always be Fitch to his friends," she reassured Eliza. "I certainly won't be calling him anything else."

Meandering through the throng of guests Rina caught snatches of conversation. Occasionally she paused to eavesdrop. She had learned as she'd got older that women of a certain age, like children and waiting staff, were often disregarded to the point almost of invisibility. They became inconsequential. Rina, at full brilliance, was difficult for anyone to ignore, but Rina, tuned down to the muted pastel of a casual sixty-something wedding guest, could be surprisingly invisible.

Ben Caprisi was talking to a man he called Alex, the younger man bending down so he could listen closely to the man in the wheelchair. As Rina skirted their group, she heard Caprisi comment that he hoped the bloody lawyers could sort things to which Alex speculated that they were paid enough.

"Which probably won't encourage them to hurry," he added.

A little further towards the house she came across two knots of guests that she didn't know. The men, suited and booted, stood apart from their womenfolk and were talking football. The four women seemed to be chatting about Mia Brewster — unless there was someone else present wearing a red dress with a drape back. The part of the conversation that Rina overheard flitted from reluctant admiration for Mia's rather beautiful shoulders and back to rumours about the will. "Uri says that Ben Caprisi says that they've got to reclaim what Mal thought was his territory. I mean, right back from when he inherited Gandy's firm. You ask me, he was losing it big time before the end and now the kids have got to fight it out. If Mia had any sense, she'd take what she's got and get the hell out."

"Mia wants more, you know that," another woman said and the others nodded in agreement.

"Oh, but you can't blame the poor girl," the first woman said. "No child of Mal Brewster's could turn out normal. He made their lives a misery from the moment they could walk, always demanding, never satisfied. If one of them made a success of something the other was supposed to do twice as well. And even then he was never satisfied."

There was a murmur of agreement and a moment of considered silence before the conversation moved on to speculation as to where Bridie had found the bridesmaids' dresses.

Rina would quite like to know that too.

She passed on. Across the lawn she could see Brian and two other men she didn't know. Brian appeared to be playing peacemaker and from the body language of the other two, neither of them seemed keen to give way. Just a drunken quarrel? Rina wondered, sipping from her near-empty glass. Or more? She could see Fitch casting uneasy glances in their direction and, none too subtly, while steering Bridie far away.

There was, Rina felt, despite the bonhomie that characterised most of the behaviour, a simmering tension that she guessed had a lot to do with the Brewsters and with the impact of Malcolm Brewster's will. Just from the point of view of idle curiosity, Rina would have loved to read that particular document.

She caught sight of Mia across the sweep of lawn. The young woman was standing close to the little copse that stood between the edge of the lawn and the chapel. She looked so isolated and lonely that Rina's heart went out to her.

Rina began to make her way across the grass towards the young woman, but progress was slow, and it was hard to keep Mia in sight as other guests drifted between and frankly got in her way. By the time she had reached halfway Mia had moved and was now standing beside one of the small gazebos and perusing the range of drinks. Judging by the scowl on her face, she disapproved of Bridie's choice of alcohol.

Rina approached with a smile and, noting how busy the waitress was, grabbed a bottle from the table and recharged her own glass. "At least the weather's held," she said blandly. "Apparently they had heavy rain until a couple of days ago."

Mia stared at her for a moment and then held out her own glass for a refill from Rina. "Why should I care?" she said.

Rina considered her thoughtfully for a moment and then said, "It must take so much effort," she said.

"What must?"

"To present such an unpleasant facade to the world all the time."

Mia opened her mouth as though to respond but they were interrupted by a woman in a grey dress asking Rina, who was still holding onto the bottle of fizz, if she would refill her glass. Rina obliged. She noted with amusement that Mia, clearly impatient to leave, was effectively trapped between herself, the newcomer and the drinks table.

"That's a very pretty necklace," Rina said to the woman and from the corner of her eye caught Mia raising a sceptical eyebrow.

"Oh, this?" The woman stroked the bright red stones in their elaborate setting. "It is rather lovely. A present from my husband on our wedding day and, just imagine, we're about to celebrate our ruby anniversary." She laughed again and hiccoughed. "I still love to wear it."

How much champagne has she had? Rina wondered. "Rubies are pretty gemstones," Rina said.

She raised her glass as though to toast Mia and then wandered across the lawn once more.

She had, she realised, completely lost track of Charlie Brewster and was very surprised to find him perched on a wall, one of the tiny fairies on his lap and other children gathered around a card table watching Tim performing magic. A handful of adult guests stood around this little group, trying to pretend they were too grown up for simple magic tricks but clearly amused and entertained.

He'd gathered a selection of props — a pack of playing cards, plastic tumblers and a handful of coins and a handkerchief he had tied into rabbit ears with a loop for his finger. The pretend rabbit seemed very popular with his young audience and he appeared to be keeping them very happily entertained.

Considering how much he had hated performing at children's parties, Rina was impressed. Charlie Brewster looked as entranced as the kids, as Tim disappeared the handkerchief rabbit and produced coins from behind ears and fairy wings. She watched the last few minutes of Tim's impromptu magic show until the tannoy announced that it was time for everyone to proceed to the dining room for the wedding breakfast.

Wedding afternoon tea, Rina thought, recalling her conversation with Bridie.

Charlie fell into step beside her. "He's very talented," Charlie said.

"He is. You should come and see some of the big illusions he performs at the Palisades Hotel, back in Frantham. He also does some really sophisticated close up when they have cabaret evenings."

Charlie nodded. "Perhaps I will," he said. "I enjoy a bit of misdirection."

Rina had the distinct impression that he was referring to her.

"You sister doesn't seem to be having a happy time," she commented.

Charlie frowned. "I don't think she knows how," he said. "Mia doesn't do relaxed or enthusiastic."

"And you do? Relax, I mean. I think you can manage the enthusiasm well enough."

Charlie laughed. To Rina's ear he sounded genuinely amused, delighted, even. "It's hard to relax when someone's checking your every move," he said quietly.

"Your father? I've heard a lot about him and if I may say, none of it good."

For a moment, observing Charlie's sudden frown, she wondered if she had overstepped. Then Charlie smiled. "No doubt all true," he said. "He's a hard act to follow."

"Maybe you shouldn't try," Rina suggested.

"Oh, Rina," Charlie said quietly. "You and I really do inhabit different worlds."

* * *

Ruari walked confidently along the short corridor and into the kitchen, carrying a box of empty bottles he had picked up at the back of the marquee and a folded tablecloth he had taken from one of the tables. He had long since realised that it didn't really matter what you did as long as you did it confidently, and a man wearing similar enough gear to the caterers and looking as though he ought to be carrying a jangling box and a wine-stained tablecloth was unlikely to be challenged or even noticed.

He was rattled though; seeing Mia talking to Regis Crick, the latter concealed from view of the other guests but very visible from where Ruari was standing, had disturbed him deeply. What if Crick had ratted him out? As he'd drawn closer, though, he'd realised that whatever Crick was saying to his half sibling, she wasn't having any of it. After a few minutes of obviously bad-tempered exchange, Mia had simply walked away, leaving Crick visibly fuming. Ruari had ducked out of sight just as he'd stormed off, leaving Ruari to wonder what all that had been about and wondering also how Mia would react when her brother Charlie ended up dead. What was the deal here?

He'd had no time to ponder too deeply, the guests had left the lawn and headed for the dining room, most of the staff with them. Ruari had waited until he judged the first course was being served and then made his way inside. Once in the kitchen, he dumped his box on the counter and dodged back out into the corridor. He opened a small door leading down to the cellar, carrying the cloth with him. Even a casual glance now would show that he had something wrapped in the cloth, but he had judged his time well and there was no one close enough to see. As he slipped through the door, he heard a rise in the level of noise and footsteps as staff emerged from the dining room, the sound cut off as he closed the door and descended into the first of the cellars.

Switching on his torch, he made his way through several basement rooms until he reached a heavy door, padlocked and bolted. He removed the bolt croppers he'd been carrying from the folded cloth and crammed that into a box of junk, one of several left in this clearly little-used basement room. It took effort to cut through the padlock; it separated with a loud crack. He opened the hasp and absentmindedly hooked the lock back over the loop, then drew back the bolt and opened the door.

There would be no need to risk returning through the house. One more door, one gate, and then he would be free and clear and the entrance from tunnels to house would be open.

Easy, Ruari thought. He emerged cautiously into the sunken garden and climbed the steep steps up to the little scrap of lawn above. Crick had already picked out a hiding place for the bolt croppers, a hollow oak providing the perfect spot.

Ruari wiped them down, despite the fact that he'd been wearing white gloves, just like all the waiting staff. He wedged the long-handled tool into the gap, hidden from sight but easy to retrieve. Then paused, his mind suddenly filled with unease at what was to come.

All he had to do was distract brother Charlie, he told himself. Crick would do the rest. But that didn't mean Ruari was too keen on seeing it done. And Charlie, of course, was only half the problem; there would still be Mia to deal with.

CHAPTER 9

At nine o'clock, Bridie and Fitch left for the airport and many of the other guests followed shortly afterwards, cars and mini-buses waiting for them on the far bank. Many would be staying in local hotels for the night with just a handful remaining on the island.

The staff began their clear-up around midnight as a few stray guests including Rina and Eliza remained on the lawn chatting and finishing the last of the champagne. Rina and Eliza sat companionably, chatting about the day, drinking in the moonlight and watching Mia and her young man beside the lake. They appeared to be arguing. Fragments of conversation drifted over to Rina; Mia appeared to be trying to persuade her companion that he should leave that night, not wait until the following day. She seemed quite intense, Rina noted; was she just bored with his company or was she expecting trouble? As Rina watched, Silas Bannerman seemed to give in. His shoulders sagged and he nodded his head. He bent to kiss her, a tender sort of kiss, Rina thought, tenderly returned. Out of character with the spiky Mia she had encountered that afternoon. Was there another side to this young woman?

She watched with interest as the couple parted; Silas Bannerman heading towards the house, presumably to collect his belongings, and Mia remaining by the lake, staring fixedly across the water.

"That is a very troubled young woman," Eliza said of Mia. "She reminds me of that other poor scrap."

"Who?" Rina asked.

"Well, young Karen, of course. George's sister. Look at what she became and yet for a very long time you had a real soft spot for her."

That was true, Rina acknowledged. There had a been a time when her love and concern for Karen had matched that which she felt for George.

"Things might have turned out very differently had they not had complete horrors for parents."

"Well, that's probably true," Rina conceded, "though Karen's mother wasn't a horror, she was as much a victim as the children were."

"True," Eliza agreed. "Poor woman, but the father was a brute."

"And George is surely proof that not everyone who has experienced a traumatic childhood turns into a reprehensible human being."

"No, of course not, but when there's no balance, no alternative to just pure survival it doesn't exactly do anyone any good, does it?"

Rina had to agree there. "And what do you think of Charlie Brewster?" she asked. "You could say exactly the same thing about him."

"Oh and I do. The difference between Charlie and his sister is that Charlie is a shark. He must keep swimming otherwise he'll drown. So he concentrates on promoting his public image, swimming around, keeping everyone on side, at least for as long as it suits him. Making everyone feel he's relatively harmless. After all it's easy to see a shark coming at you most of the time, to get out of the way if it looks like it's about to bite. Not that you can ever really tell, of course."

Rina thought about all the stories she'd heard about surfers having their boards chomped out from beneath them, but she supposed that was the point Eliza was making. If they'd seen the shark they'd have stayed out of the water and just admired the sleek lines from a distance.

"And Mia?" she asked.

"Now Mia is more of an ambush predator, but she doesn't exactly bother hiding that."

Their conversation was interrupted by the woman in the grey dress Rina had encountered that afternoon. It transpired she was one of the guests from the cottages. She introduced herself as Mrs Clark and was clearly very distressed, and Rina immediately asked her what was wrong and if they could help. It seemed she had lost the necklace she'd worn at the reception.

"I know I had it on when the dancing started," she said woefully. "I was so certain I'd still had it on when we went back to the cottage. I have this memory of putting it on my bedside table intending to get the box and put it back in the little wall safe, but then it was gone."

"And you're certain you had it at the cottage?" Eliza asked. "I don't mean to be rude, but I think we were all a tad squiffy when the party broke up. And you know what it's like, your mind tells you you've done what you always do, but it's easy to be mistaken."

"Oh, that's what my husband said, just before he fell asleep in the chair. And I'm sure you're both right, and to be honest I'd started to doubt myself, so I thought I'd come out here and have a look around."

"I'll help you look," Eliza said. "Rina, you go and check in the house, someone might have handed it to a member of staff."

This was code for go and tell Mac, Rina thought. She nodded and headed inside.

She was startled to find Mia Brewster in the atrium, sitting on the stairs, still in her red dress, a glass on the step beside her. Rina had not noticed her come back across the lawn. She glanced up as Rina entered and there was a split second when Rina glimpsed the girl behind the dissatisfied pout. A girl who was deeply unhappy.

"Hello," Rina said. "Any members of staff around? I need to see if anyone's handed in a lost necklace."

Mia frowned. "I think there might still be someone in the dining room, I heard them clattering about a few minutes ago". She studied Rina carefully. "I didn't think you were wearing a necklace today," she said. "Just your pretty brooch."

Rina was surprised at the observation. Reflexively she reached to touch the brooch, a present from the Peters sisters some years before. It wasn't valuable, this little Victorian crescent moon set with seed pearls, but she was very fond of it. "No," she said. "I've not lost anything. Mrs Clark who's staying at one of the cottages has lost hers. She was certain she'd just put it down on a bedside cabinet and when she came back, it was gone. She's now wondering if she was mistaken and lost it in the garden earlier on. She's the woman who came to get some more champagne when we were chatting this afternoon. You might remember?" Mia narrowed her eyes, as though concentrating. "Grey dress, grey hair. I spotted her later with her husband. He was spiking his champagne glass with whatever he had in his hip flask."

Rina laughed. "I noticed that too," she said. "Yes, that's the one. She was wearing a very pretty necklace that looked like it was set with rubies."

Mia's eyes narrowed. "Looked like?"

"Umm." Rina took a seat beside Mia, perching on the same broad step.

Mia turned so she could look directly at her. "You know something about jewellery? Is there no end to the talents of Rina Martin?"

Rina ignored the mocking tone. "Years ago, when I was between jobs, I worked in a pawnbroker. I learned a lot about jewellery and a fair bit about people."

"I'll bet you did. You know my dad's first shop was a pawnbroker."

"I didn't, but it makes sense. Very few pawnbrokers back in the day were much bothered by where their stock came from and if they thought it might be a bit too hot to handle, my experience was that there was generally someone out of the area they could hand it off to. There was usually some kind of quid pro quo involved."

Mia laughed, taking Rina by surprise. She would have sworn the girl was incapable.

"You're surprisingly sharp, aren't you. Doesn't explain how you spotted the rubies, though," she said.

"Well, I can't be certain, of course, but I spent several minutes chatting to Mrs Clark earlier, and was close enough to get a good look. There's something not quite right about the colour or the clarity of old pastes. Synthetics or lab grown now, they really are much harder to spot. But I did have my doubts about hers."

"You think she knows?" Mia asked.

"I imagine she at least suspects," Rina said. "If she wore the stones before they were swapped out then she'd have noticed a difference in the weight, if nothing else. And the feel of the stones, perhaps. It occurs to me, though, that a little tiny bit of research would tell her what kind of guests she might find at Bridie Duggan's wedding. It would be a perfect place to lose a paste necklace and claim the insurance value of a genuine one."

Mia regarded her with open surprise. "You're a devious old bat, aren't you?"

"I'm not the one whose lost the necklace. I've nothing to be devious about."

"No, but your brain went straight there, didn't it? To the possibility of a scam. That's not the way regular people think."

"I suppose not," Rina agreed.

Mia regarded her with what Rina felt was real interest and curiosity then seemed to make up her mind. "Leave it with me," she said. "Mrs Clark will get her necklace back. She can do what she likes on her own turf but I see no reason why she should taint Bridie's wedding."

Rina nodded, feeling some trepidation on behalf of who-ever it was who had been stupid enough to steal on an occasion like this. She was also a little surprised that Mia would care about what she referred to as a taint. "You really like Bridie," she said, unable to keep the surprise out of her tone.

Mia laughed again. "Despite what you may think, I'm capable of liking people," she said. "And yes, I like Bridie. Fitch too for that matter and I was really fond of Patrick. He was kind. He listened."

Again, there was a glimpse of the vulnerable young woman hiding behind the armoured facade but it seemed Rina had seen all she was going to of that side of Mia. She watched as the shutters came down and the girl's expression lost its openness.

Rina got to her feet, suddenly aware of how weary she felt. It had been an interesting day, a joyful one in many ways but also a long one. She had been intending to go straight up to speak to Mac. He would of course feel obliged to speak to this woman, but Rina felt that could safely be left until the following morning. Instead, she went back out into the garden where Eliza and Mrs Clark appeared to have given up their search.

"Best we have a proper look in the morning," Rina said. "And you never know, one of the staff might come across it and hand it in."

"I suppose so," Mrs Clark agreed.

"You know it's a fake?" Eliza said as they watched her walk away.

Rina must have looked slightly surprised because Eliza went on, "Oh, Rina dear, I've worn enough fake sparkle to recognise it when I see it. Agreed it was a pretty thing and very nicely made, but rubies, my eye."

"I thought the same," Rina said. "I just had a very interesting conversation with Mia Brewster," she added. "I'm sure Mrs Clark will be getting her necklace back sooner than she expects."

Later, Rina stood looking out of the window, her dark blue kimono pulled tightly round her and her fluffy slippers on her feet. She felt weary but uncertain of how fast sleep would come. So many thoughts competed for attention in her mind, so many that she was finding it hard to catch the tail of any of them. She had spoken to Mac and explained the situation and he had agreed that he should stay officially ignorant of the loss — and ramifications — until the morning. Slowly the house had settled for the night, lights had been extinguished, only the creaks and groans of an old house settling broke the silence. Rina shed her dressing gown and slippers and got into bed.

Later, much later, she was roused by a noise she could not identify. She lay still, listening to the nighttime sounds but could not work out what had roused her. Rina, too comfortable and tired to investigate further, drifted back to sleep.

CHAPTER 10

At breakfast the following morning Rina was glad to see that she was not the only one looking a little worse for wear. Mac and Miriam were at their usual table but the rest of her friends seemed to be having a lie-in. Mac definitely looked a little green around the gills and was nibbling half-heartedly at a piece of toast and marmalade, casting resentful looks at Miriam who was tucking into a full English.

Rina followed Mac's example, though she began to feel better after her first cup of tea. She was thinking she could probably manage some scrambled egg and maybe a little bacon. "I was disturbed in the night," she said. "I don't know what woke me before, but when I got up this morning, I found this hanging on the outside of my door."

She took a small paper giftbag with ribbon handles from her bag and handed it to Mac.

He peered inside. "The missing necklace."

"Quite so."

"Any idea who left it?"

"No. I expect it was at Mia's direction but I suspect if she had dealt with this personally, she would have left it without waking me. I suggest we tell Mrs Clark that it was handed in to one of the staff. It might be interesting to see her reaction."

"It might indeed, if your theory is right," Mac agreed. "Miriam and I thought we'd take the ferry and then go off somewhere for a bit," he added.

"Sounds like a nice idea. Where will you go?"

"There's a sculpture park not far away, then a pub lunch and maybe find an antique shop or something," Miriam said. "You know, act like we're really on a couple of days' holiday instead of just hanging round criminals like we usually do."

"It has been a bit of a busman's holiday so far," Rina agreed.

"Oh the wedding was lovely, wouldn't have missed it. But I definitely have this yen to go and do something lazy and frivolous," Miriam told her. "God knows when we'll next get the opportunity and as Bridie's been lovely enough to book us these two extra days, I feel we should make the most of them."

And Mac didn't seem inclined to oppose that, Rina thought. "Can you spare him for an hour while we return the necklace?" she asked.

Miriam pretended to consider. "I suppose you can have him for that long," she agreed. She glanced around the dining room. "Not many have made it down to breakfast," she added. "I may just have a second helping while you're gone."

About half an hour later, Rina having succumbed to eggs and bacon after all, she and Mac took a walk to the Clarks' holiday let, wondering somewhat belatedly if anyone would be up yet. Rina knocked gently on the door and after a while it was opened by a rather bleary looking Mr Clark. Rina handed him the bag and, bemused, he peered inside.

"Your wife's necklace," Rina said. "What luck! It was found this morning so the inspector and I thought we'd bring it straight over. I hope we didn't wake you?"

Mr Clark stared at her. "She lost it?" he asked. "I mean, yes, she lost it. But I thought—"

Rina waited, but he didn't seem to know what he'd thought. She saw the realisation dawn on him that she'd referred to Mac as an inspector and the confusion in his eyes as thoughts rushed and jostled in his still sleepy brain.

"You must be relieved to get it back," Mac said. "We'll leave you in peace now. Enjoy your day."

"You're giggling like a schoolgirl," Mac accused as they walked away.

"Oh, did you see his face? Mac, that was priceless!"

"They still conspired to commit a crime," Mac said.

"We don't have any proof of that. Perhaps you could call Sergeant Baker, or Andy and get them to see if the Clarks have a record. The house manager will have their address. It's a pity you don't have your laptop here, or you could do that yourself."

"I didn't bring my laptop because I'm officially on holiday," he reminded her. "Besides, I can't log in to a police computer from just anywhere, you know that. And if nothing else happens then I'm quite happy to ignore the Clarks until I get home. As you say, there is absolutely no proof, simply a weird set of coincidences. And now, having dealt with that weird set of coincidences, I'm going to take some time off."

Rina nodded. This had been a stressful year and especially the last few months when the murder case Mac had been dealing with had impacted them all. He deserved a break. She was about to tell him so when a piercing scream pushed all other thoughts out of her head. Mac set off at a run with Rina close behind. The sound had come from the direction of the sunken garden and had drawn others as well so that by the time they arrived, the house manager and a member of staff were only seconds behind. A young woman stood on the path, beside the fence, staring down at the area below, a tray and broken glasses on the ground beside her. Rina recognised her as one of the waitresses from the day before and guessed she had come out in search of stray glasses.

Instinctively she put an arm around the girl and drew her away from the edge but not before she had seen what had caused such a grievous reaction. A man lay at the foot of the artificial cliff, sprawling across one of the raised beds and it was pretty obvious that he was dead.

CHAPTER 11

Mac watched as Rina, now joined by Emilie the house manager, led the young woman away. She was shaking and clearly distressed. Only when they were out of sight did he descend the steep flight of steps down to the gardens.

One look at Rina's face had told him that she had recognised the victim. It was Charlie Brewster.

Mac was very conscious that he must preserve the scene. But he also knew he had to make sure Charlie was dead. He moved around to where he could see more of the head and face and knew within a second that there was no reason for him to get closer. The side of the face, pressed close against the rocks that enclosed the raised bed, was bashed so severely that Mac would not have been able to recognise Brewster from that side alone. That injury might have been caused by the fall but the blow, Mac thought, to the back of the skull was more likely the main cause of death and had instigated the fall in the first place.

"You want me to come down?" Miriam's voice from above caused him to look up.

"We're going to need photographs and call in the locals. We'll need a full CSI team."

"Already being organised. I've just logged this as a suspicious death. I had to call Frank Baker back in Frantham and get him to sort it out from there. I don't know anyone up here and I thought dialling the nines might attract the wrong sort of response from our fellow guests. Like they might be gone before our colleagues get here."

He saw her glancing up at the sky and was suddenly aware of the clouds that had not been there when he and Rina had set out for the cottage. "Heavy rain predicted in about an hour," she told him. "So, first priority is to secure the scene."

He nodded. "What about one of those small gazebo things they were using yesterday?"

"Good thinking. I'll get Tim to give me a hand. You stay there and see if you can find something to mark the route you took to get down or if not, at least get some photographs of the body. I'll see if I can find something to act as footplates. We need to get as much secured as we can, ready for when the local CSI come to take over."

Then she was gone and Mac was left with the very dead Charlie Brewster.

How long had the man been dead? Mac wondered. He reached across to touch Charlie's outstretched hand, then drew back, knowing he should not risk touching the body. Charlie had landed with one arm beneath his body and the other seemed to be reaching for something behind where Mac stood. He knew this was an illusion; Charlie's face was a mess from the fall but Mac doubted that was what had killed him. Charlie was not likely to have been conscious enough to do anything after the blow had caved in his skull, and definitely not have been capable of pointing accusingly. Even so he caught himself glancing behind as though some vital piece of evidence might lie there.

There was nothing but an undisturbed bed of lavender — now past its best — and clipped rosemary. He turned his attention back to the body, reached out again, wanting to check for rigor but then pulled back.

Best not to touch anything, not to risk any kind of unintentional transfer. Someone had murdered Charlie Brewster and though Mac was unlikely to be the one to chase them down, he had no wish to do anything that might make his colleagues' lives more complicated.

He recalled what Miriam had said about creating a single identifiable pathway that could be used by investigators, keeping the rest of the scene unsullied, but could see nothing that might be of assistance in doing that. Instead, he carefully analysed the path he had taken, descending down the steps and then skirting the raised bed, keeping close to the little wall that enclosed the next one along. He recorded it on his phone and then took some preliminary pictures of the scene.

The sky was rapidly darkening. The wind getting up, not so noticeable in this sheltered spot but visible in the increased movement of the trees above and the clouds above the trees, bruised and dark and now laden with rain. He was profoundly relieved to hear voices and then to see Miriam and Tim, carrying a folded gazebo between them, appear at the top of the steps.

"I stayed as close to the wall as possible coming down," he said. "Then I kept close to the lavender bed. Come down and I can direct you from there."

"Will do," Miriam acknowledged. She had changed from the summer dress she had worn at breakfast into trousers and a T-shirt, the closest things she had to work clothes, and to Mac's surprise, both she and Tim appeared to be popping shoe covers over their feet before descending. As they got closer, he realised these were just large freezer bags tied in place, obviously borrowed from the hotel kitchen.

"Mind you don't slip," he said, watching anxiously as they descended, the large gazebo they carried awkward and unwieldly. As they reached the bottom of the steps the first drops of rain began to fall.

* * *

Rina stared out at the pouring rain wondering if Tim and Miriam had managed to get the gazebo to Mac before the torrent began. She could no longer see the lawn, never mind the lake. The young woman who had discovered the body had calmed down a little now and, at Rina's urging, was busy writing down exactly what had happened. Rina knew just how fast true memory could become contaminated by what people thought they should have seen and done — often influenced by the questions and demands of other people. She had explained this to Emilie Trudeau, the house manager and earned herself a very odd look.

"I suppose you would know something about this," Emilie said, "when you have a police officer as a friend."

Rina agreed and noted that Emile seemed more relaxed with Rina's expertise, once she had explained it to her own satisfaction.

How much did Emilie know about the background of the other guests, Rina wondered. Perhaps she generally found it expedient not to know too much?

Rina's phone rang. It was Constable Andy Nevins from back in Frantham.

"Sergeant Baker thought you could do with an update," he said. "Local officers and CSI hope to be with you soon but apparently you're having rubbish weather up there and some of the back roads are threatening to flood, so they may be a bit delayed."

"The rain started about fifteen minutes ago," Rina confirmed. "I thought we only had deluges like this on the coast, but apparently not. I'm told it's been bad for the past week, seems we got a nice break in the weather for the wedding but now the rain is back with a vengeance. Have you spoken to Mac?"

"Sergeant Baker's just been on the phone to him. He's worried about the scene flooding. It's some kind of sunken garden?"

"It is, yes, and with very little drainage from what I saw."

"He said he and the others are sheltering in some kind of tunnel?"

"It's a sort of underground folly," Rina told him. "Though I don't imagine they'll want to be there for long. And if the locals have been delayed, well I don't really see what Mac and Miriam can do on their own, especially not in a downpour."

"Well, I'll let you know when I've got any more information," Andy told her.

She was grateful for that, Rina thought as she slipped her phone into her pocket. Technically, neither Andy nor Frank Baker needed to keep her in the loop but Rina had been involved in so many local difficulties that she supposed they were accustomed to her being around. And besides, the young constable and the older sergeant were also now good friends.

She thought about the roads they had taken to get to the hotel. They were little more than back lanes, narrow and hedged and muddy from farm traffic and soon, she imagined, running like rivers in full spate. And what about the river and the canal they had crossed before reaching the parkland that bordered the lake? The canal she assumed would be well regulated and not liable to flood. She had spotted a balancing pool at a little distance from that first bridge. The river was a different matter. She had noticed when they crossed the second bridge that the level had seemed very high but had not thought much about it at the time. Was that likely to flood and compromise access to the bridge now?

Through the partly open door she spied Ursula and George hovering in the hallway, Joy in the background. Rina checked that the young waitress had finished writing her account and then leaving her in the capable hands of the house manager, Rina went to join her young friends.

"What's going on?" George demanded. "The staff are saying someone died."

Rina ushered them into one of the other small sitting rooms and closed the door. Quickly she filled them in on the events of the past half hour — had it really been so short a time?

"And he was definitely dead?" George asked.

"Very definitely?"

"And it was Charlie Brewster?" Joy sounded awed.

"From what I saw, certainly. Of course, I didn't go down, but I've spent enough time with him that I don't think I'm mistaken."

Joy nodded. "Does Mia know?"

"Not unless one of the staff have told her. I suppose someone should, but I feel it ought to be someone official."

Joy squared her shoulders. "Look," she said, "I think maybe I should be the one to do that. Mac and Miriam have their hands full and it doesn't look as though they're going to get reinforcements any time soon, so . . . better she hears it from me than through gossip. The staff are full of it."

"The staff may not know it's Charlie Brewster. The girl who found the body didn't seem to recognise him."

"Even so," Joy argued. "Mum and Fitch are gone and so is Bri, I'm the only member of the family here. It feels like my responsibility."

Rina nodded. She didn't necessarily agree but she could see what Joy meant and understand why she might feel that way. "Then I'll come with you," she said. "Do you know what room she's in?" She'd rather not arouse interest by asking the house staff.

"I think so. If we get it wrong, we can just apologise and try the next."

Rina nodded agreement. She handed her mobile phone over to George in case Andy should call back and instructed him and Ursula to keep an eye open for Mac and the others returning so they could tell Mac that she and Joy were going to speak to Mia.

George looked as though he didn't like this idea one little bit.

"How do you think she'll react?" Ursula asked uneasily.

Good question, Rina thought. Mia Brewster struck her as the sort of woman who'd be ready to shoot the messenger. "I suppose we're about to find out," she said.

* * *

Regis Crick was annoyed at having been disturbed before he'd had time to confirm the kill. It had looked obvious enough; no one could really have survived a tumble like that — or at least, he thought it unlikely anyone could have survived the blow to the head and then the landing. A simple fall was one thing but an assisted descent something else entirely. The thought amused him. He had managed to get out of sight when he'd heard the sound of glasses clinking and a young woman humming to herself.

Ruari, he guessed, must have taken off as soon as he'd heard footsteps. Regis, already down in the garden, had retreated into the tunnels leading from the garden and now stood in the shadow, peering out through the bars of the gate.

A man hurried down the steps and came close to the body. He had heard female voices too, though not managed to catch what they were saying.

He watched the man thoughtfully; he hadn't seen his face, didn't know him from Adam, but there was something about the way he behaved that suggested this was not the first body he'd seen. He watched as the man crouched down, studied the position, examined what was left of Charlie Brewster with an air of professional interest. A momentary frisson of anxiety went through him. Who was this chap? And was he likely to come into the tunnel?

It would be too bad for him if he did, that was for certain. A sound on the path above distracted his attention and that of the man's. Two people arrived, carrying something, all poles and canvas. A tent? Things were taking a seriously strange turn.

Not waiting to see what might happen next, Regis Crick retreated further, annoyed now. If Charlie had met with his brother the night before, as planned, then things would have been very different. But Charlie had not kept the rendezvous. Instead, he had texted Ruari to casually say that if he really wanted to talk, it would have to be this morning, before Charlie left.

Ruari had been incandescent. So angry, in fact, that Crick wondered if he should just hand him the weapon and let him do the deed.

No, he thought, Ruari was all talk and no trousers. He didn't have the guts for anything that up close and personal. Better that Regis did what had to be done — and so he had, and now Charlie Brewster was no more.

One down, Regis thought, and *two* to go.

CHAPTER 12

"We can't just hang about here," Tim said. "We've done what we can and so long as the water doesn't rise higher than the raised beds, the body shouldn't be disturbed."

Mac glanced at him and then at Miriam. It might only be the end of August, but the rain felt as chill as it might in November and both Tim and Miriam were shivering, Mac knew exactly how they felt. He glanced back to the gazebo, positioned to shield the body from the rain, thankful that Miriam, who was used to setting up such protection at crime scenes, had borrowed some heavy-duty tent pegs and a mallet from the team who'd come over to dismantle the marquee. They'd arrived first thing but were now taking shelter in the house and waiting for the storm to pass.

Miriam had told them that someone had died and that it looked like an accident but that as a trained CSI she felt she should keep the body dry and sheltered. She'd had a tough time convincing the team that she and Tim could manage between them, curiosity overcoming the reluctance to get wet.

"I don't think they believed me about it being an accident," she said to Mac. "And it must seem a bit odd that a CSI just happened to be on scene soon after."

With Tim's help, they had erected the gazebo and done their best to hammer the pegs deep into the ground, just in case the wind got up and added to their problems. Then Sergeant Baker had called to tell Mac the local investigators might be delayed, closely followed by a call from an inspector called Christine Sullivan who reiterated that they were doing their best to get there.

"We should head back to the house," Mac said and saw the relief in Miriam's eyes. She'd worked her share of tough scenes but with no equipment and little space inside the small gazebo, there was a limit to her usefulness.

They left the shelter of the tunnels at a run, were soaked to the skin before they reached the steps. Mac made a last check to see if the gazebo was holding up and was relieved to see that the body was still mostly dry. That was the best they could do.

The scramble to the top of the steps left him gasping, cold rain in his face, feet slipping dangerously on the rough-hewn steps. And then they were running for the house and Mac figured that they could not have got any wetter had someone thrown them in a swimming pool. Miriam was the first to reach the house, Tim close behind her, holding the door open for Mac and then the screaming began.

Mac turned towards the sound and then yelled in pain. Bright red nails raked across his face, his neck, drawing blood, inflicting pain. Instinctively, Mac closed his eyes, lashed out, ducked away from the source of the pain. When he opened his eyes again it was to see Mia Brewster, held tightly by Tim, George and a member of the house staff, her arms flailing in their grasp and a look of sheer fury on her face.

"What the . . ."

"Who killed him? Who killed my brother? You'd better find out and find out fast or I'll have your skin. I'll—"

To everyone's shock, she abruptly ceased her struggling and collapsed to her knees so suddenly that she almost took Tim with her.

Then, as though the scene could not get any more bizarre, Mac watched as young Ursula ran across the hall and wrapped Mia tightly in her arms. He watched, stunned, as the younger woman rocked Mia, stroked her hair, hushed her.

"You'd better get those scratches seen to," Rina said quietly. "And all of you go and get out of those wet clothes. Go on, we'll be just fine."

Miriam took his arm and led him away and Tim followed, though Mac could see he was as reluctant to leave his friends with the volatile Mia as was Mac. As they reached the landing he watched as Ursula helped Mia to her feet and, arms still around her, led Mia into the little sitting room at the front of the house.

"Come on," Miriam said, "they've got things under control. Let's get you patched up."

"I thought she hated him," Mac said.

* * *

Regis Crick had waited until he was certain the others had gone and then finally emerged from his hiding place. He'd been forced to retreat further when it became obvious they were not leaving in a hurry. He had watched as the woman and the two men had set up the little tent to cover the body, even more puzzled now by their demeanour. For one person to be unfazed by a dead body might suggest experience; a doctor, maybe. But for these three strangers to be dealing with the practicalities, without fuss or drama, no screams or exclamations of horror, puzzled him greatly.

Then, when the rain had got heavier and it became clear they were heading for his place of concealment, he'd had no option but to hide himself even deeper. He wasn't worried — after all, he was the one with the gun, though he was loathe to use it in the close confines of the passageways. Three against one, when the one was armed, were perfectly acceptable odds, even though he could have done without the fallout. There'd been enough inconveniences as it was.

Certain that they had gone now, he emerged slowly from the shelter of the tunnel, gasping and cursing at the sudden shock of the falling rain, so cold and heavy it felt more suited to January than late summer.

At least, he thought, the lousy weather might keep the curious inside. Better for them if it did.

CHAPTER 13

"How are you?" Rina asked.

She bent to scrutinise Mac's face and then dropped down into the chair opposite. "That's going to be sore. I hope you put plenty of antiseptic on."

"The room reeks of it and so do I, so yes, I think so."

Rina nodded. She could hear the shower running in the bathroom and guessed Miriam must still be trying to get warmed up. "Any news of the police and CSI arriving?"

"No ETA as yet. Apparently the roads are flooded so they're trying to scare up a four-by-four to get through. Bridie was fortunate the weather held. Apparently last week was as bad as today."

"Have you contacted Bridie?" Rina asked. "We didn't like to. What can either Bridie or Fitch do? Charlie was alive and kicking when they left so they couldn't even tell us anything useful."

Mac shook his head. "No," he agreed. "There's not much they can do. I'm sure Charlie was on the jetty when we saw them off."

Rina nodded. "He was. Mia was watching from the bankside but Charlie was there with us, throwing confetti." It had, she thought, been very pretty confetti, red and purple and blue and apparently made from dried delphinium flowers. "Joy and Ursula have taken Mia to her room and are sitting with her. She seems to have calmed down." She paused, suddenly thinking of something. "I forgot to mention it yesterday but when I was keeping an eye on Mia after the photographs were taken, I spotted her meeting someone who kept very determinedly out of sight." She explained how she had watched Mia in conversation with what she thought must be a man, standing in the cover of the trees.

"It might well not be significant," Rina added, "but I thought I'd mention it."

"Worth asking her about, perhaps," Mac said. "What happened before I got back? What triggered Mia?"

Rina frowned. "I suspect that might have been my fault," she said. "As you can imagine gossip was rife about a body being found and so was all the speculation. The poor young woman that found Charlie was inclined to think he'd fallen at first. She had, of course, no sense of how long he might have been there and assumed that, maybe he'd gone for a walk late at night and maybe he was drunk and had just gone over the railing. But the more she thought about it, I think the more she realised that probably wasn't true. The fencing at the top of the garden is pretty sturdy and you'd have to try quite hard to take a dive over the top of it, so she then began coming to the conclusion that something violent had happened and believe me she wasn't quiet about that either. So Joy thought, and I agreed, that we ought to get hold of Mia and tell her what was going on before she heard it from another source."

She saw Mac nod, not necessarily in agreement but in understanding of their predicament. "So we went up and we talked to her, and she was demanding to know where you were and why you hadn't done something about it."

"Like suddenly I can see into the future," Mac said and Rina could hear the bitterness in his voice.

"I don't think she was thinking particularly clearly." Rina had expected that the young man Mia had arrived with would have been sharing Mia's room, but she soon revised that view. The room was comfortable and beautifully decorated, but the queen-sized bed, set against the wall, suggested this was never meant to be a double room. Likely, Rina thought, she had brought him as a plus one more for decoration rather than because of any relationship they might be involved in. At any rate, there was no evidence of him left in the room — it was like he had never even been there. Rina had asked about him and Mia had told her dismissively that he had left the evening before. Rina recalled overhearing their conversation and that Mia had been keen for him to go. She must, Rina thought again, have been expecting trouble of some kind and perhaps even cared enough about him not to want him involved. Whatever trouble she might have been expecting Rina didn't think Mia had been anticipating her brother being murdered.

"I wasn't quite sure how to tell her to be frank. Mia is not someone you'd like to break that kind of news to, but Joy handled it very well and explained that you and I had been returning the necklace to its owner when we heard screaming. And when we arrived, one of the waitresses had discovered a body that had fallen into the sunken gardens."

"What do you mean fallen?" Mia had demanded. "Whose body?"

"I mean his body was in the sunken garden. Mia, I'm so sorry but Rina and Mac, they could see it was Charlie."

"I have never seen anyone go so white," Rina said. "She just stood there staring at us as though we weren't making any sense. Her room is on the side of the house opposite the abbey and so when you came back up from the sunken gardens, she heard you and looked out of the window and must have realised where you were coming from. She charged out of the room before either of us could stop her and we chased her down the stairs, but you came in just as she reached the bottom. And the rest you know."

She saw Mac touch his face and wince painfully. The shower turned off and a moment later Miriam came through into the bedroom wrapped in an oversized dressing gown and towelling her hair.

"I thought I heard your voice," she said to Rina and then paused to examine Mac's face. "Anything else happen?"

"Not at the moment. Joy and Ursula are with Mia. Emilie, the house manager, has briefed her staff about the police arriving and that we're likely to have more people for lunch than they thought. The team who came to dismantle the marquee have given up on the idea for the moment and they're busy drinking coffee in the restaurant. And the whole place is buzzing with gossip as you can imagine. Tim and George have suggested that everybody writes down where they were yesterday evening and last night ready for when the police arrive and everyone seems very enthusiastic about the idea. They're still at the 'this is exciting' phase, even though it's dreadful of course, and like everyone else in this country they probably watch far too many police dramas on the telly and are expecting to be questioned."

She was pleased when Mac laughed. "I'd better go down and supervise the statements then," he said. "There's still no ETA on the police and CSI arriving so if the rain doesn't stop soon, we're going to need to go back and check on the body, I can imagine the water rising pretty quickly in the garden."

"From what I saw yesterday some of it will drain down into the tunnel," Rina observed. She frowned as it suddenly occurred to her she'd no idea where it would go from there. Would it slowly seep into the groundwater? Or had drainage been incorporated into the passageways at some point? She remembered the floor of the first section they had explored being concrete and of the passageway they had not entered having a rougher, more hewn surface.

"Well, it's likely to cause problems no matter what," Mac said irritably.

"We did what we could," Miriam told him. "But as soon as I've got my hair dry and put some clothes on, I'll have a word with the marquee crew about getting a tarpaulin or something similar, see if we can improve the protection."

She frowned. "I don't like the idea of just leaving him there. Someone should be maintaining the scene."

"I can't see anyone being keen on being out there in this." Rina gestured towards the rain pelting so hard against the window that it was like being at sea. "No, but you've got a point, of course, it doesn't feel right. How about asking the marquee people if they can suggest something, see if they can set something up on the lawn above the gardens. We've got experts on site; we may as well make use of them."

"That would be helpful," Miriam agreed.

"Do you think he died last night?" Rina asked. "I don't recall seeing him after Bridie and Fitch left."

"Initially we thought so," Mac told her cautiously.

"And now?"

"Well, for one thing he was wearing different clothes. Chinos and a lightweight sweater, not the suit he was in for the reception."

"He might have got changed."

"Could have done, but body temp was wrong," Miriam told her. "I couldn't take a proper measure. of course, but when I touched Charlie's body, it was still warm. Rina, I don't think he'd been dead for very long at all."

"You think he died this morning?"

Mac nodded. "And probably less than an hour before he was found."

"Well that puts a different slant on things," Rina commented. Though she wasn't sure what kind of slant that might be. "Right," she said, "I'll go and assess the Mia Brewster situation. Ursula and Joy will probably have had enough of her by now."

"I'll bet," Miriam said, "and we'll go and consult the riggers, see what we can cobble together. If anyone's got any decent waterproofs that would be a big help too. I don't fancy getting soaked again."

Rina, satisfied now their initial missions had been laid out, left them soon after.

Mia's room was one floor above on the opposite side of the house and Rina made her rather reluctant way there. On this same corridor was a space which had intrigued her earlier and she took a moment now to have a proper look inside. The door that she had spotted half open earlier led into what must have been a private chapel. It faced the little church that she and Tim had visited the day before and featured a deep bay window that she now recalled seeing from outside. The furnishings were simple, no Victorian stained glass in here, just a very beautiful, mullioned window that flooded the space with light even on such a resolutely grey day as this. Despite the torrential rain it seemed to cast brightness onto a small wooden altar that had an Arts and Crafts look to it and was set with a wooden cross and two brass candlesticks. The window was dressed with heavy, figured, velvet curtains tied back with gold, tasselled cords. On the deep windowsill behind the altar sat an eclectic assortment of religious objects. Two little icons, one of which was a saint killing a dragon, perhaps St George, Rina thought and one she recognised as St Michael. Beside them sat a tiny pair of silver boots — she recalled a friend telling her that in parts of Greece shoes were given as offerings to St Michaelis, who had trampled the devil with iron-shod feet. Beside them was a small statue that she recognised as a copy of one of the famous Black Madonnas, perhaps the one in Liege? And beside her, three women in a little carved boat. St Sarah and the Virgin Mary and . . . who was the third woman? Rina could not call her to mind.

Rina took a moment of quiet and breathed deeply before descending once more into the Mia Brewster fray. The air in the tiny chapel smelt dusty as though it was not often disturbed though when Rina glanced around, she realised that this was not the dust of neglect but just of age, each surface had been recently cleaned and the faint aroma of beeswax and lavender lingered alongside the underlying scent of incense. There was, she noted, no permanent seating in here, just a half dozen folding chairs arranged along the wall. Was this place used, she wondered or was it just regarded as a sweet relic of times past and its original purpose preserved purely because it was too small to be converted into a bedroom and ensuite?

Well, best get on, Rina thought and returned to the corridor. She made her way along to Mia's room and knocked softly on the door.

She got the distinct feeling that both Joy and Ursula were relieved to see her when the door opened.

"Is Mac OK?" Ursula asked.

"Miriam has cleaned the scratches and applied ointment," Rina told her. "No great harm done," she added looking at Mia. The young woman was slumped in a chair beside the window, peering out at the rain-obscured grounds. This was a pleasant room, Rina thought but she was oddly gratified to realise that her own was much nicer. This looked like a high-end hotel room while her own bedroom was still decorated with the original Chinese wallpaper, hand-painted with birds and exotic flowers.

"I'm sorry I did that," Mia said, but to Rina the apology sounded grudging.

"You were blaming the wrong person," Rina said tartly. "But we all recognise that you were distraught. It must have been a terrible shock."

Mia turned her face from the window and looked thoughtfully at Rina. "I didn't want him dead," she said quietly. "We may not have got on, but he was still my brother. And I meant what I said, I want whoever did this caught and there'll be hell to pay if that doesn't happen."

Rina didn't rise to the bait. Instead she said, "Then perhaps you can do your bit to help by writing a statement recording your movements from, say, 9 p.m. last night when the bride and groom left, until we spoke to you this morning."

She could see Mia's anger begin to rise again. She added, "We'll all be doing the same, ready for when the police eventually get here. In the meantime, we can make a start on discovering where everyone was and anything unusual any-one might have seen."

"We should do the same," Joy said.

Rina nodded. "So you should and I suggest we go down now and find a sensible space for the officers to use once they get here and purloin some noticeboards or something similar they can make use of. Are you coming down to join us, Mia, or would you like some time alone?"

She could see the surprise on Ursula's face at her tone but Mia simply shrugged. "You can all go," she said. "I don't need babysitting."

"Shall I tell Emilie that you want lunch in your room?" Joy asked.

"Who the hell's Emilie?"

"The house manager," Rina told Mia. "Her name's Emilie Trudeau."

"Tell her what you like. Soon as the ferry's running, I'm out of here."

"I don't think you will be," Rina told her. "We'll all be expected to stay until the police have established everyone's whereabouts in relation to the estimated time of death and given the foul weather, that's not going to be easy to work out." The cold rain, she knew, would have reduced Charlie's body temperature far more rapidly than might be expected for a late summer night, or morning, if Mac's speculation was correct. Not that body temperature was anything more than a rough guide at best. "The most useful thing we can all do is work out when we all saw Charlie; that will help narrow down the time of death."

Rina was aware that she sounded unsympathetic. In truth she felt deeply for this obviously unhappy young woman, but she didn't believe that Mia would respond to a soft approach. She was used to being in control; she had lost control in a very public way. Rina guessed she would now be eager for a way to move on from that; to erase the memory of it from the collective consciousness.

"We'll see," Mia said.

"It's not up to us, my dear. Not to you and not to me. Do you have a pen?" Rina crossed to the small desk behind the door and plucked some headed notepaper from the rack. "Here you go," she said setting it on the windowsill close to where Mia sat. "Start with around nine o clock last night when I know you were out there with the rest of us, watching the ferry leave."

Mia said nothing but Rina could see the mix of emotions play across the young woman's face. If she thought it would have done any good, have been accepted, she'd have given Mia a hug and told her everything would be all right. But neither of those things were acceptable, were they? She didn't see Mia Brewster as a willing recipient of physical affection — though Ursula had briefly got away with it — and it would be a lie to say that anything was all right or would be for quite some time to come. Charlie Brewster was dead and, Rina feared, there would be far-reaching and dire consequences.

CHAPTER 14

"Thanks for the rescue," Joy said. "We neither of us knew what to say or do. I mean, what do you say? I know when Patrick was killed, I was in bits for months. I still have a good cry on bad days. But I really loved my brother. What do you say to someone who hated their brother's guts and now knows there's never going to be a time to change that?"

"I don't think she did hate him," Ursula said quietly. "Or at least, not simply that."

"Neither do I," Rina agreed. "But I wouldn't really like to hazard a guess as to what she actually felt about him. I suspect it was very complicated."

Downstairs in the restaurant they found the Montmorencys and Eliza and Bethany. The contractors were gathered at one end of the long room and their manager was deep in conversation with Mac and Miriam. As she passed, Rina gathered they were discussing what equipment could be deployed to help preserve the scene. What remained of the wedding guests had assembled at the other, some were busily writing, some listening intently to something the Montmorencys were telling them and from the sheaf of paper in Matthew's hand, Rina guessed they had taken over supervision of the statement taking.

"Ah, Rina." Stephen beckoned her over. He held a notebook and was just about to take his seat at a side table set out with pens and more paper. He resembled an elderly school stationery monitor, Rina thought, a random memory from her childhood popping up from nowhere. "I'm recording contact details," he told her. "Ready for when the police arrive."

"Good idea," Rina approved, "but what might be even better is if we can get hold of a laptop or tablet. That way you can make an electronic record that won't need to be inputted again."

"Excellent idea," Matthew boomed. "I'll go and speak to Emilie."

Eliza and Bethany were sitting with the Myers, the old friends of Bridie's they had met the day before.

"This is awful," Norma Myers said as Rina joined them. "Do we know what happened?"

"Only that Charlie Brewster is dead," Rina told her. "And it looks suspicious. The police and the CSI are on their way but the foul weather is delaying them getting here." She glanced towards the window. The rain, she thought, had slowed but showed no sign of ending.

John Myers shook his head. "He seemed like such a nice young man. Who on earth would want to kill him?"

His wife, Rina noted, looked as though she thought that was a stupid question. "Well, that sister of his for a start. And who knows who else? I mean we both knew what kind of family Bridie had married into, but she was always careful to keep that side of things away from her old friends, and she brought up those children beautifully. Always well turned out and polite."

Another childhood memory bubbled into Rina's mind, this time of a young woman who had lived a few doors down from her parents. She was a single parent with three small children and no sign of a husband, but she had largely escaped censure and gained approval, and a degree of protection from the older women in the community, because her kids were always well fed and clean and very polite. It struck her as amusing that Mrs Myers should sound so much like the 'aunties' and 'grandmothers' of her own childhood. She pulled her thoughts back to the present.

"You should write your statement too," Norma Myers was saying to Rina. "You know, we had a devil of a job remembering exactly what we were doing last evening, but we think we've got it straight now."

She sounds like she'd been constructing an alibi, Rina thought, talking about getting their story straight, but being around Mac so much, she had grown used to how guilty even innocent people could feel when touched by an investigation.

"I know you were by the pier at just after nine," she said. "We were all watching Bridie and Fitch leave and you were saying how surprised you'd been when you found out he was going to be Mr Duggan."

"So I was," Norma said. "Fancy you remembering that."

"Oh, Rina has a mind like a trap and a memory like an elephant," Bethany said airily and Rina rather wished she hadn't. It was the kind of description that tended to make people feel uncomfortable.

"What are we doing with the statements when we're done?" John Myers asked.

"I think Matthew is collecting them," Eliza said. "He's filing them in alphabetical order. Emilie gave him a concertina folder."

"Right then. I suppose it's all right if we go to our rooms?" He directed the question to Rina as though she suddenly had authority over such decisions. "I think we're both rather tired after yesterday and I thought we might have a little rest before lunch."

"I'm sure that will be fine," Rina assured him. "I think we're all feeling the effects of the late night."

She looked at her watch as the Myers left. Not yet lunchtime, in fact only just after eleven, she noted. Yet it seemed as though the morning had been going on forever. She reminded herself that she and Mac and Miriam had breakfasted at a civilised seven thirty, despite the late night. Rina, because she always woke at the same time and didn't like to waste the day and Mac and Miriam because at that point, they had hoped to spend their break doing holiday things, not dealing with dead bodies.

By nine in the morning that possibility had been washed down the drain. Sometimes she felt like that poor writer in *Murder, She Wrote*, who could go nowhere without falling over a corpse.

She was aware of the Peters sisters watching her closely. "I don't think Mia did it, do you?" Bethany asked.

"We think she's capable of course, I told you as much last night," Eliza added. "But would it make sense for her to bump him off? She would know she'd be chief suspect and she doesn't strike me as being unintelligent. With all the money that must be at stake here, surely she'd just leave it to their solicitors to sort out? Being a suspect in a murder is sure to delay probate, isn't it."

"Good point," Rina said and the sisters beamed at her. "But we can't rule anything out at this stage, I suppose."

"Well, we shall just have to keep our eyes and ears open and our thinking caps on," Bethany said. "Seeing as our poor Mac is the only policeman here just now, we're honour bound to do whatever we can to help him."

* * *

Mia Brewster had waited until the footsteps had receded and she was certain Rina and the girls had definitely gone and then she dug her second phone out of the hidden pocket constructed in the lining of her bag. The call was answered on the second ring.

"What the hell were you thinking?" Mia demanded. "I never said—"

She broke off, listening, a frown creasing between her brows. "Well, if you didn't who did?"

She cut the call, well aware there would be no reply to that one, her expression stony, eyes hard and shale black as though her mood had darkened even the irises. Could she believe him? The phone rang but Mia ignored it. Instead, she switched it off and stowed it back in the pocket in the lining of her bag.

CHAPTER 15

Inspector Christine Sullivan had phoned Mac to give him an update. "I can't see us being with you until mid-afternoon," she told him. "The weather's clearing but we're still having trouble getting through. You're effectively an island in the middle of a lake surrounded by another island just now. How are you holding up? I've got to admit, I'm glad you're on scene, God knows what would be happening otherwise. I think we'd have had to get the army involved."

"The navy might be of more help," Mac told her. "The lake's halfway up the lawn and it says on the news that the river's broken its banks and you can't actually get to the bridge."

"That is an issue," Christine agreed. "The ground is already waterlogged and that's added to the problems, the water had nowhere left to go, so it's flowing down the roads. We had a sodden August until this past week and it's not the first time the roads have flooded. The CSI are worried about the scene. Anything I can tell them?"

"That we've covered the body with a gazebo and where he landed is a raised bed, so we're hopeful he'll stay clear of any rising water. The contractors who came to collect the marquee are going to erect a small tent for us on the lawn above the raised gardens and reinforce the gazebo with another tarp. Of course that means more feet on the ground, but frankly with all the wet I don't think it's going to make that much difference. The important thing is to protect the body and immediate surroundings as best we can."

"I'll pass that on, see if anyone has suggestions to make but it sounds like you're making the best of a bad job. We'll be there as soon as we can."

Mac had gone into one of the small sitting rooms to make his call and as he finished, Emilie came in with a folding table. He gave her a hand to set it up on one side of the room, shifting chairs and a small sofa to make more room.

"I've got another table coming and a couple of flip charts with stands," she said. "Your Matthew has a laptop so he can record contact details electronically, I think Miss Martin suggested that."

"Mrs," Mac said automatically. "Thank you, that's going to be helpful."

"Mrs Martin," Emilie corrected herself. "And everyone in the dining room seems to have written out their statements. I don't know about the guests in the cottages and the guest house, of course."

"I'll check on that later," Mac assured her. He had noted a reticence in Emilie's manner this morning regarding the remaining wedding attendees. Understandable, he supposed, given the sudden death, but she must have known who they were before today. Though perhaps the frisson of excitement at having some of the biggest stars in the criminal firmament attending such a glittering event had seemed exciting until things turned so sour. "Have you checked how many guests are still here?" He had asked her to make a list for him when they had first returned to the house after finding the body.

She nodded, taking a list from her pocket. "In the house we have you and your partner, Mrs Martin, Mr Brandon and Miss Duggan, Miss Brewster, of course, the two Miss Peters and the two Mr Montmorencys. Then George Parker and Ursula then Mr and Mrs Myers, so fourteen in total. Then in the guest house, there's Mr Caprisi and his son and grandson. His daughter-in-law and the grandson's fiancée left last night. They were originally all due to leave this morning but their plans seem to have changed."

Interesting, Mac thought.

"The guests in the cottages are nothing to do with . . . I mean were not wedding guests."

"Though we know that at least two of them attended the evening reception," Mac reminded her.

"Yes, that's true. There's no one staying in the flats at the Grove and Lake View. We had people in last week but they left on Friday morning, before all of you arrived. Apart from Mr and Mrs Duggan and Joy and Ursula, as you know they arrived on Thursday."

"And no one's staying in the apartments now?" Mac confirmed.

"No, we've a party of fifteen due to arrive on Monday and staying for five days. They've booked both houses for the duration. I think it's an anniversary, but they'll be leaving on Friday and then we're back to our regular changeover day on the Saturday."

She looked, Mac thought, suddenly exhausted as she flopped down into one of the easy chairs. "I'm going to have to let them all know, aren't I," she said and Mac could see she was close to tears. "I mean, no one expects something like this to happen. Guests don't get murdered in a place like this."

In Mac's experience nowhere was immune to violent death but he made sympathetic noises and assured her that he was sure the local force would try and keep disruption to a minimum.

"So," he totalled everyone up, "we've got twelve guests in the house, three in the monastery guest house, how many in the cottages?"

"Two in each, so six. I suppose we should let them know."

"Next thing on my list," Mac assured her. "What about members of staff?"

"They have rooms at the back of the main house. We've got six. The outside caterers took their people away late last night."

"So the local police will need the names and contact details for the outside caterers," Mac told her. "Let Matthew add them to the list." He realised as he said that just how unorthodox this all was. He was certain they were infringing all sorts of rules on privacy and data collection, but so far everyone had been all too eager to cooperate. It was Mac's experience that people needed to be kept busy; that they only became really troublesome when they were left idle and helpless.

"And then there's the marquee team. Five plus the manager and I already have their details. When did they do the set up?"

"Thursday."

"Right." It was unlikely they'd be detained once the investigative team finally arrived, Mac thought. "And they weren't here at all after that?"

"No, they left Thursday teatime and only came back this morning, just before the rain began."

Mac nodded, he and Rina had seen the ferry coming across when they had set out to return the necklace. "Anyone else I don't know about?"

She shook her head. "No, I think that covers it." She glanced at her watch. "You need anything else? It's going to be all hands on deck for the lunch service. The Caprisis have asked if they can have theirs over in the guest house."

Mac told her that he had everything he needed for now and let her go. It was, he noted, still only twenty minutes to twelve.

Arthur Nedham, the manager of the marquee company stuck his head around the door and said his men had readied their equipment and were ready to go. Miriam was behind him, dressed in waterproof trousers and an oversized kagoul. A pair of rigger boots finished the ensemble.

"Very fetching." Mac smiled.

"Boots are a bit big but with an extra pair of socks I can manage. At least I'll be dry."

There was that, Mac thought, wondering if they had any more spare gear. "Unless you need me, I'm going to talk to the people staying in the cottages," he said. "Let them know what's happening. Then I suggest we all get some lunch. I'm hoping the guests staying in the other house will come across."

"No, nothing you can do," Arthur told him. "Miriam here can tell us where we can or can't pitch and we'll stick some temporary flooring down so at least whoever's in there can keep their feet dry."

Mac thanked him and then thanked him again when he produced another set of waterproofs. They had the company name emblazoned on the back but Mac was prepared to live with that.

Miriam handed him some heavy-duty plastic bags. "Put these on your feet before your shoes," she said. "You don't have anything remotely waterproof with you."

As Mac went off to get ready, he reflected that they were already more than two hours into an investigation and nothing in the normal run of things had happened. The scene had not been secured to his satisfaction, though he had to admit they had done their best. He'd not spoken to half the people he knew had been on site at the time of death. He'd got unauthorised civilians collecting and collating information. In terms of equipment, he had a couple of tables and flip charts and an ageing laptop.

"Work with what you've got," he told himself sternly. "Just do your best."

Mac set off for the cottages on the headland. He passed the riggers and Miriam, setting up a substantial looking structure on the grassy area at the side of the path. He looked down into the drop of the sunken gardens, checking on the gazebo which seemed to be standing up to the rain. Miriam had been down to check and was now coming back up the steep stairway, one hand on the wall and one on the railing, she still looked uneasy, he thought, and unusually clumsy. He guessed the heavy, ill-fitting boots weren't helping.

"How's it looking?" he asked as she made it to the top. He noted her expression. "Something wrong?"

"I'm not sure. The body's staying dry and the gazebo's doing a fine job, but I'm sure someone else has been down there since we left. Nothing I can put my finger on exactly, but I'm certain the position of the body's changed."

"Changed? How?"

She shrugged, her expression uncertain. "Look, I've taken some more pictures and I'd have to compare the photos we took and it could be that with all the rain the earth has moved and the body shifted. It's subtle and I may be completely wrong, but . . ."

But she probably wasn't, Mac thought. Miriam could read a scene as well or better than any PoLSA trained police search advisor. If she thought something had changed then she was probably correct. "I should have stayed," he said angrily.

"You were soaked to the skin as it was. We did all we could, Mac, and as the only officer within what, ten miles, there was only so much you could have done. If that girl hadn't been looking for stray glasses and hadn't thought to come this far from the house, chances are no one would have realised anything was wrong. If Charlie hadn't shown up for breakfast or lunch we'd all have assumed he had a hangover and no one in their right minds would be wandering round in this lot, so no one would have found him until it stopped."

He knew she was right but he didn't feel convinced. "I should still have stayed."

"And ended up in the hospital with pneumonia or something? You off to speak to the people at the cottages?"

Mac told her that he was. Although the guests in the holiday cottages had nothing to do with the wedding they had been present at the evening reception. It was possible they had seen something unusual when returning home the night before. It was also possible they had been up early and spotted the killer. They would likely notice the activity in the sunken garden and wonder what was going on. Had this situation been normal, Mac thought, he would have dispatched a constable to appraise them of the situation and ask the

115

appropriate questions, but as it stood, Mac had no one to send.

"I'll see you at lunch," Miriam said.

"Where did they get the tent from, anyway?" Mac wondered. He'd not noticed anything of this size at the wedding.

"It's a part of the big marquee," she told him. "They've taken sections and reconfigured them somehow. Clever stuff."

Clever stuff indeed, but he was still irritated and deeply troubled by Miriam's suspicions. As he walked away, he had two thoughts. It had not occurred to him at the time that the glass collector was indeed a fair way from the house. Was it a common occurrence that people should take their drinks into what would have been a very dark environment late at night and far from the lights of the buildings or the marquee?

He could think of several reasons why people might seek privacy, but in this instance was inclined to rule out courting couples. More likely Charlie had a meeting with someone or had stumbled into something far less salubrious. Though if he'd been out there that morning and not the night before, then was that more likely to have been for a prearranged meting? And who would the meeting have been with? Had it been a guest at the wedding then would it not have been more natural for him to have met with them the night before? So, had someone else come across the lake that morning? They need not have caught the ferry, it would have been easy enough to take one of the rowing boats, left on either shore for just that purpose.

Miriam, with her usual meticulousness had gathered up the broken glass from where the young waitress had dropped the tray. What had she done with it afterwards, he wondered?

Even if Charlie had met with someone the night before, it looked as though it had been well after the reception was over. So who would he have been meeting and what was such a meeting likely to be about?

Mac knew that until just after 9 p.m. he'd been under the watchful eye of Rina and her crew, much as Mia had remained under his for most of the evening. The newlyweds had kept a careful distance, dancing and mingling with guests and avoiding the possibility of being cornered by either sibling. Then Charlie had been on the pier watching the send-off and Mia standing a few yards away on the grass. After that?

After that Mac didn't know. At ten Miriam had confessed that her feet were hurting, even though she'd abandoned her heels hours before and danced barefoot on the velvety lawn. Mac, not a dancer, smiled at the memory of Miriam, Joy and Ursula enjoying themselves, a little knot of gorgeousness at the edge of the grass. He'd felt a swell of very inappropriately possessive pride at the looks cast in their direction. George and Tim had joined them occasionally but they didn't have the stamina of their womenfolk. Besides, Mac had got the distinct impression that the three women wanted to be left alone to enjoy themselves without the men getting involved.

But where had Mia and Charlie been?

Casting his memory back, he recalled Mia and the young man she had come with, the actor, Silas Bannerman, standing beside the small gazebo that was now being used to shelter Charlie's body. Bannerman had been getting her a drink, Mac thought and he remembered feeling that the atmosphere between them seemed a tad frosty. He must have left last night as he'd not been on Emilie's list.

Charlie . . . Charlie had been talking to Ben Caprisi at around the same time but after that Mac had lost track of both siblings. Bridie and Fitch had left and Mac had seen his duty to the couple settled so Charlie and Mia were no longer an issue. Then Miriam had returned to their table having 'danced her feet off' and Rina had joined them. For the next hour, they and Tim and George had chatted about the day and indulged in the kind of random conversations that happen between good friends, particularly when they'd imbibed too much champagne and Pimm's.

He vaguely remembered a conversation with George about whether or not Noah would have needed to take plesiosaurs on the Ark, or if they could have swum along-side, but the context was lost in a pleasant haze. He just about recalled the conversation becoming more and more absurd and George attempting an impression of a plesiosaur thrashing around on deck.

In the present, Mac had reached the cottages now and stood dripping in the porch as he rang the bell. This was the cottage next to the one the Clarks were staying in and had been rented by a couple called Prentice according to Emilie's list. The lady Mac assumed must be Mrs Prentice came to the door and stared at him. He must cut an outlandish figure, Mac supposed, all done up in heavy waterproofs, soggy train-ers with plastic bags sticking out of the tops and running with water from hood to toes. He'd had the forethought to stick his ID in a plastic bag and put it into a pocket of the water-proof jacket. He produced it now, and introduced himself, gently explaining the purpose of his visit — that one of the guests had fallen into the sunken garden and died and that there would be a police presence for a few days.

"Oh," she said. "Well, I suppose there'll have to be an investigation. Obviously the railing isn't high enough, not if someone's fallen. Do you think the family will sue?"

It was an angle Mac hadn't even thought of in terms of explanation.

"Who is it?" a man's voice asked and Mac had to explain the situation all over again.

"I expect they'll sue," Mrs Prentice said sagely.

"Silly fool probably had too much to drink," Mr Prentice said and wandered back to doing whatever he'd been doing before Mac arrived.

Well that was a different reaction, Mac thought as he left the porch and went to knock on the Clarks' door. The rain had eased a little and from the door of the cottage Mac now had a view of the lake, though the view was reminiscent of looking through a heavy net curtain. He knocked again. No response. Had the Clarks left? Had the incident with the necklace spooked them? If they had been planning an insurance con then having a police officer, even an off duty one, turn up at their door might cause panic.

Realistically, Mac didn't see when or how they could have left; the heavy rain had started just after he and Rina had been returning to the house and the ferry had not made the short trip across since then. The lack of visibility made even that little distance between the jetties unwise if not impossible.

He knocked again and this time the door of the third cottage opened and a man looked out.

"Can I help you?" he asked.

"Mr Brent?" Mac introduced himself and explained why he was there.

"Someone died? That's dreadful." He looked as though he meant it.

"We took up the offer and went to the evening reception," he went on. "Had a lovely time. Though I was glad we had a torch when we came back. You forget how dark the countryside can get."

That was true, Mac agreed. He was aware of a sudden frown on Mr Brent's face. "You say he fell into the sunken gardens? How did he manage that? Was he trying to go down the steps in the dark? I can see how that might be a bad idea, but the fence along the top is pretty sturdy." He regarded Mac with a slightly challenging look now.

"We don't really know what happened," Mac said. "And in this weather all we've been able to do is secure the scene and wait for the CSIs to get here."

"Odd though, isn't it?" He grinned suddenly as though something struck him as funny. "Handy, you being here. Maybe you'll make like Poirot and get everything solved before reinforcements arrive."

Mac smiled tightly and wondered if he should remind this man that Poirot had not been a policeman and was in any case fictional. "Any idea where the Clarks might be?" he asked.

"They're in as far as I know. Who'd want to go out in this?"

"No one with an ounce of brain and a choice," Mac agreed with feeling. Despite the plastic bags that kept the wet at bay, his feet were freezing cold.

"Maybe pop round the back in case they're avoiding you," Mr Brent said. "You were here earlier, weren't you?"

Mac agreed that he was. "Mrs Clark lost a necklace. Fortunately it had been handed in," he explained.

"Lucky."

"You mentioned going round the back?"

"Oh, yes. Go round the end of the garden wall and there's a little path that leads to the back gates."

Mac thanked him and went on his way, noticing that Brent waited until he'd turned the corner around the garden wall before closing the door. Mac paused. The cottages backed onto woodland, narrow paths leading into the density of trees and just for a moment Mac got the distinct impression of . . . what? Someone watching him? Someone moving in the undergrowth? He took a few cautious steps towards the line of trees and peered into the mirk, then some instinct encouraged him to step back and focus on the job in hand. He had to admit that he'd be very glad to be back at the main house and out of the blasted rain. Resolutely turning his back on the wood, conscious still of the prickling feeling at the back of his neck, the vague sense of being watched, he continued along the access path at the back of the cottages.

The first gate he came to was obviously to the garden that backed the Brent cottage. Through the slatted gate he could see that the back garden was small, a patch of lawn, tiny patio, trellised area for the bins. The Clarks' garden much the same. Mac made his way up the path and noticed that the back door was ajar. Now who would leave the back door open on a day like this?

Filled with misgiving, Mac pushed it open and shouted a hello. "Mr Clark, Mrs Clark, it's Inspector MacGregor. Your door was open."

So was the door between kitchen and hall. Mac leaned so that he could get a better view of the narrow space. He swore softly.

The first thing young officers were told when dealing with a suspected crime scene was that if they are the First Officer Attending, the FOA at a crime scene, then their duty is to preserve the scene. The only thing superseding that duty was the preservation of life. Though every instinct told Mac that it was far too late for that, he knew he had to make sure. If there was even a tiny chance . . .

Slowly, taking a route he ascertained looked clear of blood spatter, footprints and anything else of an evidentiary nature, Mac dripped his way across the kitchen floor, horribly aware of the muddy footprints he was leaving in his wake. Mrs Clark lay across the threshold between the hall and sitting room. Blood had pooled around her head and she was clearly dead. Her face was turned towards the front door affording Mac a view of the gaping wound in the back of her head. She'd have been dead before she hit the ground. When Mac and Rina had returned the necklace earlier that morning, Mrs Clark had been wearing the blue dressing gown she was wearing now, there had not been time for her to dress before the killer had struck. So how long after he and Rina had left had this happened?

Her husband lay slumped in a heap beside an easy chair as though he had just risen and turned before being felled, his head caved. Had he heard his wife cry out and tried to come to her aid? Mac looked again at the wound at the back of Mrs Clark's head and decided she wouldn't have even had the chance to cry out. The single blow would have felled her before she had the chance and Mac could see no obvious defence wounds; he got the distinct impression that she had not even been aware of her killer. More likely, then, that Mr Clark had heard the blow and then his wife fall, but the killer had struck before he'd had time to do more than begin to rise from his chair. He too was still in his nightclothes and the striped pyjamas and dark red dressing gown somehow added a level of pathos to the scene, made the pair look even more defenceless.

For a moment or two Mac stood in the hall unable to do more than just stare at the bodies. The house was very still, a heavy silence filling the space. He found he was listening hard, half afraid that the killer might still be close by. What if he had heard Mac come in and was now upstairs?

Briefly, Mac wondered if he should go up and find out but he immediately thought better of it. Whoever had killed Charlie Brewster, whoever had killed the Clarks, was a very dangerous individual and this was no time to be playing hero.

Mac swore softly and, knowing he must record the scene, quickly took what pictures he could on his mobile phone. He then retreated the way he had come, the vague sense he'd had that he was being watched had intensified now. He found himself hurrying, glancing fearfully back at the woods, dense and overgrown, an army could have hidden among the brambles and fallen branches and he not know about it. Impatiently, he shook the thought away and seconds later was hammering on the Brents' door. "I'm going to need you to pack some belongings and come with me," he said. "I'm taking you and the Prentices up to the main house. Now, please."

"What?" Brent looked at him at first puzzled and then concerned. "What's happened?"

"I'm afraid Mr and Mrs Clark are both deceased," he said as calmly as he could, aware that his voice was shaking. "I'm going to take you to the main house. Please just pack your things."

A few minutes later he was escorting a loudly complaining Mr Prentice and his wife and a quieter but very concerned pair of Brents back through the gardens and past the first crime scene. The riggers had finished their job and someone had placed a CCTV camera in waterproof housing, positioned to monitor the path while a second covered the sunken garden. Mac presumed there would be batteries powering a recorder in the tent and once again felt grateful for the presence of Arthur Nedham's team. And then he thought that the presence of the riggers just added to the number of people he now felt responsible for and wished that they had already left. He sighed, there wasn't a lot he could do about that right now.

Whoever was monitoring the cameras would see their little procession, Mac thought and wonder what was wrong.

Plenty, Mac thought. Just what had they stumbled into?

CHAPTER 16

"What's happened?" Miriam demanded. She had met Mac and the others by the door and they now all stood dripping on the black-and-white tiles of the floor.

"He says the Clarks in the next cottage, they're dead," Mr Brent's voice quavered.

Emilie Trudeau came out of the dining room, presumably attracted by their voices, and Mac beckoned to her. "Could you get Mr and Mrs Brent and Mr and Mrs Prentice some coffee and maybe something to eat? And if there are spare rooms available, that would be a real help."

She frowned, puzzled, but to Mac's relief just nodded and led the two couples away.

"The Clarks are dead?" Miriam asked. "I'm taking it that it's not natural causes."

"Murdered, looks like blunt force trauma, on the face of it the same as Charlie Brewster."

"What the hell is going on, Mac? The Clarks weren't even meant to be at the wedding."

"Maybe they saw something they shouldn't have done. Maybe that little scam with the necklace attracted the wrong kind of attention. I just don't know."

"I should get over there," Miriam said.

"Not a lot you can do except drip on yet another floor," Mac said with feeling, "and I think I've done enough of that for both of us. I've photographed the scene best I can and secured the house. The back door was open, that's why I went inside. I stopped at the kitchen door. It was pretty obvious both were dead and there was nothing I could do. The back door key was still hanging on a hook by the door so I used that to lock up. I think the chances of the killer having touched it are remote but I got the Brents to give me a sandwich bag to put it in."

He delved into the pocket of his borrowed waterproofs and removed the large old key.

"Get it labelled and add it to the box," Miriam told him, indicating their makeshift incident room. "I've been in touch with DI Sullivan but still no ETA on their arrival. I've sent her all the photographic evidence we've got so far and electronic copies of the statements, contact details and anything else we've put together so far. Matthew's a dab hand with the scanner and the laptop and Emilie has got everyone to sign the release forms they use when people allow their photos and reviews to be used in the publicity, just so we're covered for data protection, not that I see anyone making trouble but you never know, do you?"

"I bet it was fun explaining to DI Sullivan who Matthew Montmorency is." Mac grinned at her.

"I think she's just grateful we're on scene," Miriam said.

Mac shed his waterproofs and parked them beside the front door, certain he'd need them again. He followed Miriam into the incident room. It had developed a bit since he'd been gone. Arthur Nedham had set up a card table in the corner and was monitoring the cameras not just overlooking the body but at several other locations around the house and gardens.

"Emilie let me access the CCTV camera feeds," he told Mac.

"I didn't realise they had any in operation," Mac said, a little annoyed with himself for not thinking of that earlier.

He'd not noticed security cameras the previous day — and he habitually looked for them out of professional interest.

"Strictly speaking they don't, but they do have five different trail cams and three of those are capable of remote operation. The other two are the motion sensor kind you have to retrieve and download and we'll get to those later, but I've got the remote access up and running from a central point now." He shrugged. "The quality's a bit iffy, but you never know."

"Good thinking," Mac applauded. "What are they usually used for?"

"They've had a pair of ospreys nesting at the very tip of the island for the past few years. One camera monitors the nest and another looks back towards the other jetty."

"Towards the jetty," Mac said. There was a chance that one might have caught any action happening close to the cottages.

"Yes, the first year the birds nested, some bastard rowed over and tried to steal the eggs. The third camera and fourth cameras are just set up to watch feeding stations closer to the house. Both belong to Jill, a member of staff who just likes watching the birds." He pointed to two of the feeds recording an area of the garden Mac assumed must be at the back of the house. The bottom edge of a window frame was just visible and Mac guessed that the cameras must be inside the staff quarters. The rain blurred the images but it would still, Mac guessed, be possible to make out movement and general shape should anyone be caught on camera.

"It's certainly better than nothing," Mac agreed. He indicated the two feeds from the cameras Arthur's team had set up close beside the gardens. "You must have seen us coming back."

Arthur nodded. "Guessed it meant more trouble?"

Mac nodded, quickly filled him in on what he had found. "I'm not sure how long they'd been dead, but it can't have been very long. We were with them just before Charlie's body was found. I don't suppose you saw anyone else?"

"Sorry, no. We're still working our way back through the earlier footage on the off chance."

"Emilie has tried to persuade the Caprisis in the guest house to come over and stay in the main building," Miriam told him, "but they're not having it. They say they can look after themselves."

"And they could be right," Mac agreed uncomfortably. Speculating on what resources the Caprisi might have was not reassuring. "Though I'd personally feel happier if everyone was under one roof and didn't have the opportunity to wander off."

The sound of shouting broke through their conversation.

"Something kicking off in the dining room," Arthur said.

It certainly sounded like it, Mac thought as he and Miriam crossed to where the argument and the shouting seemed to be escalating. He glanced quickly around the large room. Arthur Nedham's team were still ensconced at the far end of the room, coffee cups now joined by a pack of cards and a pile of what looked like poker chips.

Matthew, Steven and the Peters sisters were clustered together in one corner, Eliza looking indignant and Bethany concerned. Rina, unsurprisingly, seemed to be where the action was, standing beside the Prentices and attempting to placate Mr Prentice who was shouting very loudly and demanding "something should be done".

"And just what do you suggest?" Rina asked him, her voice utterly calm.

Mac went over and stood beside her. "Mr Prentice, if you and your wife and Mr and Mrs Brent would be kind enough to make your statements, then I'm sure you'll be able to go to your rooms and rest."

"Statements? What do you mean, statements?"

"I'm sure you can understand, Mr Prentice, we need to get a complete picture of where everyone was when . . . different events happened. When the wedding guest, Charlie Brewster, died and now when the Clarks were—"

"Murdered," Mrs Prentice said. "Murdered."

"Yes, Mrs Prentice, it does look that way."

"And this wedding guest, this Charles . . . what did you call him. He was murdered too?"

"Yes, Mrs Prentice, it appears that he was," Mac confirmed.

"And you expect us to just go to our rooms and wait for our turn? Where are the other officers? When will the police arrive?" Her voice broke suddenly and she slumped back in her chair, staring at Mac as though it was all his fault.

"No, Mrs Prentice," Mac said quietly, "I expect you to help with the enquiry and make a statement for me. I would like you to describe everything you did yesterday evening from about 9 p.m. until my visit today and anything that happened that might have struck you as odd."

"Odd. Two people were murdered only a few feet away from where I was probably sleeping and you talk about 'odd'!"

"Did you hear anything strange," Mac persisted. "When did you last see the Clarks? Anything you can tell us would really help us understand what happened and how. And as to where the other officers are, the roads are flooded and that's delayed them. But they are on their way."

"And in the meantime," Rina spoke now, her tone firm, "we can all be grateful that a very experienced detective and an equally experienced CSI happen to be here already. Once the full team get here they will at least have a head start and the more information you can supply the more help that will be."

Mrs Prentice stared at her and then nodded. "All right," she said, sounding cowed and tearful. "I'll do what I can."

Mac left the Prentices in Rina's capable hands and moments later they were seated at separate tables, at least attempting to write. Their demeanour reminded Mac of exam students, afraid to look at one another in case they might be accused of cheating. He had already organised the Brents who both looked pale and shocked but were more cooperative.

"Do you think we're in any danger?" Mrs Brent asked softly, glancing at her husband as though afraid that he might hear.

"We've brought you all together here to try and make sure you're not," Mac reassured her. He sat down opposite and gratefully accepted a cup of hot, strong tea. "Did you know the Clarks before you got here?"

She shook her head. "No and we didn't really have much to do with them. They arrived a day or two after us, so on this past Monday. They seemed friendly enough but we didn't exchange more than a few words. We were out on Monday and again on Wednesday and Thursday, we took the ferry across the lake. Tuesday was fine so Keith took the kayak out and I had a lazy day sitting by the lake with my book and we had a bit of a picnic. We didn't really see much of them at all."

She leaned confidentially across the table. "We saw and heard more of the Prentices. I'm afraid they seem to argue a good deal."

Mac nodded his understanding. "So," he repeated the earlier instructions. "If you could write down what you did and anything else that occurs to you, between 9 p.m. last night—"

"That was when the bridal couple left."

"That's right, yes."

"We saw them go. We'd been having a bit of a walk before bed."

"Did you come to the evening reception?" Mac could not recall seeing them but then, his attention had been focussed on Mia Brewster.

"For a little while. It was so nice of the bride and groom to extend the invitation. Her dress was so lovely. But the bridesmaids. Don't you think that was a little bit shocking? All that black and gold. For a wedding?"

Mac smiled. "Bridie likes to do her own thing," he said.

He went over and asked the same questions of the Prentices, and got very similar responses. No they had not known the Clarks and no, they had not had occasion to do more than pass the time of day. They thought the Clarks had just used the cottage as a base and been absent for most of the time, once even staying away overnight.

Mac got the distinct impression that Mrs Prentice had been keeping a close eye on her neighbours, but he suspected that she was what his mother would have called a curtain twitcher. It was odd, Mac thought, that the Clarks should have spent so little time at the cottage. Surely if all you wanted was a base from which to explore an area, there were more convenient locations than a cottage on an island in the middle of a lake with a ferry that only ran between eight in the morning and seven at night usually? Yes, it was possible to row across at any time but the Clarks had not struck him as the type to inconvenience themselves in a damp rowing boat.

Returning to the incident room with Miriam he took her through the photographs he had taken at the scene and then sent these to DI Sullivan. Then he called her.

"We're hoping to be with you by 3 p.m.," she told him. "And we've got someone else joining the team. A DS Terence Pritchard. His orders have come from high up; any guesses what that's about?"

"My guess is that there's already an operation underway that no one's bothered to inform us about."

"Oh." She suddenly sounded cautious and Mac got the feeling this was a conclusion she had also reached. "What makes you think that?"

Quickly Mac filled her in his meeting with the chief constable and coffee table man before he had come to the wedding. "That I'd be asked to keep my eyes and ears open was not entirely unexpected," Mac told her, "but I had the distinct feeling there was a lot that wasn't being said."

"And that's really pissed you off," she said and Mac realised belatedly that he must have allowed his frustration to creep through.

"You could say that," he agreed. "No one suggested I should be on high alert."

"I doubt anyone figured you would end up having three murders to deal with. I'll see what we can find out about the Clarks and be with you as soon as I can. Looks like you're doing a good job of holding the fort in the meantime."

Mac set his phone on the table and skimmed through the pictures he had uploaded onto the laptop. The inside of the cottage had been dimly lit and his phone had defaulted to flash mode for some of the initial shots. He'd then repeated the shots with the flash off, hoping post-processing would take care of the exposure issues. He reminded himself that the CSI photographer would be arriving with Christine Sullivan's team and that these initial images were primarily for his own purposes. Even so, he liked things to be right.

The images taken with the flash were stark, oddly unreal, all deep shadows and sharp edges. The bodies looked artificial, like obsessively accurate mannequins. The pallor of the skin and the redness of the blood adding to the sense that this scene had been staged and that at any moment the director would call 'cut' and they would get up and walk away. The later images, though flattened by the dimness in the room nevertheless emphasised the reality of events.

The blows that had killed both had been delivered with full force and intent — that much was evident even on the swiftest of examinations. Mrs Clark had been attacked from behind, her skull had been caved in. The thought came back to him that she had probably been dead before she hit the floor. Mr Clark seemed to have been struck at a more oblique angle, which fitted with Mac's theory that he had been rising from his chair.

Whoever had killed them had been cool to the point of coldness. Efficient, ruthless. He wondered what it was that made him feel so sure there had only been one person involved, that there had been no second, perhaps with a gun, to keep the victims under control. Perhaps, he thought, it was the appearance of efficiency. The killer had come in, struck Mrs Clark, then must have stepped over the body almost as she fell and killed Mr Clark as he was trying to rise from his chair. Had there been a second person present then Mr Clark would not have tried to get up, the blow would have been struck from a different angle.

He ran his thoughts past Miriam, and she agreed that it sounded feasible.

"No footprints at the scene." Miriam was looking over his shoulder.

"No, the killer kept clear of the blood. And as I've said, he must have moved quickly and carefully. And there were no other prints from what I could see. Mine are all over the kitchen floor." He pointed to the wet and muddy track he had trailed across the tiles and then carefully recorded as he had followed the same pathway out.

"So we can assume he went in before the rain began. Even if the footprints had dried they'd have left some mud behind. The path to the cottages is filthy and the grass is no better now."

Mac nodded. "I should have checked for rigor," he berated himself.

"And risked disturbing the scene further? Mac, I was gloved up and able to touch the back of Charlie Brewster's hand without disturbing anything else but you couldn't do anything of the sort. You didn't even have gloves with you. If Andy or any other of the officers you've been in charge of had gone poking about you'd have given them what for. You did exactly the right thing, and you know that. You checked that life was definitely extinct, and let's face it, no one could have survived that kind of skull-crushing blow. You got out and secured the scene then moved vulnerable civilians out of the way. I'd have liked to take Charlie Brewster's temperature, but the only thing available was a meat thermometer in the kitchen and I've no way of knowing how accurate that might be."

Mac grimaced. For some reason the idea of using something intended for the Sunday joint to test the liver temperature of a corpse made him feel slightly nauseous. "You know," he said, "I had the distinct feeling that whoever had killed them was still close by. Call it an overactive imagination if you like, but I just had this feeling I was being watched all the time I was there."

"It's bound to have spooked you," Miriam said. Then seeing Mac's expression, she added, "You think the killer is still on the island? You think he was actually watching you?"

"Both rowing boats were tied up to the jetty. I didn't see the kayak." He realised suddenly that he hadn't asked Brent if he'd moved his kayak away from the water's edge. That would be the next thing to do.

A quiet knock interrupted his thoughts. Rina stuck her head around the door. "The Brents and the Prentices have finished writing their statements," she said. "Matthew has scanned them into the other laptop. You can pick them up on this one from the shared file. Steven sorted that out. Miriam already has the password."

"They've done a brilliant job," Mac said. "I'm grateful."

"They're like the rest of us, happier when they're doing," Rina said. "I think the rain's slowing down," she added.

About bloody time, Mac thought.

Before the Brents had time to disappear into their rooms, he went and spoke to Mr Brent and asked him about the kayak.

"I left it on the jetty," Mr Brent said then paled. "Oh my lord, you think the killer took it?"

Mac tried to reassure him that as yet they really didn't know but he could see from Brent's face that he would never again get the same pleasure from his innocent and pleasurable little hobby and that somehow he now felt almost like an accomplice.

CHAPTER 17

The rain was not slowing down on the motorway. DS Terry Pritchard had driven fifty miles with his windscreen wipers on full, peering through the murk, exacerbated by the spray from lorries that seemed unwilling to make any concessions to the filthy conditions. He swore as yet another pulled out to overtake his car, sending another wave of heavy spray to join the downpour already impeding his view. Visibility stretched not much further than the bonnet of his car and he was relying on the satnav to warn him of upcoming junctions; there was no way he could see the road signs until he had almost passed them by.

The call that had catapulted him onto this journey — only a hundred odd miles in distance but a thousand times that, if miles could be measured in reluctance — had come less than two hours before and there had been no resisting it.

"Charlie Brewster's dead," he was told and then later, while he had been driving, hunched forward, peering through a windscreen awash with tidal volumes of rain, came the news of two other deaths. A holdall containing clothes and other necessities rested on the back seat but that had been the sum total of his preparation. There was no one at home to tell, no relationship to take account of and his family were far away and well used to not hearing from him for weeks at a stretch.

Terry swore as the lorry that had pulled out now pulled back across, settling just yards ahead of his car, adding yet more depth to the flow of water across his screen. He was profoundly relieved when the clipped female voice on his satnav told him that his junction was just a half mile ahead.

Off the motorway, along the slip road, crossing the round-about, second exit. A short stretch of dual carriageway and then a turn onto an A road before another onto something much narrower, high hedges rising on both sides. His windscreen wipers only had the rain to contend with now and seemed more able to cope with the task. He could see a little further ahead though, it turned out, not far enough. He screeched to a halt, car slewing sideways and almost ending up in the thick greenery of the hedge, his front wheels axle-deep in water.

Gingerly, Terry reversed, straightened himself up, got out of the car and stood with the rain pouring down the back of his neck as he stared at the lake that now occupied the space his satnav told him should be road.

Terry sighed. *Now what?*

He got back into his car and reversed until he found a farm gate and was able to turn around. Sitting in the car, parked half on the verge, he called DI Sullivan and was told that this was a problem the whole team was facing. She gave him directions to an assembly point they had set up further down the motorway and then it was back to the spray and the lorries and racing of inadequate wipers across a flooded screen until, five miles further on, he pulled into the services and spotted what must be Sullivan's team in one corner of the lorry park. For one fleeting moment he thought about turning around and heading back onto the motorway, taking the slip road south and heading for home.

Why should he care if Charlie Brewster was dead? And as for the other two, he'd never even heard of the Clarks.

Then someone got out of a four-by-four and waved at him and the moment was lost. Terry sighed, drove slowly towards the woman who was now sheltering under a very large umbrella. She was tall and blonde with a narrow face that looked austere until she smiled at him and extended her hand for him to shake. Her handshake he noted, was firm. The smile genuine — as was the curiosity in her eyes.

"So, you're the mysterious DS Pritchard," she said. "We're waiting on the CSI team so we've got time for a coffee before we set off again and you can tell me why you're so damned important."

CHAPTER 18

Terry Pritchard cradled his coffee and gathered his thoughts. It was clear that the DI wasn't going to help him out by asking questions, she was waiting on an explanation and a full account. Leaning back in her chair and unwrapping a pack of shortbread biscuits, she had the look of a woman who was willing to wait all day if she had to.

He knew the impression was illusory; she'd be as frustrated by the delay as he would have been had the job involved anyone other than the Brewsters. As it was, he was the one willing to wait, preferably until she got bored with him and left him sitting at the services.

"So," she said, tilting her head to one side and regarding him with what he took to be an encouraging expression.

Terry took a deep breath. "I don't know what you've been told," he began.

"Presume I know nothing. I was just informed that you'd be joining us. That you had information that would be useful to the enquiry. So, do you?"

"I don't know," he admitted. "Maybe. Look, I was undercover for six months, since a couple of months before Malcolm Brewster died until a few weeks ago. Then a man I'd befriended within the organisation, Graham Stevens . . . Gray, he—" He broke off, the memory of that night flooding back into his head until it was all he could see.

"Take your time," she said and he was grateful for the calm and even tone of her voice.

"They thought he was . . . disloyal. I knew they'd kill him and there was nothing I could do. I knew it was only a matter of time before they took a closer look at me so I asked to be withdrawn."

Asked to be withdrawn. That sounded so civilised, so controlled. It hadn't been like that, had it. He'd run like hell, sat shivering and trembling in the yard at the back of the pub until someone had come to collect him and even than he'd not been sure if the right people had come for him. If he was really safe.

He was suddenly aware that he'd spilled hot coffee on his fingers. That his hands were shaking. He swore, softly, angrily and set the cup down.

"Here," she said.

He took the tissue she was offering and cleaned the coffee from his hands.

"I'm sorry about your friend."

He nodded, not quite trusting himself to speak, thinking that was the last thing he had expected her to say.

"It looks like the CSI team is here," she went on, "so time to move out. You need a minute?"

"No, thanks, I'm fine. I'll be fine."

"Look," DI Sullivan went on as they stood once more under the oversized umbrella, "this is going to be hard on you. I'm going to need you to prepare a proper briefing for the team, once we know what we're dealing with. But get to know the rest of your colleagues first and when we understand the situation better I'll be better able to ask you the right questions and you'll have a better idea of what we need to know. In the meantime it seems we struck lucky in one respect."

"How so?"

"One of the wedding guests is a DI and his partner is a CSI and they've been busy doing some of the basic prep. Hopefully we can hit the ground running."

"Ah. Yeah, I know."

"You know?"

"DI MacGregor. I . . . um I met him briefly a few days before the wedding."

"Right. So you must have been the mystery man who gave him the file."

"That would have been me, yes."

She laughed. "Then you should know he's a trifle pissed off with both you and his boss. He thought he was attending a wedding, not a massacre. Could you not have given him more of a heads up?"

Terry glanced at her, not certain how to react, then saw that she was trying not to laugh. He relaxed.

"So, do we have an ID on who killed your friend?"

He nodded. "Man by the name of Regis Crick. Worked for Brewster senior for years and latterly acted like his second-in-command. But he's gone to ground. Neither of the kids liked or trusted him and he knew his days were numbered. The past couple of months I got the impression he was asset stripping, so he's probably off somewhere with no extradition agreement and living the good life."

"So, who was he taking his orders from after Malcolm Brewster died? Or had he set up on his own account?"

"Officially Mia Brewster was his boss, but you know the kids are in dispute? Their dad's will was guaranteed to put them at one another's throats. Mal Brewster was a bastard, it gave him some kind of a kick to see them fight for his approval."

"And now Mia Brewster is presumably the winner of that particular fight . . ." Christine Sullivan said.

CHAPTER 19

Mac was just grabbing some lunch, sitting on the stairs in the hallway in a vain effort to get a little thinking time as well as food. The dining room had become the focal point for speculation and argument, emotional outburst and grim determination to keep the upper lip appropriately stiff. He really did need to escape from that, just for a few minutes. He'd thought of retreating to his room, but that seemed like a step too far from the action.

Emilie came to tell him that Ben Caprisi had asked to speak to him immediately. This had in fact been Mac's next thing on the to-do list, but he finished his sandwiches first and had a second cup of tea. What was he trying to prove? He asked himself, wryly amused. That he was the one in control?

Miriam emerged from their incident room and beckon for him to follow her inside. "I was right," she said, pointing at the computer screen.

Mac could see that she had laid out the images side by side. Those she had taken when they had first found Charlie and those Mac had taken before Tim and Miriam arrived with the gazebo and then those she had obtained when returning to the scene with the team setting up the little tent on the lawn above the garden.

Mac studied them intently and nodded agreement. Someone had definitely moved Charlie Brewster's body. The differences were not major, the person committing this act — Mac found himself thinking of it as desecration — had obviously taken notice of the way the body had been lying and had done their best to reposition Charlie's body in as close approximation as possible. But there were differences that could not be accounted for in terms of simple slippage of the ground beneath, or as the body settled.

"The right hand and arm are definitely in a different position," Mac said. "Different by several degrees and the fingers of the hand are stretched out, palm down whereas before the hand was twisted at the wrist and the palm was partly turned up originally."

Miriam nodded. "There are other small changes too but that's the most obvious and nothing can account for the hand being turned over, apart from someone disturbing the body."

"They were looking for something, something they thought he might have in his pockets," Mac speculated. "We should have checked his pockets before leaving."

"And had we done that we'd have disturbed the body. Protocol, Mac. You know the rules, the CSI examine the body, the doctor pronounces death, only when they've examined everything in situ can you turn the body over. Besides, we were more intent on getting the whole scene covered up and protected while not catching pneumonia. What on earth would make us suppose that there would be someone out there waiting for their chance?"

An odd stiffness in her posture suggested to Mac that there was something else wrong, something beyond anger and irritation. "What?" he said.

"What if they were watching us, waiting for us to go away? What if you were right when you went to the cottage and you felt someone was keeping you under observation. The thought that the killer was hiding somewhere close by . . . Mac, I can't get that out of my head."

He opened his mouth to say something reassuring and then shut it again. Chances were, she was right and there was nothing he could say that would not come across as trite and unconvincing. "OK, so we now have a good idea of where everyone was this morning and we can crosscheck their statements, see if it's possible one of the guests or one of the staff was close to either the cottages or the gardens. If they were, then they become definite persons of interest. If no one was out there . . . well, we'll have to deal with that. The full team will be here soon. Can't be too soon as far as I'm concerned."

Miriam nodded agreement. "I'm certain there's someone else out there, someone we can't account for because we don't know who they are. This might be a small island but there are plenty of places to hide."

Mac opened his mouth again; then shut it. He nodded. He was pretty certain she was correct. "I'm going to talk to Ben Caprisi," he said. "Do you want to come?"

She shook her head. "I'm more useful here. I'm going to give DI Sullivan a ring and bring her up to speed, unless you'd rather?"

"No, you do that. Send her the photographs and explain what is going on. When the weather clears she might be able to get hold of a helicopter or a drone, it would be easier to search a place like this from the air, especially if they can get an infrared camera in play. Have a chat to her about anything else that is going to be needed. It's not exactly easy to get here or get equipment across."

He left Miriam and headed for the guest house and Ben Caprisi. The grandson had been looking out for him and unlocked the door, then locked it again behind Mac. He led the way along a corridor to where his grandfather was waiting.

Mac had met the old man once before though he doubted Ben Caprisi would remember. He was wrong, the old man did. As he shook hands Caprisi said, "You gave evidence against Ricky Belmont, almost a decade ago. You were a sergeant back then. We exchanged a few words in the corridor on the way out of the courthouse."

Ricky Belmont, Mac remembered, had been an armed robber. He'd also being a little trigger-happy and badly wounded one of Caprisi's lieutenants, a young man who happened to be a distant relative. This was not to be endured by the Caprisi family and a tip-off had led to his arrest. "You have a good memory," Mac said. "But yes I was a sergeant back then."

"And a hard time you've had of it since," Caprisi went on. "The death of that child was a terrible business."

Mac realised that the old man must have seen the look in his eye because Ben Caprisi then said, "But we'll leave that, shall we, I doubt it's something you wish to discuss. Though you should be proud of yourself for the justice you managed to bring for the family."

Mac shifted uncomfortably. Justice, he thought, had been long enough coming and the outcome had almost cost more lives. He sat down in the chair opposite Ben Caprisi and accepted a cup of coffee poured by the grandson. The door opened and Gianni Caprisi came in and took up a position at his father's side on the leather sofa. Ben's wheelchair stood beside the door plugged into a charger.

"So," Mac said, "why particularly do you need to see me?"

"Because I see you floundering," Caprisi told him frankly. "You came here as a friend, to celebrate a wedding and you find yourself in the middle of a mess."

Mac did not feel he could argue with that assessment. "And do you have anything to tell me that might stop me floundering?" Mac asked. "Three people are dead, at first sight they seem to have all died the same way so it's not beyond the realms to speculate that the same person is responsible. Two were not even guests at the wedding. I am aware that Mia and Charlie Brewster were at odds, but they've been at odds for a very long time. Even given the circumstances surrounding their father's will, I find it odd to think that Mia might have taken it into her head to have her brother killed, or to kill him herself, here and now when presumably she's had plenty of opportunities prior to this."

"You don't think Mia was responsible?"

Mac considered; should he be discussing any of this with the likes of Ben Caprisi? The thing was, there was probably not much he could tell the old man that he didn't already know, or suspect. The Caprisis and the Brewsters had every reason to know what was going on in the opposing camp, it was just basic business sense.

"Mia has to be at the top of the list, but I have my doubts," Mac told Ben Caprisi. "She seemed genuinely shocked to hear he was dead. She could just be a good actress, of course. If she is responsible, then she had an accomplice. It would have been difficult for her to go and kill the Clarks and her brother and make it back to the house with no sign of having been out in the storm and with no one seeing her, in time to do this." He touched the side of his face where Mia's nails had raked his cheek.

Ben Caprisi showed no sign of surprise that Mia had been responsible and Mac guessed he had already heard about her attack on him, perhaps from Emilie. There had been a number of witnesses after all.

"I thought your daughter-in-law and, is it your grandson's fiancée, intended to stay until this morning," Mac said pointedly. "They left early. Were you expecting trouble?"

Ben Caprisi considered for a moment and then said, "We were expecting conflict, we weren't expecting murder. My daughter-in-law was feeling unwell and Elizabeth simply went with her to make sure she was all right. The two have become close, despite the difference in age. From here we are all going to stay with friends, they simply went a few hours early."

Mac waited but it was clear that this subject was closed and so he asked, "What can you tell me about the will? And what can you tell me about what Mia and Charlie wanted from you, from Bridie, from others attending the wedding?"

"The young woman has a sense of entitlement," Ben Caprisi said. He shifted uncomfortably in his seat. "My back is aching, you will forgive me if I don't keep you for long but I need to lie down."

He looked frail, Mac thought, but he still had presence and mentally seemed to have lost none of his acumen. Mac wondered about reminding him that he had been the one to issue the summons but decided against. He had a feeling that Ben Caprisi was inclined to be his ally, at least for the moment and that he should make the most of that. Instead he merely nodded.

"I had my lawyers email certain documents and Emilie was kind enough to print them for me," Caprisi said. "I don't know if this will help in your murder inquiry, but it might give you some background, at least an insight into who wanted Charlie Brewster dead — apart from his sister."

"And you believe she definitely wanted him dead," Mac asked.

"I believe that she may have done but now he's gone I believe she may wish him still alive. They had a complex relationship, not the kind of relationship that siblings ought to have. Malcolm Brewster did them a great disservice. In many ways he was a revolting man and the legacy he has left to them is disgusting and obscene."

He took a handkerchief from his pocket and mopped his face. Mac could see that he was in a great deal of pain. He stood, knowing it was time to go. "Thank you for your time," he said. "And for the information."

The grandson crossed to a little table at the back of the room and picked up a sheaf of paper in a clear plastic wallet, he handed this to Mac.

"I'll see you out," he said.

As they walked to the door Mac asked, "How ill is he?"

"His doctors say he might make it to Christmas but not to plan his New Year celebrations. He's had a good life, he knows that, and he'll be missed. He knows that too. But he's in a great deal of pain and none of us wish for the pain to get worse. He enjoyed the wedding and is very happy to have made it this weekend. He's fond of Bridie and thinks she's made a good match."

"Well, we can agree on that," Mac told him and earned himself a genuine smile.

The door was unlocked and then opened and Mac stepped outside. He turned to shake hands with the grandson and then both hit the deck as a shot rang out.

For a moment Mac stayed prone, expecting a second shot, turning his head to try and discern where it had come from and what had been hit. He realised he had heard shattering glass and looked upwards towards the house. And then he was on his feet and running into the woods, the two younger Caprisis at his side.

The two men broke left and right and Mac continued straight on, breathing hard, his pounding footsteps seeming very loud even on the muddy ground. He could hear what he assumed were the two Caprisis crashing through the woodland undergrowth on either side of him but had no sense of who might be up ahead.

Mac reached a clearing in the trees and came to a halt. He turned back to look towards the house now hidden behind the trees, though beside a fallen branch he could see heavy footprints from booted feet. Other tracks led off into the woodland. He was about to follow when Gianni Caprisi emerged from the wood to his right. Mac indicated the footprints and Gianni crouched down to examine them and he too looked back towards the house.

"From down here you have a clear sightline," he said and when Mac crouched beside him, he realised the man was right. The gun man had probably fired from a prone position, Mac realised, using the fallen log to steady his weapon and fired upwards. From here he could see the shattered window. Whose window? He would put money on it being Mia's.

The grandson appeared in the clearing. "I caught sight of someone," he said. "Tall, heavyset, running towards the cottages. He turned back and aimed his weapon in my direction and frankly I thought . . ." He shrugged.

"Sensible," Mac commented. "We could do without another death. I think three is more than enough for one weekend."

Gianni patted him on the shoulder. "We could head towards the cottages," he said.

"We could, but chances are our man has disappeared and as Miriam pointed out to me earlier there are plenty of places to hide on the island. If we go back the way we've come, hopefully we won't trample on any evidence," he added. "I think my next move needs to be to speak to the detective who will be SIO and suggest she brings armed officers with her."

"That would seem to be a good move," Gianni agreed.

The three of them walked back towards the guest house, examining the ground as they went, finding more footprints crossing the path they had taken as though someone had moved back and forth, quartering the terrain to find the best position. Mac retrieved the folder he had dropped when the shot had rung out. Then he waited until the two men had gone inside, reassured Mac that nothing had happened to Ben Caprisi in their absence, then locked the door. Mac hurried back towards the house.

Miriam was waiting for him. She threw her arms around his neck and Mac could feel that she was trembling. "When you didn't come back, I thought . . . I don't know what I thought."

"I'm OK. We found footprints in the wood and the location the shooter was using," Mac told her. "There was a clear view of the window. Mia's window? Was she hurt?"

"A few cuts from the broken glass but nothing serious. Mac, this changes things dramatically, doesn't it?"

He nodded. What had previously been a dire situation had now become more volatile. "I'll come and speak to Mia in a moment, I want to get straight on to DI Sullivan, we're going to need armed officers."

* * *

Terry Pritchard could see that Inspector Sullivan was clearly worried after her conversation with DI MacGregor and then with the Gold Commander, requesting the armed response. The previous situation had been bad enough but now to add firearms into the equation raised the stakes considerably. It had already become apparent that they were dealing with someone cool, calm and calculated, able to get close to his victims and attack with deadly accuracy. But if this man also had a gun, that definitely upped the ante. He didn't have to get close. He could target anyone, anywhere and the fact that he had already used the weapon meant that he'd decided stealth and silence were no longer required.

"Any details on the weapon?" Terry asked when Sullivan had briefed her team on this latest development.

"A rifle, he assumes. Judging from the distance and angle of fire. No brass left on scene that he could see but with luck the bullet can be recovered from the room."

"Do we wait here for the Armed Response Unit?" someone asked. Terry remembered that he was a DS and that his name was Dean Petty.

"No, we head out as planned. They'll rendezvous with us before we cross to the island. We've been ordered to wait until they can secure the perimeter." She was, he could see, clearly angry at this delay but knew as well as the DI did that this was protocol. No sense risking other people getting shot.

"DI MacGregor needs our backup now," she said irritably. "We've been delayed long enough. And now more sitting on our hands."

Terry could feel the tension among the other officers in the four-by-four and feel the frustration pouring from her; a sensation he shared. She had relayed the information to those in the other two vehicles, other police officers and the CSI team. He sensed that no one wanted to wait. That it just added to the feeling of helplessness and that sense that they just weren't doing their jobs. Terry, who had seen enough of firearms this past few months, who would be happy never to encounter any kind of gun for the rest of his life — not even one as innocuous as the fairground shooting galleries he and his sister had loved when they were kids — felt a guilty relief in being told they must stand off until the area was made safe.

On the other hand, he could imagine how DI MacGregor and the rest of the wedding guests must feel when they realised that the promised relief would not be arriving any time soon.

CHAPTER 20

Mia was sitting in Rina's bedroom, on the opposite side of the house to the room where her window had been shot out. The Peters sisters had brought extra chairs and were close by, sipping tea and offering biscuits and telling stories about their time on the stage to an unresponsive and glowering young woman. She would have to learn, Rina thought, that Eliza and Bethany would not be put off by any such simple attempt to ignore them. In their youth they had worked every end-of-pier show, every back street theatre and working man's club on the circuit, both as part of someone else's act and then as their own, before they began to make names for themselves and play the better houses. A studied silence was nothing compared to the catcalls and fights and occasional missiles aimed in their direction that they'd learned to cope with back then.

Rina also knew that sooner or later even Mia would find herself forced to make some kind of response, the sisters had a way of wearing listeners down and almost tricking them into conversation. She was slightly surprised that Mia had made no attempt to depart in a huff. She was either genuinely shaken by events, Rina thought, or she had reason to want witnesses to her whereabouts.

A quiet knock on the door announced Mac's arrival. Rina poured coffee for them both.

Mia glared at the new arrival. The Peters sisters announced their intention to leave Mac to do his job and then spent several minutes checking that he was all right before doing so.

"Miriam said you chased after the gunman!"

"Oh really, Mac. You should be more careful. He might have fired at you."

"Did you see the villain? What was he like?"

"I'm afraid I didn't," Mac said. "Only his footprints."

Eliza and Bethany kissed him, one on each cheek, leaving faint traces of pink and coral. Once they had gone, Rina handed him a tissue and Mac, wise these days to the after image of the sisters' kisses, wiped the lipstick traces away.

He sat down opposite Mia. "I'm told you were cut," he said, "by the window glass." Rina could see him examining Mia and satisfy himself that whatever injuries she had received were minor. Mia had been lucky, Rina thought, she'd been lying on the bed and out of the direct line of fire and broken glass. The heavy curtains had absorbed much of what might have come her way. This puzzled Rina. Why would anyone shoot into what must have looked like an empty room. Had the gunman thought he'd spotted a figure before he'd fired?

"I want to get out of here," Mia growled.

"As do we all. But that's not going to happen for a while yet."

"Why not!" Mia demanded. "The rain has stopped, the ferry should be running. I demand you get the ferry here to take us off."

"I can't do that," Mac told her, his tone reasonable and quiet. "The ferry won't come across while there's a chance of someone shooting either at the ferryman or the passengers. We just have to sit tight and stay inside and away from the windows. The doors are locked and everyone is gathered in the main body of the house. We just need to stay calm and wait for help to arrive."

"Will there be armed police?" Rina asked.

Mac nodded. "That's being organised, and DI Sullivan's team are expected within the next hour. They've got orders to stay on the other side of the lake, and well out of range, until the Armed Response Unit gets here but help is on the way and we'll hopefully be off the island by this evening."

"It's just one man!" Mia burst out. "You think I'm afraid of just one man? What's to stop me taking a rowing boat and leaving anyway?"

"Strictly speaking, nothing," Mac agreed. "But I'm not about to let you. Miss Brewster, your brother is already dead. Two other guests on the island are also dead. An attempt was made on your life, so I'm not about to let you take a rowing boat and make yourself into a target."

"And how are you going to stop me?"

She stood now and Mac did the same and for a moment they were toe to toe and Rina wondered if she'd be needing the antiseptic again.

"So, how?"

"By locking you in a room if I have to."

"I'll get out of the window."

"The room I had in mind is an old pantry. No windows and a very solid Victorian lock on the door. Admittedly, it's not the warmest place, but with a blanket or two you should survive."

"You wouldn't dare."

"Try me."

Rina's thoughts were drawn to what Bridie had said about the flowers before the wedding. That she planned to keep them in an old larder, that they'd be cool in there. Was that what Mac had in mind? She was relieved when Mia, either believing Mac or feeling she had made her point, threw herself into the chair and went back to glowering.

"So, apart from you, who would want your brother dead?" he asked.

"I didn't want him dead. I just wanted him out of my way," Mia spat back.

"Well, let's leave that for a moment. Who else would want him dead?"

"How the hell should I know? There are always jealous people, unreasonable people, people who want what others have got."

"Like you do?" Mac questioned. "I'm told that both you and your brother believed that the Caprisis and the Donovans and the Duggans owed you something, just because they once had business dealings with your father."

"Damned right they do."

"Legally, no they don't. Not so far as I can make out. Ben Caprisi has had his lawyers go through your claims with a fine-toothed comb and found you don't have a leg to stand on. It's very likely the other families have done the same. It's my experience that crime families are very careful not to owe favours or have debts that might be called in, not unless they've got equally big favours or other debts they can call in for themselves. No one wanted to do business with your father, Miss Brewster. Hadn't done for decades, not since well before you were born. He was not a man anyone trusted and this from a community that probably wouldn't trust their own grandmother. He even played you and your brother off one another and he's still doing it now, even though he's dead and buried."

Rina knew Mac well enough to understand that he was really angry with the situation they now found themselves in. Angry and frustrated and losing patience with Mia, a young woman he certainly didn't like. But she was also conscious that he would always strive to be fair. Rina said, "Trust him, Mia. If someone is trying to kill you, then it's likely you know the reason why. Mac can't protect you unless he knows who and what he's protecting you from."

To her great surprise, Mia began to laugh. It wasn't hysterical laughter or suggesting any kind of lack of control. It was simply, Rina realised, that the girl found the whole question absurd.

"You think you can do anything?" she said. "Oh my God, you really do, don't you? You really think you can make any

152

bloody difference. You're just one man. You're just one bloody policeman. Who the hell do you think you're kidding?"

Rina could hear the bitterness in her voice and, she thought, the fear. Mia wasn't simply being scathing, she was speaking the truth, as she saw it, and Rina considered that she was probably right.

"Let him at least try, Mia," she said quietly. "You can trust Mac to do all he can."

"Can I? Look, Rina, I know you all mean well but you're all out of your depths here. Charlie's dead. Those other people, the Clarks, they're dead, no one stopped that happening, did they?"

She's really scared, Rina thought. "Trust us. You must have an insight into what's going on, into who might want you and Charlie dead. I mean really want it as opposed to those people who would just find it convenient."

Mia laughed again but this time it was a genuine sound and she regarded Rina with what seemed to be amusement. "You really are a strange woman," Mia said.

Mac sighed, he sat back in his chair and regarded the young woman thoughtfully. "It's only a matter of time before the investigative team get here and the armed officers and then I won't be just one man, there'll be others to help find the gunman and to protect you from harm. And I'm sure they'll do their best to make sure you get off the island safely. But I ask you this, Mia, what happens then? Are you going to shut yourself away from the world, surround yourself with walls and locked doors and employees you just have to hope you can trust? From what I've seen of your family, none of you have gone out of your way to generate any goodwill or loyalty. I suppose you'll just have to hope, whoever you have to put your trust in to keep you safe, that you're paying them enough. Perhaps it's time you allowed someone else to help you. Perhaps, despite what you might think, I can."

Rina could see that the words hit home from the sudden pallor that showed on Mia's face. Harsh, she thought, but probably all too true. And Mac hadn't finished with her.

"I believe Emilie managed to find you another room," he said. "I've checked with her and the sash windows are locked off at just six inches above the sill, so I doubt you'll be able to get out. I suggest you keep the curtains closed. If you want to join the rest of us downstairs, then you'll be very welcome, I'm sure. And if you decide you want to talk to me and tell me who might top the list of wanting you and your brother dead, then come and find me."

He got up and held the door open. Mia's eyes flashed hatred and, Rina thought, genuine hurt. She wasn't used to being spoken to like this, to being disregarded — though Rina knew Mac was doing no such thing. She watched as Mia got up and left the room, taking the atmosphere of deepest discontent with her.

"Do you think she's ever been happy?" Rina asked when Mac had closed the door and resumed his seat.

"You have to wonder if she'd even recognise the feeling," Mac agreed. "But I get the feeling she wants to be and hope-fully, one day, if she survives that long, she might just figure it out."

"Mac, one thing puzzles me."

"Just the one thing? No, sorry, go on."

Rina reached for the coffee pot and refilled her cup. She was already far too caffeinated, she thought, but somehow hot drinks were comforting. "The gunman took a shot at Mia so presumably thought he saw her in the room. But Mia says she was lying on the bed, not standing where he could see her. I've been into her room and the bed is on the left-hand side as you come in. The door faces the window. There are heavy curtains and even when they are open they'd absorb a lot of the flying glass, which is probably why she escaped any serious injury, though she still sustained some nasty cuts. But there's no way the killer could have seen her, as according to Mia, she had been lying on the bed reading a magazine for a while before the shot. I don't think there's any question about her not being there. She was cut by the flying glass, and there were fragments in her hair and caught up in her clothes. So, I suppose my point is, what was he shooting at?"

"It's a good question," Mac told her. "It's possible he spotted something he thought was someone moving in the room. From the angle the shot must have been taken I don't think it was possible to have seen anyone unless they'd actually been standing at the window. I suspect, Rina, that he shot out the window in order to frighten rather than to kill. He might have got lucky, which from his perspective would have been a bonus. He'd also have to know that window was Mia's which suggests one of two things."

Rina nodded. "That he'd seen her standing in her room earlier or that the aim was simply to terrorise and he didn't particularly care whose room it was."

CHAPTER 21

Mac had insisted everyone gather in the hotel dining room. The Caprisi family had come over from the guest house and Ben Caprisi had reluctantly agreed to remain in the main house. He would have to use the service lift to reach his room; as Emilie had explained, there had been nowhere to install a guest lift when the house had been restored and therefore guests with mobility issues had generally been accommodated in the guest house. The old man seemed quite sanguine about the situation but Mac could see that he was plainly exhausted. He promised to deal with his briefing as quickly as possible.

The staff had also made it plain to Mac that they were not happy to remain in their quarters. They were in a ground-floor and somewhat ugly extension, built some decades before and with no thought to aesthetics — or, for that matter, for security. Emilie had told him that the rooms had been refurbished when the present owners took over and had taken Mac to view them. The rooms were small but clean and light and well-equipped, but, Mac agreed, impossible to secure. The single-storey extension stuck out at the rear of the main house. The windows could be locked but Mac could see that they'd be easy enough to force and were certainly not bulletproof. Moreover, the rear door, an emergency exit, though solid enough, would not, he felt, be enough to afford protection to the women staying in that disconnected little wing.

He had agreed with Emilie that space must be found for them in the main house, even if that meant camp beds or shifting the guests around. Hopefully, they'd be well away from the island before sleeping arrangements became a concern.

The mood, Mac thought, was not good; at best frosty and at worst mutinous.

Everyone wanted to leave — understandably. They had no wish to be left on an island with a murderer on the loose, and Mac could not fault them.

"But we can't leave until the ferry is running again," he told them. "The rain may have stopped for now but the ferry won't make the crossing until it's considered safe to do so and that won't be until the Armed Response Unit arrive and secure the scene."

"And how long is that going to be?" Emilie asked. She'd been holding up well, Mac thought, but the strain was beginning to show.

"DI Sullivan expects to arrive in around twenty minutes or so and the armed unit isn't far behind. In the meantime, we'll just have to sit it out. What we can most usefully do in the meantime is pinpoint where everyone was when the shooting occurred. Anything we can do so that DI Sullivan's team can hit the ground running is going to be helpful."

"You're treating us all like suspects," Mr Prentice accused.

"No, I'm treating us all like witnesses," Mac told him. That was true but his instinct was also to keep people occupied. All of the doors had been locked, he had brought them into the dining room, the only windows here were facing out towards the lake and anyone trying to approach their position could be seen as they crossed the lawn. The cameras had been repositioned so they were on the first-floor windowsills, covering as much of the exterior as possible. Arthur, the marquee man, was monitoring the cameras from the laptop he'd set up on a corner table. It wasn't perfect but Mac hoped it would be enough to give them some warning of any hostile approach. It was the best he could do.

He pointed to the two flip charts he had brought in from the incident room and on which he had drawn up two rough plans of the ground floor of the house and the first-floor bedroom. He'd illustrated the other two floors and the ground floor of the abbey guest house on the next pages of the charts. He had copied these basic outlines from the fire escape instructions on each floor of the house, a simple map that that showed the basic layout of each floor and position of the exits.

"The shot was fired at two fifteen," he began. "Many of you will have heard it. So cast your minds back to that moment and tell me where you were." He paused and then said, "I was standing in the doorway of the abbey guest house with Simon Caprisi." He found the appropriate page on the flip charts and marked two crosses, adding both names.

"I had gone to my bedroom," Ben Caprisi told him. "My son was with me, checking there was nothing I required."

Mac thanked him and added the two names to the plan.

"George and I were in our room," Ursula said. "Tim and Joy were with us."

Four more names went onto the plan.

Rina and the sisters had been in the hallway, crossing from the dining room to the small sitting room. Rina had immediately run up the stairs and arrived at Mia's room at the same time as Tim, the others close behind.

It seemed that they all assumed Mia had been the target. Mac wasn't sure whether to commend their bravery in running towards gunfire or berate then for their risk-taking. Wisely he held his peace, reminding himself that he too had hurtled towards danger, in pursuit of the gunman. Instead he asked Miriam, in her role as recorder, to add this information to the notes.

"I was in the kitchen," Emilie said. "We were clearing away. Most people had finished their lunch so we'd made a start on the washing up."

She had been in the kitchen with four members of staff. Two others were in the laundry room preparing to make up beds for the additional guests Mac had brought from the cottages.

Slowly the plans filled up with names and Miriam's notes fleshed out the details.

Mac's mobile rang. DI Sullivan's team had arrived on the lakeside. He felt the collective sigh of relief in the room as he relayed this information. The armed officers were only half an hour behind.

Mac went to the front door, unlocked it and opened it cautiously. He waved at his colleagues on the opposite bank: two police Land Rovers and a large white van belonging to scientific support. He counted a dozen people in all.

"Everyone OK?" Christine Sullivan asked, continuing with the phone call, rather that attempting to shout across the water. "I've got minibuses arranged to take witnesses away ASAP. We should have you out of there soon."

"We're all very relieved about that," Mac told her.

* * *

Terry Pritchard looked across the lake at the man he had last seen in the chief constable's office and wondered what he'd think when Terry turned up.

He surveyed the scene. The sun had broken through the heavy grey cloud and sparkled on rough water, stirred up by a fractious and surprisingly chilly breeze. The house sat four square and was positioned straight ahead across the water, the door wide and broad, set between two equally large and imposing bay windows. To the left was another structure he figured must be the religious buildings he'd been told about, but a stand of trees got in the way of a full view. More woods behind. Not easy ground to search or to protect.

He glanced around to where the DI had a map spread out on the bonnet of one of the four-by-fours, and went over to look.

"So the island is a rough teardrop shape," she was saying. "If you can imagine, this is the fat end, with the house and monastic buildings, chapel, guest house." She pointed to each in turn as marked on the OS map. "We could do with a Landranger map", she said. "This shows the area but doesn't have the detail I'd like. You can see though that the island stretches back beyond the house and ends in a kind of peninsula, tagged onto the end of the teardrop. That's where the cottages are and where the bodies were found."

She brought up the image on her phone and Terry did the same. Having the large-scale map helped orientate him and Google Maps on his phone allowed him to hone in on the detail without getting confused about where he was looking. He'd always envied people who only had to look at a map to figure out exactly where they were and how to get to where they needed. He always got his bearings in the end but Terry did subscribe to the school of thought that said you should turn any map to face the direction you were going. It seemed only sensible.

"And these must be the holiday flats," one of the other officers said. He too was studying his phone and comparing what he saw to the OS map.

"No one was staying there," Sullivan confirmed, "So we have to wonder if our killer is using one of the houses as a base."

"Is everyone in the main house?" Terry asked.

"Yes, Detective MacGregor has got them all together. Apparently there was a bit of opposition in certain quarters."

Her phone chimed and she checked her messages. Smiled. "The armed response team are just crossing the bridges. The minibuses are parked up on the road just beyond. The water's still too deep for them to get through. We might have to ferry anyone that can't walk that far."

"Ben Caprisi uses a wheelchair," Terry said, earning himself a curious look from one of the other officers.

"You met him?" DI Sullivan asked.

"I did, yes, but that was on another case." He had liked the old man but thought that was probably not information he should share at this point. He was saved from further questions by the sound of an engine coming up the drive, announcing the arrival of their armed colleagues.

Terry looked back across the lake. Who was out there? Was it someone he had run across while he'd been undercover? That seemed likely or at least possible. Would he be recognised? Of course he would. Twice he had been in the company of Mia Brewster. In the background certainly, but he had no doubt that the young woman was possessed of an encyclopaedic memory, and though his appearance had changed, she would remember him.

And if the man in the woods, the man with the gun was also known to him, would that make him more of a potential target?

Probably.

Knowing there was nothing in the world he could do about any of it, Terry joined the others in welcoming their colleagues.

* * *

For the next hour, Rina watched from her bedroom window as people and equipment were ferried over, each trip guarded by two armed officers while others watched, on high alert, from the jetty and the lawn. She guessed there would be others out of her sightline, closer to the woods and that one would probably take up position in the bell tower of the little church. Rina thought about that, wishing she and Tim had taken the opportunity to climb the steps and see what the view might be like. From what she remembered the openings at the top of the tower were slatted, but it might be a suitable position for a sniper's nest. She was irritated with herself for not knowing for sure, but reminded herself that when she and Tim had been exploring, they hadn't, even in their wildest of speculations, expected there to be a murderer loose on the island.

She'd counted eight of the armed officers, Specialist Firearms Officers, she reminded herself, in full body armour, helmeted and if she remembered right, they would be armed with Heckler and Koch 9 mm and probably Glock 9 mm pistols. Six other officers, the first three to cross less distinguishable from their colleagues now that they too had donned protective gear. Four CSI, still waiting on the far shore with the three remaining, regular police. They seemed to have been ordered back into their vehicles by the leader of the tactical unit and those vehicles had been backed up and parked behind a small stand of trees. Rina figured this would be so they were out of easy range of any gunfire. A capable sniper with a decent rifle would still be perfectly able to take down any officer on that further shore, but having seen the damage to Mia's window and the penetration of the bullet into the wall — not deep, capable of removal from the plaster and brick into which it had buried itself — Rina wasn't of the opinion that the gunman had used anything particularly high-powered.

She'd not visited the location in the woods from which he'd taken his shot but had got a very amused Simon Caprisi show her the approximate location on Google Earth and, allowing for the changes on the ground since the mapping had been done and which showed a more open location, Rina figured that any half decent shot could easily have taken out Mia's window.

She had said so to Ben Caprisi. The old man chafing against the pain and boredom but unwilling to go to his room and be out of the loop, had taken up residence in the second of the small sitting rooms and they had settled him comfortably on the deeply padded sofa.

"And are you a decent shot?" he had asked, clearly amused.

"Actually I am. Only target shooting and clay pigeons, you understand. I've rarely had the opportunity to do more than that."

"Rarely?" he'd asked and then laughed. "I don't think I'll ask."

Actually, Rina thought, it had only been the once and the circumstances had been oddly similar to this, apart from the season. On that occasion she and Tim and Joy, attending a conference Tim had been invited to in his magician persona, had been cut off by snow. A man had died, there had been shooting . . .

"Thank you for distracting him," Simon Caprisi had said a little later, when his grandfather had fallen asleep on the sofa and Rina had fetched him a blanket.

"He's in a lot of pain, isn't he," Rina said. "Hopefully it won't be long before you're all out of here. I know Mac will give him priority."

"You don't think we're suspects, then?"

"For Charlie or for the attempt on Mia?"

"Either."

Rina had considered the question. "Well, when the shot was taken at Mia's window you were standing conveniently close to Mac. I don't think your grandfather could hold a rifle steady enough and your father would have had to nip out of the back door at a run, zip round the chapel, into the woods, settle himself in position and take the shot all in the minute, probably less than two, it took you to walk Mac to the door and say your goodbyes. I don't recall anyone telling me he was an Olympic athlete."

"And Charlie Brewster?"

"Ah," Rina said, "I don't think any of us have a decent alibi for that. We don't even know when he died."

She thought about the conversation now, about who could be ruled out and who very definitely could not. She knew that no one in the Frantham contingent was involved in either death. It was probably fine to discount the marquee riggers. Was it possible that a member of staff might be involved? It didn't seem likely, on the face of it, but they couldn't be completely ruled out, of course. The four women and two men, plus Emilie, were able to go practically anywhere and no one would really notice them; there were few locations where they would be considered out of place. The catering company had taken all of their people away the evening before but, Rina wondered, were those staff who remained regular, long-term employees or, as with so many hotels, agency staff who might only work on short-term contracts?

Jill, the young woman who had served Rina breakfast, had mentioned she had worked at the house for several years and lived in. Because Rina had been interested, she had confided that a marriage breakup had effectively made her homeless and when this opportunity had come up, with accommodation, it had seemed perfect. Rina recalled that Jill was also the one with the cameras set up to watch the birds and other wildlife.

She hoped the experiences of the weekend would not completely ruin the sense of security this place must have provided for the poor girl.

The sound of a helicopter caused her to look up, craning her neck to watch as it overflew the house. It looked like the police were taking advantage of the break in the rain to do an aerial search.

"Good luck with that one," Rina muttered. There were so many places on this little island that a man could hide. So many unlocked doors and empty buildings. The little chapel, with its pretty bell tower, the monastic buildings she and Tim had wandered through the morning before. Even the guest house, now the Caprisis had acceded to Mac's request and come over to the main house. Then there were the cottages, now emptied of guests — and it occurred to Rina that as Mac had not ventured upstairs when he had found the bodies, that the killer could even have still been on the premises. She shuddered at the thought. Mac had mentioned the sense of being observed while he was there, what if he'd been observed at even closer quarters than he imagined?

Then the two houses at the end of the headland, currently unoccupied, but easy enough to get inside. Not to mention the tunnels.

The helicopter was all well and good but, given the lay of the land, it would be about as effective a technique as attempting to search out a rabbit that had already dived back into a warren. This wasn't really open country, was it.

Bored with watching from the window, Rina made her way downstairs and was immediately conscious of the level of noise, rising to her as she reached the first floor.

Someone sounded cross, she thought. The voice was more petulant than angry — though it wasn't the only one raised in concern and irritation. Rina found the Peters sisters seated on the mezzanine landing, gazing intently down into the hallway, calling to mind pastel-clad emperors, observing the drama in the circus below.

"What's going on?" Rina asked, peering over the balustrade. The noise level, now she was here above the chaos, was actually quite intense. Mac and a female officer, she assumed must be DI Sullivan, were pretty much surrounded by a very anxious crowd, all asking variations on the same question. When would they be allowed to leave. To their credit, Rina thought, both Mac and the unfamiliar DI were handling things calmly and with great restraint. They urged the guests to go back to the dining area or to their rooms, assuring them that as soon as it was considered safe the ferry would take them over to the shore in small groups, accompanied by armed officers.

"It's been very exciting," Bethany said. "Mr Prentice lost his temper with Mac and started calling him names. He said he was a jumped-up little Napoleon. Can you believe that? It seems like such a silly thing to say."

"Napoleon wasn't really even that small," Eliza added. "Obviously, not as tall as Mac, but he was taller than Nelson and only a little shorter than Wellington. Stories about his height were just false news!"

Rina hadn't known that but assumed Eliza was correct. She was, as a rule, very good at trivia. "I've not heard anyone use Napoleon's name as an insult in a while."

"It's definitely a tad old-fashioned," Bethany agreed.

"Where is everyone?" Rina asked.

"Oh, the youngsters are in George and Ursula's room watching a film. Matthew and Steven are still in the dining room. They're explaining Matthew's filing system to one of the young officers that came with DI Sullivan."

Rina nodded. She was rather proud of her people, she realised. They had stayed calm, done their best to be useful and were now quietly keeping out of the way and not adding to the general melee. Rina could understand the urge to leave, the desperation of individuals who had never before met with gunfire and were certainly unprepared for this level of existential threat, but shouting about it wasn't going to help.

Over the din she heard the boat engines as the ferry arrived, presumably with the final contingent of officers. The CSI came into the reception area a few moments later, laden down with more equipment, accompanied by the final three officers, also burdened with technical supplies.

The noise level dropped as everyone turned to appraise the new arrivals and to Rina's surprise, Mac stepped away from DI Sullivan and marched towards one of the newcomers. He had kept his temper with the civilians, but it seemed to Rina that all the pent-up irritation exploded now, aimed at a young, dark-haired man, cradling a metal case as though suddenly he needed it for protection.

"You!" Mac exploded. "I think you owe me a bloody explanation, don't you?"

CHAPTER 22

DI Sullivan had left the job of placating the guests to her other officers and now Mac, Christine Sullivan and a very uncomfortable DS Terry Pritchard were crammed into one of the smaller rooms beneath the mezzanine and Terry was certainly the centre of attention.

"So, what the hell's going on?" Mac demanded. "Did you have any idea of the level of threat when you handed me that damned file?"

Terry shook his head. "I knew things could get messy, so many rival interests in the same place and the Brewster siblings in the middle of a fight, but no, I had no idea anything like this would happen."

"Three murders and an attempted fourth," Mac snapped back at him. "And a gunman loose on the island. So, talk!"

Terry Pritchard looked away as though he was too ashamed or embarrassed to meet Mac's gaze. Mac realised with a slight shock that the young officer was in fact just trying to gain control of his own emotions before responding to Mac's.

He looked exhausted and deeply uncomfortable. Mac sighed, decided to cut the younger man some slack. "So, what can you tell me?" he said. "We've got three dead and what we have to assume was an attempt on the life of a fourth. I don't suppose you've run across the Clarks before, know why they might have been targeted?"

"The dead couple at the cottage? No, the name rings no bells."

Mac had deleted the crime scene photographs from his phone as soon as they'd been downloaded. He had no wish to wander about with such bloody scenes sitting in his gallery. "As soon as I've done with you, go and see Miriam and she'll show you the crime scene photos. It might be you've run across them under a different name and they somehow figure in this mess. Or they might simply have been in the wrong place at the wrong time. Or seen something the killer thought might identify him." He paused. "And you've no idea on that score either, I imagine. Who we might be dealing with?"

"You seem pretty sure it was a man," DI Sullivan observed. "Why not the sister, she had the most to gain. From Charlie Brewster's death, anyway."

"It's possible," Mac conceded, "but the force of the blows makes me think otherwise. Certainly, a strong woman could have done it, I'm not certain that Mia could have."

He watched as Terry took a deep breath. Mac motioned him to a chair in the corner of the room and seated himself opposite. DI Sullivan took the third chair, closer to the door. Mac noted she was watching with interest but seemed disinclined to intervene. He doubted she'd had much time to interrogate the DS either, and Mac realised a little self-consciously that interrogate was pretty much what he was doing. He tried to modify his tone, aware that he still sounded irascible. "So, tell me," he said, "just what is your involvement in all this?"

Terry closed his eyes for a moment and Mac could tell that he was finding everything very hard. That he did in fact look very unwell. "Should you even be here?" he asked bluntly. He knew that look; it had faced him in his own mirror for months after the Cara Evans case had ended so badly. He had watched a child die and been unable to intervene and that had nearly destroyed him.

"Probably not. Sick leave wasn't doing me any good, so I requested a return to light duties. I was supposed to be making a soft return, desk duties only. Then all this blew up."

"So, they threw you back into the wolf pit," Mac said, his tone registering both understanding and a certain distaste. "Had you been undercover?"

Terry nodded. Mac listened as he explained, as he had earlier to DI Sullivan, what he had been doing and how his stint had ended. How he had walked away, knowing that his friend, Gray, would be killed. Known he had no choice. Mac watching both Terry and the DI could see the watchful concern on Christine Sullivan's face. She felt deeply sorry for this young man. She also needed him, fighting fit and able to contribute.

Mac got up and opened the door, managed to attract the attention of a member of Emilie's staff on their way to the kitchen and asked if they could have some coffee.

"How are you all holding up?" he asked gently.

"Keeping busy, can't wait to be out of here." Her smile was forced but he returned it with as much reassurance as he could muster. "It won't be long, now," Mac told her, hoping that was true.

She returned quickly with three mugs of instant, milk and extra sugar plus some biscuits. "The commander or whatever he is, the man in charge of the guns, he's said we can each take a small bag, that they'll be sending men to look after us while we pack and we'll be leaving in the next hour or so. I think they want to get the gentleman in the wheelchair off first. He's looking really poorly."

Mac thanked her and set the coffee on a tiny table between the chairs.

"First priority is going to be evacuation," DI Sullivan said. "We've got arrangements with a couple of local stations to get interviews done there. The less people we have knocking around here, the better."

"Agreed. It's not going to be an easy location to search or to secure," he said. "What about the bodies?"

"Soon as we can, we'll get to them. But priority is the living. Get them to a place of safety, or at least get that process underway. I know the CSI manager is itching to get on scene. It's if and when we can do that safely."

Mac glanced back at Terry. The brief redirecting of the conversation seemed to have given him a breathing space and he looked calmer. "So, this Regis Crick, you think he's behind the attack on the Brewsters?"

"He'd be my first guess. He was bitter that when the old man died, he didn't leave him a share in the business. After all he'd been running a good chunk of it in recent years, knew all the ins and outs. Where all the bodies were buried, literally and figuratively. Crick figured he was owed."

"This whole scenario seems made up of people who think they're owed," Mac observed. "And he'd be acting alone?"

"He has the usual crew of loyal hangers-on. Loyal while the wind blows the right way. Trouble is, when he had assumed he'd get rewards in the old man's will, so did everyone else. Then, when that didn't happen, well he lost face, felt he'd been made to look a fool."

"So certain of his hangers-on would start drifting away?"

Terry nodded. "So all of a sudden proving your loyalty became a big thing. He became obsessed. Gray fell foul of that, but the truth is, it should have been me. He'd done nothing wrong."

Mac let that pass. This was not the time to be indulging self-recrimination or guilt. "So, who might be working with him? You think he'd take on a job like this in person?"

"I'd bet on it. This had become personal, especially when Mia laughed in his face when he suggested her father had made certain promises. She told him that no one in their right mind would believe anything Mal Brewster said and followed it up with a few more observations about Crick's brain power. She's not a girl who bothers to even look like she wants to be friends."

"Unlike Charlie," Mac observed.

"I didn't have anything to do with Charlie Brewster. One thing that became obvious was that you worked for one or the other and to the exclusion of the other. But from what I heard, his tactics were different to hers, yes."

Mac nodded. "And the will directed both of them to reclaim territories Brewster believed were rightfully his. The one that gained the most was outright winner?"

"I didn't see the will, but I think that was the gist, yes."

Mac considered. "What about the third sibling? Ruari. I know he is theoretically not part of this mess, but . . . what?" Terry's expression told Mac he'd hit on something.

"Thing is, everyone believes that Ruari Brewster is legit. That he doesn't figure in any of this. But he came over for his father's funeral and for the reading of the will. I saw him and Mia at it hammer and tongs afterwards. I reckon it's not beyond the bounds of possibility that Ruari Brewster is working with Regis Crick. They seemed friendly enough at the funeral and there are rumours about both. That Crick is using Ruari to stake a claim stateside, using his connections there. But no way could I prove anything solid and so far no one's taken the idea particularly seriously."

"Did you have any dealings with Ruari?"

Terry shook his head. "No. I saw him at the funeral and at the wake. That was where I witnessed the argument. They were standing in the garden and not bothering to keep their voices down. Mia was telling him that he'd had all he deserved and that he wasn't even a proper member of the family. Ruari was reminding her that their father had always acknowledged him and that he deserved his share. That was the gist, anyway."

"And Charlie wasn't involved?"

"Charlie stood on the terrace and watched for a while, then he seemed to get bored and went back inside. He didn't look ruffled; didn't even seem that interested."

"And do you have any sense of Ruari's relationship with Charlie?"

"Not really, no. From what I heard they didn't actually hate one another and in a family like the Brewsters that practically passes for affection."

"But if Ruari killed his half siblings, he must know that he'd be a suspect, must know that he'd not benefit if his involvement could be proved," DI Sullivan objected.

"True, and as you say, that would be a problem *if* his involvement could be proved. But how much of what the Brewsters are known to have done can be or has been proved? Ruari may have left the fold, or at least appeared to do so, but you can bet he's as twisted as the rest of them."

"Appeared to have done so . . ." Mac said thoughtfully. "You think it was just a front?"

Terry shrugged. "I don't know. I got curious about Ruari Brewster, so I looked him up. He's done some really interesting work, mostly documentary and short films and mostly about social issues. But the more you dig the more you realise his role has been as producer and distributer. Other people, usually film students looking to make a name for themselves, do the actual grunt work. The research, the interviews, the actual production. He claims to be some sort of mentor on his website and the films he oversees have done well. I mean there's a fair few awards on his CV, but, I don't know, none of it's big budget stuff, mostly films for the festival circuit. Yet he's got a place in Los Angeles up on the edge of Laurel Canyon that seems, well . . ."

"Like he's living beyond his means," Mac said.

Terry shrugged. "Officially it belongs to the company. It's got a great name, the company. He calls it Little Toad Films. The house has a big plot of land at the back, complete with a small studio and production facilities and there are rumours about the kinds of films that get made there."

"I suppose pornography makes bigger bucks than socially aware student documentaries," DI Sullivan said. "But it's not *necessarily* illegal. I suppose Mal Brewster may have claimed a share of the profits."

"It's the kind of thing Regis Crick was into, officially on the old man's behalf. I don't imagine all the money flowed into Mal Brewster's pocket, though. Especially not towards the end when his grip on business was virtually non-existent. It was Mia that was running things, according to Crick."

"I don't imagine Charlie was happy with that," Sullivan commented.

"No, he and Mia rowed about that at the funeral. He accused her of sucking up to their father just so she'd get a bigger share."

"Well, that didn't work out so well for her," Mac said.

"No, it didn't, but the will was made when he was still fully compos mentis and at his ruthless best. I think if Mia knew what he'd got in store for the pair of them she'd have skimmed as much as she could while she was in control and then walked, left brother Charlie to pick up the pieces."

He shrugged. "I don't know. Mia Brewster and her brother were a mystery, even to the likes of Regis Crick, I think. He reckoned to understand the old man, to be in favour with him, but in the end he got nothing. He was left dependent on the favours of one or other of the kids and that left him mad as hell and twice as mean. It's not something he was prepared to forgive and forget, I know that."

"But something else bothers you about the family," Mac said.

Terry nodded.

"And I'm guessing it's why a man like Mal Brewster, not exactly known for his altruism or fatherly affections, even bothered to acknowledge Ruari. Never mind take charge of him, pay for boarding school, finance him through his studies and then gave him money to get started on his own when he left film school."

"It does seem unlikely," Sullivan agreed. "So why did Brewster take such an interest?"

"Maybe we should ask Mia?" Mac asked. "Seeing as she was so adamant that Ruari isn't a proper member of the family. Perhaps she meant that literally. Perhaps she knows something about Ruari that we don't."

"We don't know for sure he's involved in any of this," Sullivan reminded them. "So far all we've got is speculation, based on an argument at a funeral and that he seems to be living beyond his means, and that might easily be explained by money earned from the films he doesn't advertise."

"But it's something to bear in mind," Mac said.

A knock at the door recalled Sullivan back to her duties and Mac took Terry to meet Miriam so he could view the crime scene photographs of the Clarks. Mac watched him as he studied them carefully, noting the pallor and the sweat breaking out on Terry's face. He hadn't met the Clarks and didn't know them from Adam, he told Mac, but it was clear that the images affected him deeply. Mac recalled his first crime scene after coming back to work from sick leave. To his embarrassment, he'd nearly thrown up — something that hadn't happened since his days as a rookie in uniform. He sympathised with Terry but felt strongly that he should be nowhere near an investigation. He needed to be back on sick leave, be giving himself time to heal no matter how much that might have rankled or what his superiors deemed was necessary. But he held his peace; the officer was here now and nothing could be done about it and he sensed that Terry, his guilt overwhelming him, quite desperately, wanted to be useful.

CHAPTER 23

George and Ursula had been sprawled on the bed watching an old film when Tim and Joy knocked on the door.

"We're bored," Tim announced as Ursula let them in. "So bored I've forgotten we're supposed to be scared. So we thought we'd come and annoy you two for a bit."

Ursula laughed. "Bored enough to be watching *The Wizard of Oz*?" she asked.

"Oh my lord, no." Tim glanced at the television and shuddered. "I'm never going to be that bored."

George turned the television off. "We've both drunk too much tea, been down to the kitchen twice for cake and that was after lunch. It would be all right if we could be useful, but we're just not used to hanging around and doing nothing. It's not as if we can go outside."

"Not outside, no," Joy said, "but there's no one saying we can't explore the house."

Ursula was puzzled. "Explore what?"

"Well, the cellars for one thing. Emilie was telling us about the cellars under the house and how the tunnels from the sunken garden made them unsafe. It had to be underpinned. It's all fine now," she added, "but we thought we'd take a look. We're curious about how close the tunnels came to the basement and if there's any signs. Actually, Tim just wants to know if there are secret passages."

"Guilty," Tim agreed.

"You are such a child," Ursula told him. Sometimes it was easy to forget that Tim had a decade on George and herself.

"Guilty again," Tim agreed cheerfully.

"Well, it's better than sitting here," George said.

Ursula wasn't so sure, but she nodded agreement. It wouldn't be like the tunnels, she thought, this was just the basement of a house, not a narrow channel, cut through solid rock and with absolutely no escape should the roof cave in. "Best take a torch just in case," she said.

"Emilie said there's electric light," Joy told her. Then added, "But a torch is a good idea."

Joy was aware that Ursula suddenly looked worried. "Sure you'll be OK?" she asked quietly as they all trooped out of the room.

Ursula nodded. "Like you said, there'll be lights. I'm fine, really I am. It's just . . . It's just that suddenly I'll get scared or silly about something that would never have bothered me before. And it's not like it's reminding me of anything. It's just . . ."

Joy squeezed her arm. "I get it," she said. "Everyone warned me I might get flashbacks from when I was taken aboard the boat or about Pat being killed but it wasn't like that. I'd be fine and then suddenly something random would just knock me sideways. Like the first time I caught a bus, I got this really bad panic attack. It felt like someone was chasing me and I couldn't breathe. You know those dreams you get when it's like running through treacle?"

Ursula nodded.

"And then on Bonfire Night, with all the fireworks. I suddenly remembered seeing the flare and the ship and the sea and everything being lit up and how scared I was and how cold and how absolutely certain that we'd been seen and someone would start shooting at us. You don't have to apologise, you know that. You don't have to worry that we won't understand."

"Thanks," Ursula said. "I do know that, and it does make it better. I'm just not used to not being prepared for things, you know?"

Joy laughed at that. "No, that must be really tough," she agreed.

Being prepared was what Ursula did. She studied and she wrote lists and she organised, she protected herself from the unexpected and being unable to do that made her feel terribly vulnerable. The strange thing was, the death of Charlie Brewster, and the attempt on Mia's life had left her oddly unperturbed, or if not unperturbed — she was aware that sounded callous and cold — then certainly no more afraid. She told Joy this and Joy just nodded.

"I know what you mean. It's like it's not real because they aren't real. Charlie was all surface and Mia is not someone you can get to know because she won't let you and besides, they aren't exactly your ordinary people. People who live like the Brewsters often come to a bad end. You kind of expect it. It was like when my dad was killed, there'd always been that risk, that someone would want him out of the way. That's why our mum was trying so hard to make everything legit. Pat, though, Pat was his own person and would never have been involved in anything criminal or underhand, but it didn't stop him getting shot. That made us all feel really helpless; like it wasn't possible to get things right, no matter what you did."

"I feel sad for the Clarks though. They only came here on holiday and they wound up battered to death."

Instead of heading towards the main staircase, Tim had led the way to what must have been the servants' stairs and was now marked as a fire exit. They had used the stairs before, as a quick way to access cake and other comestibles. Emilie, stepping back from her role as house manager and into one focussed on maintaining morale, had shown them where the biscuits were and the extra tea and coffee. Jill had produced cake and suggested sandwiches if they were hungry. The staircase came down close to the kitchen, accessed by the corridor that ran back under the mezzanine and, glancing back along the corridor to the entrance hall, Ursula could see a mix of guests, armed officers and other police milling about. Miriam was chatting to what Ursula guessed were other CSI. It seemed to Ursula that there was an irascible, impatient mood prevalent among those gathered. Guests were obviously champing at the bit to leave — understandable, but not a good idea if they were likely to be shot at — and the officers were almost visibly impatient, wanting to get on.

"Through here," Tim said and opened a small door that Ursula had previously noticed but assumed was a broom cupboard.

To her relief there was indeed a light switch and the narrow, open stairs were well illuminated. At the bottom of the stairs was a storage area for the kitchen, filled with cans and dried goods. It was chilly but when Ursula touched the walls, surprisingly dry. The whitewashed walls looked sound and recently painted. She felt a surge of relief.

A doorway led through to a network of rooms, the first two clearly still used for their original purpose. Wine stored in tall racks, carefully labelled with ancient looking metal tags and more recent adhesive labels stuck onto the woodwork.

Tom pulled a sketch map from his pocket. "Where did you get that?" George asked.

"From Jill, in the kitchen. She hasn't been into the back rooms but she gave me a rough idea of what was down here. She reckons it's haunted."

"Of course it is," Joy muttered. "Murderers and ghosts."

Ursula realised that Joy was here only because of Tim's enthusiasm and because she didn't want to be left behind. With all that had happened, she was probably as uneasy as Ursula. Silently, she took Joy's hand.

They walked through the wine cellars and into a space that seemed used as a general dumping ground, filled with broken chairs, cardboard boxes and tea chests. At the end of this was a new-looking wooden door, it was closed but not locked. Tim pushed it open. Behind it was an accumulation of more rubbish and an air of dampness that spoke of it not being used for anything important, perhaps for years. At least there was electricity here, a light switch by the door illuminated a single low wattage bulb and Ursula was glad they had brought torches. George had switched on his phone, using the torch function to stumble across a stack of magazines in the corner. Ursula looked curiously at the sepia pages, they were dated to the 1920s and seem dedicated to the art of fretwork and home woodworking. She wondered if she could take a few of them up to her room and have a look later, not because of any particular interest in fretwork but out of historical curiosity.

"There's another door," Tim said. "And it looks fairly new."

Ursula shone her torch towards the door. This new door was of solid, heavy wood, and equipped with a sturdy looking bolt and a padlock. Cautiously, Tim stepped forward and shone a light on the bolt which Ursula realised had been drawn back. The padlock too, although it looked formidable it was not fully closed and had simply been hooked through the hasp. On closer inspection, it was obvious the hasp had been cut through. The door could be opened.

Ursula felt trepidation as Tim reached out and swung the door wide. The cold hit them, a chill like winter even though outside it was late summer and the house was warm too.

"Is that a well?" George asked.

"Be careful!" Ursula felt quite frightened now though she could not have explained exactly why.

George was standing beside the low parapet and looking down into the well. "I wonder how deep it is?"

"I can live without knowing," Joy responded and Ursula was inclined to agree. She was relieved when George stepped back and instead shone his torch around the walls. Ursula suddenly realised what was making her so anxious. "I think we're in the tunnels," she said. "Weren't they supposed to be blocked off?"

She hadn't let go of Joy's hand and she was grateful now of the fingers tightening around her own.

Tim, gung-ho as ever, had circled the well and shone his torch down the passageway. "I think it is blocked off, I'm going to look."

Fear suddenly flooded Ursula. "No, don't!"

He turned to look at her, his eyes concerned but she could see he was still itching to explore. She sighed. "Alright, just a quick look and then we go back. Please."

He nodded. "A very quick look," he agreed.

The three of them watched as Tim went a few paces along the rocky floor into the narrow passageway and shone his torch around. Then he turned abruptly and came back.

"What is it?" George asked, though Ursula felt she could guess.

"It's not blocked off, is it?" she said.

"There's an opening," Tim confirmed. "It looks like they've run cabling and plumbing into the house. I suppose when they did the underpinning they maybe had to divert some of the old utilities and so they made use of the existing tunnels, that would make sense. I can see another gate, like the one we saw when we went down with Rina. I don't know if it's locked."

To Ursula's relief, and she knew to Joy's, Tim did not seem inclined to go and find out. They retreated to the room with the magazines and closed the door.

Tim hesitated. "Do you think we should lock it?" he asked.

"I'd feel happier if we did," Joy said.

"What about fingerprints," George wondered.

For a few moments they all stared at the heavy wooden door and then Ursula took their room key from her pocket and used it to push the bolt home. "Mac needs to see this," she said. She could feel the sense of collective relief as they returned through the wine cellar and back up the stairs. In the reception area things were quiet once more, guests having withdrawn to either their own rooms or the dining room, Ursula guessed. She could not see Mac.

As they emerged from beneath the mezzanine, Ursula looked up. Rina and the Peters sisters gazed down at her. "Have you seen Mac?"

"In the little sitting room with Miriam," Rina told her.

The place they were using as the incident room, Ursula thought. She was aware of Rina coming down into the hall, no doubt the sight of the four of them all together and looking anxious piqued her curiosity. Ursula knocked on the door. A man she didn't recognise opened it and then Mac came to the door, pulling it closed behind him but not before she had glimpsed images on the laptop set on a table. She was grateful that she'd caught only a glimpse; that had been enough.

"Problem?" Mac asked.

"Maybe. We were bored, we went down to explore the cellar. We found something you need to see."

* * *

Mac and DI Sullivan examined the now bolted door. Ursula had described how she had closed it, just using the rigid edge of the keycard. Tim admitted to having touched the handle to open the door. Fingerprints would need to be taken, with Tim and the others submitting theirs for elimination. One of the armed officers who had accompanied them now slid back the bolt, using a pen borrowed from Mac. Mac and DI Sullivan watched anxiously as the two men slipped through the gap and set a powerful lamp on the floor of the chamber beyond. The well was set in the middle of the chamber and Mac felt curious. Had it served the house once upon a time? He peered upward and was rewarded by a view of a narrow shaft, now capped off, that he assumed might have led to the room at the back of the kitchen that Emilie had told him had been used for laundry. One of the old coppers used for heating water was still there, kept as a curiosity.

Did the water from the well come from the lake, or were there natural springs on the island? He had vaguely thought of it as being manmade but now realised that was an absurd idea. It was far too big. No, more likely a water course had been diverted to create the lake around a natural rise in the land and the island created as a result of that. The house did sit proud of the gardens, he thought. The lawn sloping down quite dramatically before levelling out. It was quite possible that the well was fed from natural springs.

He was seeking distraction, Mac realised. The idea that the killer could have come into the house from the tunnels was a disturbing one — and not something he had previously considered, believing that the passageways had long ago been blocked off.

The two officers now returned. "There's a gate just down the passageway, closed but not locked and a door about thirty feet beyond that. The padlock had been cut off. It looks as though it's designed to be used as an access way, in case the plumbing or electrics need maintenance."

Mac nodded. He guessed that the utilities must eventually come out above ground, somewhere at the back of the house. Did that make them vulnerable? He made a mental note to speak to Emilie and find out.

"We need to secure both gate and door and reinforce the entrance into the house," DI Sullivan said.

"Emilie Trudeau will know if there are any spare padlocks," Mac said. "If not, we'll have to improvise."

Leaving the armed officers in the last cellar, with the door bolted, Sullivan and Mac retraced their steps through the cellar and back up into the kitchen corridor. "Do these friends of your usually go off exploring?" Sullivan asked, a touch of asperity in her voice.

"Perhaps it's as well they did," Mac said. "We were given to understand that the tunnels under the house had been sealed off, not just locked down. It's something I should have checked out myself, but there's not exactly been the opportunity. The important thing is that we now know about that door. The alarming thing is that someone inside the house must have opened that final lock into the cellar. That couldn't have been done from the tunnel side."

"So, a member of staff or one of the guests?"

"Either way, the sooner we get everyone out of here the better."

"Agreed." She glanced at her watch. "Four fifteen. We still have a good amount of time before it starts to get dark. At least we're not doing this in the middle of winter."

"Small mercies," Mac said. Four fifteen. Was that all? He felt as though he'd been on the go for days since they'd found Charlie's body just after nine that morning and then discovered the Clarks close to one. It just felt a whole lot longer than that.

As though reading his mind, she said, "You and Miriam must be knackered. You want to take a break?"

He shook his head. "Miriam might, but I doubt it. She's been frustrated by the wait since first thing. And I'm much happier if I'm doing."

Sullivan nodded. "You've already got a relationship with the house manager. Talk to her, see if you can sort out some means of securing the doors and the gate, get her to tell you about the staff. I'll get someone onto the PNC to do some formal checks but gossip is always helpful."

It was, Mac thought. There was some information the Police National Computer could not supply. "If she doesn't clam up once I tell her about the door," Mac said. "Everyone is on already on edge."

"Apart from your friends, it seems."

Mac looked curiously at the DI. They had reached the kitchen corridor now and a buzz of noise from the hall reached them. At least no one was actually shouting, Mac thought. "I'm not sure what you mean," he said, suddenly deeply irritated by her tone and by whatever she happened to be inferring.

"I mean just about everyone else has been either gathered in frightened little groups or they've been shouting the odds about leaving. Your lot, on the other hand, well the

Montmorencys or whatever they're called have been falling over themselves to be useful and I have to admit they've done a good job. The old women have been sitting up on the landing, watching like all this is just entertainment laid on for their amusement. Then there's those four going down to nose around in the cellar and Miss Martin with her tête-à-têtes with old man Caprisi. You've got to admit they are at the very least an odd lot."

Mac glared at her, his temper threatening to flare. "They are, none of them, people given to panic," he said finally. "But if you're trying to form some kind of accusation, then I suggest you keep it to yourself."

Sullivan's eyebrows raised, she lifted her hands in mock surrender. "OK, keep your hair on. No doubt you're used to them, but from an outside point of view, they are a bit weird. I mean you look at the other guests at the wedding and you have to wonder what their game is . . ."

"I was the best man," Mac said coldly. "Perhaps you'd like to wonder about that." He left her standing and headed into the kitchen. Yes, he admitted, perhaps the Frantham contingent were . . . unusual. Perhaps he had also thought they were bloody odd when he'd first had dealings with Rina and her unusual little household. But once he'd got over his shallow prejudices, he'd found a level of acceptance and affection the like of which he'd rarely experienced in his life. Not to mention loyalty and sheer, undaunted courage when required. He would not hear a word against any of them.

Emilie, Jill and two more of the staff — he recalled that one was John and the other Maryam — were sitting at the kitchen table sharing a well-earned pot of tea. Emilie looked up as he came in. Mac motioned for her to stay where she was and pulled up a chair.

"Are the others anywhere about?" he asked.

"Billy and Mo have gone with one of the officers to collect their things. We've been told we can take one small bag. Tina's holding the fort in the dining room. Why? Do you need to speak to them?"

Mac had intended to speak to Emilie alone but he now decided that would just add to the tension. If one of the staff had been responsible for cutting the lock and opening the bolt, then it was possible they'd give something away. Besides the formal interrogations and statement-giving would be DI Sullivan's concern. "In a minute," he said. "I'll start with you four." He paused. "Look," he said, "we've just discovered something that's potentially quite disturbing. How familiar are you with the layout of the cellars?"

Looks were exchanged, puzzled and a little wary. "We use the first one for storage and the second two for wine," John said. "I can't say I've been any further than that. I did have a poke around the next room when I first came here. I was curious, you know, but there wasn't anything in there apart from a load of old junk."

Mac nodded. "And you've been here how long?"

"Two years," Emilie said. "Or will be next month."

"And do you live in?"

John shook his head. "I sleep over when there's an event, or if I'm on lates, otherwise I get the ferry. Depends what shift I'm on."

"I've been down there," Jill said. "There are I think two more rooms and there's a big, locked door. Billy told me it led to the new plumbing and electrics they put in about five years ago. That was just before I came here. I got the job a couple of months after Emilie arrived. She did my interview."

"Billy's been here longer than I have," Emilie said. "He doesn't usually live in, he comes and does the day shift, he helps out in the kitchen. He's mainly our maintenance man. He sees to all the repairs and odd jobs here, in the guest house and rentals and in the garden. We have a gardener come over with his assistant twice a week, but Billy takes care of any day-to-day stuff. He also stays over if we need an extra body for events." She winced at what she realised might be seen as an inappropriate phrase. "The caterers hired the marquee company as part of their package this time, but for some events we do that ourselves. Billy organises that and he and

John and usually a couple of casual staff erect the smaller marquees."

Billy must be the older man Mac had noticed, he thought. He nodded.

"Mo is the head chef. Maryam and Tina work in the kitchen, Jill is mainly front of house and we have part-time staff who do different shifts as and when we need them. Some just do a few hours a week and others do more."

She frowned at Mac, clearly wondering where this was going. "It's not like a regular hotel," she went on. "Most of the guests come to stay in the self-catering accommodation. The only time we need more than a handful of people is when we've got a big event on."

Mac nodded. He supposed that made sense, but he was no expert when it came to the hotel business.

"The padlock to the external door had been cut," he said. "The bolt had been opened. From the inside."

He watched their faces, saw only shock and fear and incomprehension. "You think it was one of us?" Emilie shot back angrily.

"No, no, I don't. I don't hold any particular suspicions. But everyone who had access has to be viewed as a possible accessory. We must assume that the door was opened so that someone could come in. Possibly so that the killer of Charlie Brewster could gain entry. We have to assume that Mia might be his next target."

Emilie looked stunned. The others distinctly sick.

He had the other staff summoned to the kitchen and put the question a second time. All knew that the basement level was there, had been down into the main rooms of the cellar. Only Billy had been through that outer door. He knew about the well, had liaised with the outside contractors who had come to replace the utilities. He stated that the other gate and door had been locked when they had done and as far as he was concerned, had stayed that way ever since. No one wanted guests or staff wandering down into an area that, though now made safe, led to a room that housed a deep and dangerous old well.

"So, it was put about that the tunnels had been blocked off, mainly for safety reasons?" Mac asked.

"Pretty much, yes. The gates were kept locked to stop people going down there and we always tell guests the tunnels are blocked off just after the first gate, on the garden side. You can't see far enough down, even with a torch, to know any different. The owners talked about doing it for real, but once that side of the house had been underpinned, the surveyors attached these little monitor things to the walls to check for further movement. So they needed access to those. And seeing as the tunnels were already there it made sense to use them for replacing cabling and plumbing in this back section."

"Are there plans available?" Mac asked.

"Sure, we can dig them out for you. Emilie put them in the fireproof cabinet in the office, I think, along with all the schematics for the new utilities."

Emilie nodded.

"Can you bring them to me?" Mac asked. "I'll be with DI Sullivan. And the outer doors and gate will need securing."

"I can sort something out. You want me to go down there?"

"Absolutely not," Mac said.

CHAPTER 24

The padlocks had been reinstated and the keys delivered to DI Sullivan. Emilie and her team had been instructed to bring anything they might need up to the kitchen and a final padlock had been applied to the cellar door.

You'd have to be very determined, Mac thought, to get through all obstacles. Although the locks back in the tunnels could be disabled with the aid of a pair of bolt croppers, it would be hard to get through the final door into the cellar and then the one to the kitchen without making a hell of a lot of noise.

He reminded himself that they were dealing with some-one who had killed three times at close quarters and, if it was just one man they were dealing with, had attempted a fourth with a calmness and purpose that Mac found chilling.

If it was just one man. Mac was rapidly coming round to the idea that two individuals were involved. One who had no qualms about dealing with their victims in about as direct a fashion as was possible. The other who didn't have the stomach or the skill or the confidence for that, who preferred to take their shots from a distance.

It was not a reassuring thought.

It was almost 5 p.m. when he knocked on Mia Brewster's door. She was sitting on the bed, watching television, pillows behind her and a discarded magazine at her side. She looked thoroughly bored.

"They're hoping to start the evacuations soon," Mac said. He indicated a chair set by a small desk. "May I?"

She shrugged. "Sure."

"It's been decided that Ben Caprisi and his family will go first. He's not at all well. Then DI Sullivan will schedule the rest of you. I just wanted you to know that each trip will be accompanied by armed police."

"Which won't stop a sniper," she pointed out.

"The area's been searched both on foot and with drones. A perimeter has been secured as far as that's possible. The layout of the house and grounds makes it impossible to be one hundred per cent certain of anything, not with the forces we've got. DI Sullivan had requested more officers, but it might be a while."

"If she gets them at all." Mia sounded scathing.

"We'll do all we can to ensure everyone gets across safely," Mac said. "Mia, do you have any idea who might be behind this?"

"Why should I?"

"Why wouldn't you? I don't imagine you or your brother were without enemies. With those who, as you said earlier, feel entitled to what you've got. People like Regis Crick, for instance."

Her mouth twisted in disgust. "That loser."

"Was he a loser? Rumour has it your father led him to believe he'd be a beneficiary when he died. Did your father make him promises? Did he then renege on them?"

"If he believed a word my father said then he's an even bigger idiot than I thought. Listen to me, DI MacGregor, or Mac or whatever it is other people like to call you, my father never saw a lie he didn't like, never made a promise he didn't break, never got bested in a deal, or if he did, he always made sure he got the upper hand the next time round. And he could wait, could Mal Brewster. Wait and plan and keep everything logged in that brain of his. Every little betrayal, every little weakness, everything he thought he was owed."

"And what did you owe him?" Mac asked.

"I owed him nothing," Mia said flatly. "You know the crazy thing? The bastard actually loved me. Didn't think much of Charlie but he reckoned we were cut from the same cloth."

"And are you? Were you?"

Mia actually laughed. "Hell no. Charlie was more like him, truth be told."

"And yet he had the two of you fight it out over his will. Over his little empire."

"A far larger empire than you'll ever have, Mr Policeman." Mia sighed. She looked suddenly weary. "Look, Dad wanted to leave everything to me. I told him that wasn't right. It was one of the few times I went up against him but I knew what would happen if Charlie was done out of his fair share. So he had the will drafted so that we had to fight it out. This way Charlie would feel he'd got what he deserved and I'd still come out on top. This was before he fell ill. I've often wondered what might have happened if he'd not fallen ill."

She looked suddenly bereft and very young, more like a lost child than a fractious and unfriendly young woman. Mac wondered what was really going on behind that facade and if she yearned to let it drop. If she even knew how, anymore.

"From what I've heard the will was a winner takes all situation."

"There are provisions for the loser. They're up to the discretion of the winner, but—"

"And you were confident of winning?"

"Confident enough that I didn't have to kill my brother to make it happen. Understand this, Mr Policeman, our father first showed signs of being unwell four years ago. Within six months he was so sick and so wrapped up in getting treatment that I was running the show. Charlie was just running around and looking like he cared, like he was capable, but the truth is Charlie was just . . . decorative." She spat the word as though it was deeply distasteful. "Not a business bone in his body."

Mac let that pass; he had no immediate way of judging the truth of that. Instead he asked, "And what about Ruari?"

"What about him?"

"I heard he came over for the funeral and he was not best pleased at being cut out of the will."

"What did he expect?"

"Your father acknowledged him. He paid for his education, gave him money to set up in business, behaved with more generosity that I'd have expected from Mal Brewster."

She was laughing again. "You don't understand a damned thing, do you?"

"So, explain."

"I thought you were the detective. Why would a man like my father bother with someone like Ruari?"

Mac had already thought about that but come up with no definite answer. In truth, he could see no reason. Had he been forced into a corner? But the thought of that happening to someone like Mal Brewster was absurd. He would either have killed his way out or paid someone else to do it. The best outcome anyone could have hoped for was that he'd have bunged the mother a few grand and made certain she knew to disappear. And could Mac imagine him even doing that?

"Ruari wasn't your father's son," he said finally. "Mal Brewster was acting on someone else's behalf."

"And why would he do that?"

"I don't know. It would have to be either someone he wanted to protect or someone he was afraid of. Either scenario is hard to imagine."

She smiled but gave no clue as to which, if either, was correct. Mac however felt that he was onto something. "Does Ruari know?"

She seemed to hesitate and then said, "He might well suspect. Though the fact that he was demanding a third of all Mal owned makes that unlikely."

"Then why not tell him? A simple DNA test would clear up any doubt."

She shook her head. "Because then it would make Mal look weak. Like you said yourself, most people would assume he was scared of the father, that's why he gave his name to Ruari."

"I seem to remember offering a second option."

"Respect? Who are you kidding."

"Fear it is then."

She was looking at him as though he'd just proved what a fool he was. What wasn't he getting right?

"Or profit. I can see your father lending his name to someone else's boy if the price was right."

This earned him a slow handclap. "Well, bravo that man."

"So, how did you find out?"

"As I told you, I ran my father's business for the past three, nearly four years. And a bloody good job I did too. I had access to his papers, to his legal team, to all his records."

"Did Charlie know?"

"No, Charlie didn't know. Why would he? My brother liked to pose, Inspector, he was what you might call averse to the real hard work."

"And yet you persuaded your father to let him fight you over the will."

"And he would have lost. I'd have paid him off, kept him happy."

"You think so?" Mac really doubted that. "I think you're being naïve."

That earned him a very sceptical raised eyebrow. "And I don't think you know what you're talking about," Mia said.

Mac shrugged. He stood up. "You can take one small bag across with you," he said. "I'll let you know when it's your turn to leave."

CHAPTER 25

"Who the hell are they?" DI Sullivan demanded. "And who the hell notified them?"

Mac peered out through the front door at the little knot of figures on the far shore. Their cars were parked close to the police vehicles and the sound of engines signalled others making their way up the drive. He was relieved that the ferry was on their side of the lake; he'd have made a bet on someone trying their hand at firing up the boat and coming across.

"It was inevitable really," he said, "that the press would get wind of this. A police convoy, complete with technical support and then a serial of armed police making their way along the back roads, through the villages. It was bound to arouse someone's curiosity. They could have spoken to the minibus drivers. We've had them hanging around with nothing to do for the past several hours. And that's without the possibility of someone among the guests contacting the press. You've a couple of dozen very bored and very scared people with nothing to do but worry. The idea of getting the media involved was bound to occur."

"Do you always have to sound so damned reasonable?" she asked him. Then, more seriously, she added, "You reckon they're out of range over there?"

"Depends on what weapon our shooter has and where he is. Look, we're wasting time worrying about the media. Let's get the Caprisis and maybe some of the house staff out on the first run, you go over with them and do your media relations bit or at least get them moved further back. Our priorities haven't changed, we've just got an audience."

He glanced up at the sky. "Looks of things we'll be getting more rain before long, I'd be happier if we'd got everyone out before it starts again. You quite literally couldn't see the other bank in the last downpour." Half the lawn was still under water.

She sighed. "You still want to go with the CSIs?" she asked.

He nodded. "I don't want to leave the body overnight, especially not if the weather does close in again. The Clarks' bodies are at least under cover, but Charlie Brewster's completely exposed to the elements."

"Ok then, but be careful."

"I'm never anything but."

"Like I believe that."

Mac left her to deal with the evacuation of Ben Caprisi and his son and grandson. Two armed officers would travel on board on every crossing. Two others would now be leaving with himself, DS Terry Pritchard, the CSI team, including Miriam, to the first of the crime scenes. The other four would be maintaining the perimeter. One had settled in the church tower, two more on either side of the lawn, one operating a drone and monitoring the surroundings from overhead. They had two drones with them, Mac had been told, each could remain in the air for around half an hour before they needed their batteries changed out.

Mac could not help but think that where the wood was densest the drones would be of little use. He still allowed himself to be mildly reassured by their presence.

A few minutes later he had strapped on his protective gear and he and his team had left through the kitchen door, heading for the sunken gardens.

* * *

Back in her room, Rina watched as the Caprisis and the Myers, Bridie's old friends, and two members of the household staff were escorted to the ferry. They looked very anxious, Rina thought, and she too felt somewhat trepidatious, waiting for her turn to come.

The Peters sisters and Matthew and Steven had gathered in her room, bringing their bags with them. Rina too was packed and ready. The view from the window was exceptional and Rina had no real worries about stray bullets from this angle. There were armed police visible on both sides of the lawn and two in the ferry. Others, she knew, had been deployed overlooking the house and close terrain.

"Tim and the others really should not have wandered down into the cellar," Matthew fretted. "Given what we now know, they might have encountered the killer."

"Someone should have checked them out earlier," Bethany countered. "We were told that no one could get into the house that way. Mia might have been murdered in her bed."

It was interesting, Rina thought, that it did not occur to Bethany — or probably the others — that anyone else might have been at risk. Personally, Rina was not so certain that Mia was the target. Or at least, not the sole target. Though perhaps it was just the death of the Clarks that was making her so uneasy. Had they a role in this mystery or had their deaths been just a question of chance; something seen, or something overheard that made them into a threat?

The ferry cast off and began its slow progress over the lake.

"I see Inspector Sullivan has gone with them," Steven commented, coming over to stand beside her.

"I expect she wants to deal with the media," Rina said. "At least get them to back off. They're putting themselves in danger where they are. You can just imagine the fallout for Sullivan if the killer starts taking potshots at journalists."

"Who do you imagine leaked what is happening to the press? Do you think it was Mia?"

"I think it's possible. Though my money's on the loud man from the cottages," Matthew commented.

"Prentice," Rina supplied. "I wouldn't be surprised." She shifted position, trying to see where the drone was overflying but it seemed to be over the woods and was out of sight from this window.

"I'd like a drone," Eliza said unexpectedly, apparently realising what Rina was looking for.

They all turned in surprise to look at her.

"What? I think it would be rather wonderful. George showed me a little film on YouTube. Apparently you can get a Virtual Reality headset so you can control it and see exactly what it's seeing at the same time."

That did sound appealing, Rina thought. The closest a human could get to seeing what the birds could. Perhaps they should look into the possibility. "I think you need to go on a course," she said, "get a license, but I agree that it's a rather lovely idea." Rina sighed, suddenly bored with the view from the window. An idea struck her. "Do you think it's possible to get up into the attic rooms?" she asked of no one in particular.

This time all attention shifted to her.

"The backstairs," Eliza said. "They'd probably be the ones the servants used." She shrugged. "It's better than hanging around here, waiting for our turn on the boat. Mac will be making sure the most vulnerable people go first, so we'll be way down the list."

Rina blinked. In any other universe, their age might have implied that the Peters sisters and the Montmorencys be classed as vulnerable, but she would not have liked to be in the shoes of anyone who might suggest that.

She led the way along the corridor to the back stairs and up to the second floor. From there, a door opened onto another stairway and up to what must have been servants' quarters, she supposed, when the house was a private home.

"Dusty up here," Matthew commented. "It looks like it's just used for storage now."

The dormer windows were high up, set into the roof space but an assortment of boxes and a small table provided the necessary lift. Rina climbed up and peered down. As she had hoped, the view she gained was of the woods and the edge of the sunken garden. She spotted Mac and the CSI team, accompanied by two armed officers and the drone above them, momentarily, almost at eye level with Rina before lifting above the treetops again. She wondered how long the battery would last before it needed to be charged.

"What can you see?" Eliza demanded.

"Nothing very exciting," Rina admitted. "Mac and the CSIs are going into the sunken gardens, I expect they'll want to get Charlie's body out before the rain comes back. The clouds are starting to look very dark."

She surrendered her place to Matthew who provided a running commentary for several minutes about the drone and the view and the glimpse he caught of the armed officers, then he too gave up his place and Bethany took her turn.

"What's bothering you, apart from the obvious?" Steven asked, settling on a box beside Rina. His knees were not up to clambering onto the improvised stepladder of tables and boxes.

"Truthfully, I'm not sure. I maybe just don't have all the pieces and so much has happened in what has really been such a short time. Maybe I'm looking for something that isn't there. I could understand Mia wanting her brother out of the way and vice versa, but who would kill Charlie and then want Mia dead?"

"Someone who wanted to take over the entire Brewster business, I suppose," Steven said. "Someone else in the criminal fraternity."

"Agreed, but why here, why now?"

"Why not? If they want to get to both Charlie and Mia in one fell swoop, then I suppose here is as good a place as any. I don't imagine they're both available, in the one location, all that often."

Maybe not, Rina thought.

Bored again, they headed back to Rina's room and watched as the ferry made another crossing. This time it took the riggers across and it occurred to Rina that one of Arthur's

197

team could have been responsible for summoning the press. After all, they'd got mixed up in this by sheer fluke. It was entirely possible that one of them might see potential profit in selling an eyewitness account. She was a little surprised that Arthur's team should be leaving ahead of others, but she assumed it was because DI Sullivan was trying to clear the least important witnesses first. Or maybe it was just that they had further to go and would give their official statements to the local police when they got there.

The media had moved back, Rina noted, and others had joined them. She supposed even journalists in search of a story were averse to getting shot.

Rina looked up at the sky, watching the rainclouds moil and roil and gather in threatening masses. Would they all get to leave before the rain began again? And at what point would DI Sullivan decide it was time to ship Mia out? Had the choice been Rina's, Mia'd have been on the first boat to cross, then been bundled into a fast car and driven far away.

* * *

Mac had not been into the sunken gardens since that morning and he now felt oddly vulnerable, despite the two armed officers watching their progress from above. If anyone could get close enough to fire down at them it would be like shooting fish in a barrel. That he was not alone in his unease was emphasised by the many glances up towards the lawn above, the tendency of the CSI team to keep close to the walls. The sense that everyone was watching their backs.

To his relief Charlie's body was as they had left it. The water had risen — he could see that from the wetness on the stones around the raised beds — but not risen high enough to disturb the scene too badly. Though any evidence that might have lain on the paths would have long since been washed away or at least displaced.

Miriam was talking her colleagues through her findings. They had seen the comprehensive set of photographs both she and Mac had taken and what scraps of evidence they had been able to collate. A stiff breeze had risen as they had climbed down into the gardens and the sky was now purple and grey and heavy with rain.

"They'll want to get him moved, soon as," Terry commented.

Mac nodded. "It's going to be fun getting him up the steps."

It was all very messy and unorthodox, Mac thought. Ordinarily, everyone would have stood down until a police surgeon had pronounced life extinct but no one had been available to come with Sullivan's team and death would likely not be pronounced until the body was in the mortuary. The coroner's report was going to be an interesting one, Mac thought.

"We're about to turn him over," Miriam said. "Then get him on the stretcher."

Mac went over, Terry beside him. Miriam and another CSI turned Charlie onto his back, preparing to lift him onto the split stretcher that lay, in two bright yellow halves, beside the bed. It was, strictly speaking, a spinal board, Mac knew, but of a type often used to move bodies from awkward locations. Easy to carry, light in weight and equipped with broad straps.

Charlie was tilted onto his side and then laid flat and Mac understood then what had happened to have caused the body to move. Muddy scuff marks stained his jumper on one side, a merest trace of shoe print at one edge. "Someone kicked him," Mac said. "Kicked him in the side, and that lifted the body. It dropped back but not in quite the same position."

Miriam nodded. "It looks that way. Then they realised that we'd notice the body had been moved and they tried to put things back the way they were."

"Why kick a dead man?" Terry asked. Then answered his own question. "Whoever it was really must have hated Charlie Brewster."

"I'm guessing that particular list is a long one," Mac said.

Just as they had that morning when Charlie's body had first been discovered, heavy drops of rain began to fall. The CSIs moved quickly to get the body bagged and strapped to the board. Then it was all hands on deck to get it up the steps and onto level ground, Mac and Terry lending a hand, one at the head and one at the foot of the stretcher, pushing and pulling up to the top.

They turned back towards the house, cold rain falling on bare heads and necks. Mac wished he'd donned his water-proofs again.

Back at the house, DI Sullivan elected that the body be taken over to the waiting mortuary ambulance before the ferry took its next load of passengers.

"Well, that's one out," Mac said as they watched the boat with its sad cargo dock on the far side. It was then loaded onto the gurney for its journey to the local hospital where the official pronouncement of death would be made and the post-mortem carried out. "I'd feel happier if we could deal with the Clark scene."

"Commander Elwood is confident they can secure the cottages for you," Sullivan told him. "But they need to check out the holiday flats before anyone goes near the cottages."

Mac nodded agreement. The ferry was returning and the hotel staff now gathered behind him, waiting for their turn to leave. He wondered where Rina and the rest had got to. They were no longer camped out on the mezzanine.

Emilie and her staff took off at a run towards the ferry. The rain was now falling in earnest, though not as heavily as it had that morning. It was still possible to see the other shore. The journalists had, he noted, now retreated to their vehicles and one of the minibuses had managed to make it from the lane up the drive and onto the bank. Having seen what the weather could do earlier that day, Mac suspected that they'd have to leave pretty sharpish before they got cut off again. He watched as Emilie and the others piled into the vehicle and were driven away. The ferry was returning and the two remaining couples from the cottages, together with George and Ursula, now waited to leave. Tim and Joy hovered in the background.

"We've been trying to get the elders to go first," Tim said. "But they're insisting we go. I think they all want to cross together."

Typical, Mac thought, but he nodded. "Best get going," he said as the ferry pulled alongside the jetty. He watched as the two couples from the cottage and the four from Frantham ran across the lawn and clambered aboard. So, the Peters sisters, Steven and Matthew, Rina and Mia next. He had a horrible sense of why Rina had elected to go last. She'd been feeling responsible for Mia, in that way Rina had of being responsible for anyone who crossed her path. The Peters sisters and the Montmorencys, consciously or otherwise, always took their lead from her.

He glanced around; the two armed officers on either side of the lawn looked like drowned rats and the two in the boat thoroughly miserable. Their protective gear might stop a bullet but it was bugger all use against the weather. The drone was no longer able to fly and that troubled Mac greatly. Visibility from the woods and the bell tower would be minimal. He voiced his concerns to DS Terry Prescott. His watch told him it was only just after six but the depth of cloud made it feel like late evening.

"Hopefully that means visibility will be crap for any would-be shooter," Terry said. "It will at least be as uncomfortable for them as it is for our lot."

They watched the ferry dock and everyone scramble into the minibus Mac had driven up from Frantham. Tim was now at the wheel and moving off fast. A few of the hardier journalists had left their vehicles and run towards the minibus, but Tim was already heading down the drive. Seeing it leave Mac felt suddenly pained, as though he'd been deserted, left in hostile territory. He told himself not to be an idiot and just hoped the lane had not flooded again already.

The rain eased momentarily as the ferry docked again. Even to Mac's untechnical ears, the engine sounded to be misfiring. As it touched the dock it cut completely and Mac could see the officer who'd taken over ferry duties from the civilian ferryman, fiddling with the controls.

"All we need," Mac said.

Sullivan spoke to the officer on her airwave. It was clear from her expression that he had no idea what was wrong.

"Best call the ferryman," he said. "See if he can suggest what might be happening."

Sullivan nodded. "Tell everyone the evacuation's on hold," she said to Terry who nodded and ducked inside the house.

"Perhaps we can use the time to check out the other scene," Mac suggested. "I'd at least like to take a look at the holiday flats on the peninsula."

"They've not yet been secured."

"And the drone's spotted no movement from that end of the island."

"And if they're holed up in one of the cottages or either of the houses, then we won't know until they come out shooting, will we?"

Mac sighed, frustration at the enforced inaction really getting to him now. "They?" he questioned.

"I'm inclining towards the theory that Ruari Brewster might be involved and not alone. As you pointed out earlier, two distinct MOs for the killer or killers would point to two very different personalities. And if that is the case, we can't rule out the possibility of more than one weapon."

More than one gun, she means, Mac thought. He nodded reluctantly. Then swore, softly as the rain returned, pelting down so suddenly and thickly that even the ferryboat blurred into near invisibility.

If the killer or killers are out there, Mac thought, now would be the time to move in closer to the house. While attention was distracted by the ferry and the rain and the men on guard at the edges of the lawn would be soaked through and miserable, moving instinctively into what little shelter was offered by the treeline and the man up in the bell tower would be unable to see any damned thing. He could almost see the same thoughts running through Sullivan's mind as she moved restlessly, willing the man on the ferry to get the engine fired again.

* * *

"Apparently there's something wrong with the engine," Rina told George. The rain was so loud against the window she'd had to move into the corridor to use her phone. "But you're all OK?"

"Fine, we're being put up in a B&B close to the police station. Um, I'm not exactly sure where, Tim was told to follow a police car once we'd got to the road. The rain's so bad we can barely see their taillights. The windscreen wipers couldn't cope. We'll all feel a lot happier when everyone else is out."

Rina had to agree with that. "You're breaking up a bit," she told George. "Call me when you've got a better signal and try not to worry, we'll all be fine and we'll be with you soon."

She returned to her bedroom where the sisters and the twins were waiting. The mood had shifted, Rina thought. It had lifted when the evacuation began but now everyone was in the doldrums. Rina had been to check on Mia when Terry had come to tell them that plans were on hold. The young woman seemed as down in the dumps as the rest of them and Rina had suggested she might like some company. She had been rebuffed but not with as much acidity as Mia usually employed.

"I'm going to wait downstairs," Rina announced. "I know we can't do anything to help, but I'm starting to feel very cut off here. Besides, I feel like making a decent cup of tea. In a teapot, rather than just dabbling a tea bag in a cup."

Eliza brightened visibly at the idea and it clearly appealed to the rest. Rina led her little crocodile, carrying their bags, down onto the mezzanine and then she and Matthew made their way to the kitchen. It was terribly quiet, apart from the drumming of the rain. The officer on duty by the cellar door looked bored, Rina thought, but also grateful to be out of the rain. He accepted her offer of tea.

"What's your name?" Rina asked.

"I'm DS Dean Petty, ma'am."

"A DS standing guard over a door." Rina was amused. "But I hate 'ma'am'. I'm Rina. Any news on when the ferry will be ready?"

"Apparently not," she told the others as they prepared the tea and raided the cupboards for biscuits. Out in the hall she heard the crackle of DS Petty's airwave. She eased closer to the door, but the man was listening rather than speaking. Rina sighed. When you were set on eavesdropping it was very disappointing when no one said anything for you to overhear.

"I think they have rodents in the wall behind the pantry," Matthew commented as he emerged with several packets of biscuits. "We will have to tell Emilie. We wouldn't want her to have trouble with the health inspectors."

"Rats?" Rina questioned. "What makes you think that?"

"Oh, a sort of scratching sound coming from somewhere behind the wall."

Intrigued, Rina went to listen and of course the whole contingent followed her into the narrow storeroom. A second led off from this one, the flagstone floors still intact and a cold slab of white marble set into the wall. Rina wondered if this was where Bridie had kept her flowers before the wedding and if it had also been the room Mac had threatened to shut Mia in when she wanted to escape and steal a boat. She wondered what would have happened had Mia called his bluff, there being no door to lock on this second room.

"There, did you hear that?" Matthew said. "That was the sound again."

Rina listened, aware that everyone else was straining their ears as well. A faint scratching seemed to be coming from beneath the floor . . . or was it inside the wall? Rina turned her head, trying to pinpoint the sound which did, on first hearing, sound very much like claws.

Like, but not exactly like, Rina thought. There was something oddly metallic about the sound. Then it stopped and although they stood there for several minutes more, it was not repeated.

"What's below us?" Steven asked.

"I'm really not sure. I think the cellar goes the other way." Rina frowned and then returned to the hall where DS Petty had been stationed. Bethany followed her.

"Are you sure the cellar is still secure?" she asked him.

She was met with a puzzled look.

"There are odd sounds coming from under the floor. Metallic sounds," she told him.

Puzzlement was followed by a look of misplaced sympathy.

He thinks I'm just some anxious old biddy who doesn't know what she's talking about, Rina thought.

"Look," he told her gently, "I know you're worried. Who wouldn't be. But there are padlocks on the gate and on both doors and on this door too. We'll have you out of here as soon as we can and in the meantime you're perfectly safe. I promise you."

"You should never make empty promises," Bethany told him tartly. "Rina, we should go and find Mac."

"Mac? Oh, you mean Inspector MacGregor. Well, ladies, I'm sure you understand that the inspector is going to be very busy just now and—"

Rina ignored the young man. As they had come down the stairs, she had spotted Mac standing beside the front door. She headed there now, long strides and squared shoulders communicating her disapprobation.

Mac heard her and turned. One look at her face obviously telling him that Rina was displeased.

"Problem?" he asked.

"Possibly. Do you have a moment?"

He followed her back to the kitchen and into the pantry. Listened as instructed but much to Rina's chagrin there was nothing to be heard.

"Inspector, I'm sorry." Petty stood in the kitchen doorway looking profoundly embarrassed. "I did tell the ladies that you were too busy to be—"

"If Rina tells you something is wrong, then it's worth taking notice of," Mac told him.

"It might not be a bad idea to have an armed officer in the house," Rina said quietly.

"There are three locked doors and one gate to get through," Petty objected.

"Two of which have previously been cut through," Mac reminded him.

"And any damned fool can shoot a lock off, even through a wooden door," Rina added.

"I'll have a word with DI Sullivan," Mac promised her.

Rina nodded. "Any progress on the boat?"

"I think so, yes. The officer on board has been speaking to the ferryman and he's suggested things to try. Hopefully we'll have you all out of here soon."

CHAPTER 26

It was gone half past six when the engine was finally working again and the final load of passengers were told it was their turn. Mia sailed down the stairs and passed close to where Terry Pritchard was standing. He willed her not to pay attention to him, but Mia's gaze took in everyone and everything in her path. She paused.

"I know you," Mia said, studying Terry through half closed eyes.

Terry made no response.

Mia passed him by and headed towards the door where the others were waiting. Then she stopped and turned and said, "And now I remember where from."

Terry felt a chill run through him.

"Right now none of that matters," Rina said. Mia switched her attention to the older woman and Terry felt relief at the distraction. Mia must be remembering him from her father's funeral when he had been in company with Regis Crick.

But she hadn't finished with him. Ignoring Rina now, Mia turned and walked back in his direction. She paused a few feet away and regarded him with what he could only describe as malevolence. "And I don't like traitors," she said.

He watched, frozen in place, as she spun on her heel and headed towards the massive entrance door. His chest was tight and he could feel his face burning.

The weight of her judgement should not have bothered him. Mia Brewster was not someone he would ever have wanted to impress, a woman who did not deserve and had never earned his regard and yet he felt his body tremble under the weight of her contempt. He had been in many situations, particularly in his uniformed days, when insults and, on a couple of occasions, half-bricks and bottles of urine, had been thrown in his direction, but somehow those paled into insignificance at the level of threat implicit in Mia's words. He remembered the day that Gray had died and he had run. He had run but he had not escaped.

He drew a deep and shaky breath, thrust the anxiety and shock aside. He had known this was likely to happen, that at some point he'd come face to face with Mia Brewster and the odds were that she would recognise him. There was nothing he could do about that now; later there would be time for assessing the level of threat and implementing the appropriate action.

Assessing the situation in those terms helped him to gain a level of self-control. He was aware that Mia had now stepped outside, the two older ladies in front of her and the two men, Steven and Matthew, who had done such a solid, if unconventional, job of gathering statements, just behind her. The two armed officers accompanying them were alert and anxious. They were hurrying through the pouring rain, now halfway across the lawn. He was aware that the woman Mac was so friendly with, Rina, had hung back and had turned to speak to him. Whatever she had to say was lost in what happened next.

A shot rang out and then a second. Terry saw Mia go down, saw the two armed officers react, turning to try and get a sense of where the shots were coming from, urging the Peters sisters and the Montmorencys forward towards the ferry.

"Run," Rina shouted. "Get to the boat."

Terry was running too, instinct and training propelling him to those in need of protection. A random thought struck him that whoever had taken the shot, in these conditions, certainly knew what they were doing.

The armed officers returned fire. Not because they could fix the location of the shooters. Shooters, plural, Terry realised with shock, on opposite sides of the broad lawn and deep in tree cover. But in the hope of pinning them down and gaining time for the innocent to reach the boat. The Montmorencys and the Peters sisters were moving fast but it was clear that one of the men — Steven, Terry registered — was struggling and the others were not going to let him fall behind.

Terry reached them, grabbed Steven's arm and pulled it across his shoulder. Matthew did the same, and between them they half dragged Steven towards the boat. The officers from the ferry had run towards them to help and with relief Terry handed the older man over to them. Behind him shots still rang out and he was horribly aware of how little cover there was as he turned back towards the house. Just what the hell had he been thinking?

The boat engine gunned, taking off from the jetty, heading fast across the lake. Terry began to run, back towards the safety of the house and then it happened. The shot, the pain, the blackness. And then nothing at all.

CHAPTER 27

"Oh Rina, Rina that was so terrible." Eliza's voice was shaking and in the background Rina could hear Bethany's sobs and Matthew's calm voice as he tried to comfort her.

"None of you are hurt?" Rina asked again. She had watched in horror from the doorway as the scene unfolded before being dragged inside by the armed officer they had brought in to protect the cellar door. He had pushed her into the dining room with terse instructions to "stay down".

"We're all fine," Eliza reassured her. "We're not hurt, Rina, just very frightened."

Rina's body sagged with relief. She had retreated now from the dining room back to the mezzanine floor, out of the way but able to observe as the officers brought Terry and then Mia into the house. Two officers, one from the armed police and one of Sullivan's, clearly well trained in first aid, were working on Terry. His face was dead white and he was utterly still but he must, Rina thought, judging by the action around him, be in with a chance of surviving. The same could not be said of Mia.

Mac came up to the mezzanine to check on her. "I'm fine, Mac," she told him. "And the others are being taken away to somewhere safe. They're terribly upset but will be all right."

Mac nodded. "I'm sure they will."

"Will he make it?"

Mac glanced down to where they were still working on Terry Pritchard. "I don't know. He's unconscious but it looks like one bullet just grazed his skull, the other hit him in the arm but went straight through. It was bleeding like crazy but the bullet missed the brachial artery and it looks like they've managed to stop the bleeding now. Hopefully, the head wound *is* just a graze."

Rina nodded. "I was watching, Mac, he was targeted deliberately. It wasn't just random stray shots."

"You can't be certain of that."

"Oh yes I can. It was when he turned back from the jetty and they . . . whoever it was . . . had a clear shot. When he was helping Steven he was moving fast and the armed officers were firing, pinning the shooters down. The shots from the left-hand side of the lawn stopped, just briefly and then Terry was hit and Mac, I'm sure the gunman fired from a different angle. He'd moved further down towards the lake. Mac, I might be being fanciful, but I don't think so. I think the shooter changed position so he could get a better shot at DS Pritchard."

She was grateful that Mac didn't ask her if she was sure. He knew her too well for that. Instead, he nodded. "I want you to talk to Commander Elwood, the team leader," Mac said. "Tell him what you observed."

She nodded. Mac went back down the stairs. Terry was being lifted now, four officers taking care to keep his body supported as he was carried through to one of the side rooms. She hoped that their careful handling of him meant they hoped he would recover. So why target that particular officer? Rina wondered. She could only think of one reason; Mia had recognised him from somewhere and she was furious about it but perhaps she hadn't been the only one. The shooter knew him too and was equally incensed to have seen him here and realised who and what he was.

211

CHAPTER 28

DI Sullivan looked up as Mac came in. She was seated at the computer desk that Arthur Nedham from the marquee company had set up and was watching one of the screens intently. She was, he realised, in communication with the three armed officers they had sent down, after the shooting on the lawn, to check on the security of the cellar.

Sullivan pointed to the screen. "Your friend was right," she said. "The two outer locks have been bolt-croppered again and there's an odd thing. They've noticed smears of blood and a few grey hairs adhering to the metalwork on the gate."

She enlarged the image and Mac peered at the smears. "Someone injured themselves when they were cutting through the locks?" he wondered. "Or . . ." He thought about the wound to the back of Charlie's head and the extensive damage inflicted on the Clarks. "You think the bolt croppers might have been the weapon used?"

Sullivan shrugged. "It's one of a range of possibilities," she said. "Whatever, they must very quickly have realised the lock on the inside of the cellar had been replaced. There are signs that they tried to break through and, as your Rina pointed out, any fool could shoot a lock off a door, but presumably that would have made too much noise."

Mac smiled, realising that Rina's comments must have been repeated to Sullivan by DS Petty. "So they took the other option and waited for Mia to leave the house. Terry Pritchard too."

She looked up sharply. "You think he was deliberately targeted?"

"I think it's possible." He told her what Rina had noted and whereas, an hour or so ago she might have dismissed this as anxious imaginings, she now looked thoughtful.

"So, Mia definitely recognised him."

"Looks that way, she challenged him when she saw him in the reception hall and she figured out what he'd been doing when she last saw him."

"If Ruari Brewster is involved, it's possible he saw Terry at the funeral, which is when Mia most likely encountered him. He was there with Regis Crick," Sullivan told Mac. "It was in his report."

"You've read his report?"

"Skimmed it. There's not exactly been time for a detailed study."

"No, there's really not."

"It's on the computer if you want to take a look. Of course, Regis Crick would have recognised him straight off." She glanced at her watch. "Elwood wants a meeting in ten minutes' time. He's called his entire team back to the house, apart from the two that are across the other side with the ferry. There's not much point the others staying out there in this downpour. He wants my team, you and the CSI in the dining room. You may as well bring your Miss Martin and she can tell his team what she thinks . . . what she saw."

Mac went back up to the mezzanine to speak to Rina but she wasn't there. He glanced back down to see if he'd missed her in the hall. Elwood's team was assembling there, those whose duty had left them standing in the rain now dripping onto the black-and-white tiles of the floor. The two who had accompanied the passengers in the ferry had remained on the other side of the lake and taken refuge in the police vehicles, hopefully with the heaters on so they could dry out. At some point they would have to bring the ferry back across and in the meantime they could ensure the media kept their distance. It bothered Mac that they were now two men down.

Rina appeared at his side. She carried a bundle of men's clothes in her arms and she headed down the stairs with them. Mac followed. Rina addressed the officers who'd been most exposed to the elements. "You need to get dry," she said. "I've put towels in the little meeting room next to the stairs. I'm sure you can take it in turns to get yourselves sorted out."

Mac blinked. God but that was so Rina, he thought. Elwood looked from Rina to the dripping officers and shrugged. "Thank you, Miss Martin, that's thoughtful."

"Mrs," Mac said automatically to no one in particular. He watched as Rina led the way to the side room and deposited the dry clothes on a chair.

"I chose the least flamboyant of Matthew and Steven's jumpers," she said to Mac when she returned. "The boys won't mind. Apparently they're now in the B&B with Tim and the others. So at least we know they're safe and sound."

Mac nodded. The front door had been closed and locked now, and he guessed all entrances and possible means of ingress had been secured. Somehow seeing that front door locked unnerved him.

Rina, being Rina, seemed to catch his mood. "It's like being in a castle under siege," Rina said, her voice reassuring and calm. "But at least we have supplies and arms."

CHAPTER 29

Rina settled at a table at the back of the dining room. She thought how odd the white-clad tables looked now, how out of context. The table at which she had seated herself was still set with a little vase of fresh flowers left from the wedding, now past their best but still pretty. The vast arrangements Bridie had commissioned still decorated the hall and great swags of ribbons and roses hung somewhat limply above the windows. How quickly things could change. Her little wristwatch told her that it was now half past seven. Only twenty-four hours ago she and the other guests had still been enjoying the wedding breakfast, happy, relaxed and celebratory. Miriam spotted her and came over to sit at her table.

"How are you holding up?" she asked.

"I'm fine, happier now I know the family is safe, though I wish you and Mac were with them."

"And we wish you were." Miriam squeezed her hand. "We'll all be fine," she said. "My feeling is that they'll have left the island by now. They'll have achieved what they came to do."

"If the shooters are Ruari Brewster and this Regis Crick, then how do they hope to get away with it? The pair of them will be top of the suspect list."

Miriam shrugged. "A solid alibi can be bought," she said. "Proving they were here will be harder, unless there's DNA evidence."

Elwood, Sullivan and Mac stood at the other end of the room waiting for everyone to settle. The officers Rina had found dry clothes for now had blue and purple sweaters beneath their protective vests. It struck Rina that no one had removed their protective gear. Even Mac wore a stab vest, albeit a less chunky model than the armed officers. Rina felt distinctly underdressed.

Missing were the two officers who were looking after Terry Pritchard and she wondered how he was doing. She hoped the young man would survive. Hoped that he would also survive whatever demons were pursuing him.

"As you know," Sullivan was saying, "another attempt was made at entering the building via the cellars. It seems that was abandoned when it was realised that the inner door had been re-secured and they must have realised we'd be guarding the route into the house."

With just one officer who wasn't armed and not even convinced there was a problem, Rina thought, recalling DS Petty's scepticism. Just as well the gunmen hadn't known that.

"Unfortunately, they seem to have achieved their objective by other means and as you also know DS Pritchard was seriously injured and Mia Brewster killed."

That felt like an afterthought, Rina thought grimly. Was anyone actually going to miss Mia? The thought that perhaps no one would filled her with sadness, even though she had barely known the young woman. She felt that, given time, she could have encouraged the young woman to accept the friendship that was offered. It would have done her good.

"We now know that there are at least two shooters, so this is unlikely to be over yet."

"Assuming the intention was to assassinate Mia Brewster, do we even know that they're still on the island?" someone asked, clearly of the same mind as Miriam. Rina didn't know the man's name, but he was one of Sullivan's team.

Elwood replied, "No, we don't know that. I'm informed there are rowing boats on the other side of the island so it's quite possible they've left, even though conditions are still difficult. We've got roadblocks in place and as soon as the weather clears the helicopter will be back up and we'll make full use of the drones."

"So, in the meantime we're holed up in here," someone else complained.

"No one likes feeling helpless," Miriam murmured. "They all came here to do a job and so far no one's been able to do anything except get shot at."

Rina nodded. She listened as they were told that backup was on the way and in the meantime they had been told to stay inside and wait until the weather cleared enough for the helicopter to be drafted in.

By which time it would be dark, Rina thought grimly. She wasn't keen on the idea of spending another night on the island.

The talk moved on to an analysis of the shooting and to Mia's death and Terry's injuries. Priority was to be given to getting him away and there was talk of getting a search and rescue helicopter in to take him out. There was nowhere suitable for the helicopter to land, unless the lawn might be suitable though Rina gathered that was a decision for the crew and not anyone presently in the room. She'd seen coast-guard helicopters land on postage stamps of clear land but whether the lawn might be a suitable landing site, Rina had no idea and, as Elwood pointed out, it was going to be a hard ask for a crew to come in when there might be men with guns at large, ready to take potshots at them.

Rina raised her hand, feeling like she was back at school. "How is DS Pritchard?" she asked.

"He's conscious," Elwood told her. "He was unlucky to get shot but damned lucky not to have been killed."

Rina nodded. "You know he was targeted, don't you?" she asked, aware that to the room she must seem like just a random, elderly civilian who knew nothing about the matter.

Elwood frowned. The murmur of curious conversation that had greeted her announcement subsided as he spoke again. "We've reached a similar conclusion," he said.

"The gunman shifted his position so he could get a clear shot when Terry left the jetty," Rina said. "I was standing in the doorway, I got a very clear impression of what happened."

She felt the mood shift, the curiosity intensify, redirected towards her.

"My men on the boat observed the same thing," Elwood agreed. "I'm told Miss Brewster spoke to him before she left."

"She did. She said she recognised him and that she recalled where she had seen him before. She told him that she hated traitors. Perhaps whoever was shooting at Mia also recognised him and also felt betrayed."

"Would anyone have recognised him?" Petty asked. "It was pissing it down out there, you could barely see halfway across the lawn."

"I imagine they may have observed him before this," Rina suggested. "Anyone that knew him would recognise him, even through the rain."

Petty looked about to argue but Elwood said, "We're working on that assumption. We're also cognisant of the fact they may really want to make sure he's dead. That they might try and make certain, which is why we're being so cautious about bringing in the rescue heli."

"You think they may try to get into the house?" one of the CSI asked.

"We think we need to be prepared."

As the meeting broke up Mac and Elwood came over to Rina and Miriam. "I'm told the two of you and Mac have had a chance to look over the house," he said. "We're looking for vantage points to post guards, just in case we end up spending the night here. Mrs Martin, Mac suggests that your room might offer a good position."

"It might," Rina told him. "You can see the jetty and most of the lawn on both sides. There's a little chapel on the same side as the abbey guest house, up on the second floor.

It has a deep bay window that gives a good view out towards the sunken gardens and the path beyond. And there are attic rooms that look down on the rear of the house. The back wall is practically windowless, the servants' stairs run down that side and into the kitchen so I suppose there was no need of a view or of much in the way of natural daylight." There was a skylight at the top but electric light was necessary from about halfway down, even in daytime.

"The dormer windows in the attic are quite high up, but I noticed some steps in the back pantry. You could probably improvise something."

Mac smiled at her as he and Elwood went on their way.

"I hope we don't get stuck here all night," Miriam said. "If Mac and I ever decide to tie the knot it's going to be . . . on a bridge over a really busy motorway, with clear escape routes and no chance of anyone taking potshots at us."

Rina wondered abstractedly if there were any bridges licensed for weddings. She rather liked the idea though perhaps not the motorway bridge option. Perhaps they could start a trend. "I'm hungry," she said, "and very much in need of tea."

She glanced at her watch again. Gone eight o'clock. Before leaving the dining room she took a chance to twitch one of the dining-room curtains aside and peered out into the gloom. "The rain is slowing again," she said and, as so often happened in Rina's experience, when it was too late in the day to want to be bothered with it, a narrow shaft of sunshine was doing its best to break through between the heavy clouds.

* * *

The police officers had come in to eat in shifts. Rina, Miriam and the other CSIs taking over kitchen duties and keeping the kettle going and the sandwiches supplied. Emilie had left a good supply of various sandwich fillings in the fridge and taken extra bread out of the freezer and Rina was grateful for her foresight. There were also tins of soup in the pantry and this was as gratefully received as it would have been on a winter's evening rather than one in late August. Food was ferried up to the officers who had taken up their positions in Rina's room and the little chapel. A platform had been cobbled together in the attic space so that it was possible to look down onto the path leading to the cottages and the end of the island.

Rina took supplies in to the two officers who were looking after Terry.

He was conscious, though looked sick and dopey, settled in a big armchair and wrapped in a blanket. Rina was relieved when he accepted tea and thought he could manage a biscuit. His right arm was supported by a sling and was heavily bandaged. In the corner of the room the television was on and Rina was slightly shocked to discover that the events on the island had become 'breaking news' with a live feed. She had, of course, been aware of the journalists but not given much thought to what they might be reporting.

Rina watched for a few minutes as the reporter tried to patch together the events of the day. There had been a murder and a shooting or perhaps more than one. There were still police officers and an unknown number of civilians pinned down on the island and the journalist seemed to want to call them hostages but wasn't sure if that was appropriate. Rina gathered that reports were coming directly from the media on the bank opposite the hotel and also gathered that no one knew anything much for certain which meant that speculation was rife.

She could imagine the headlines, Rina thought, when it emerged whose wedding it had been and the nature of some of the guests. Gangland slayings would no doubt feature and no doubt Bridie would be described as the widow of a crime boss or some such — which while technically true only told part of the story.

Mac intercepted her as she crossed back to the kitchen. "I just wanted to tell you that you won't be able to get hold of any of them for a while," Mac said, "they've all had to surrender their mobiles."

"Oh?"

"Apparently Prentice was caught trying to contact one of the tabloids. His phone was confiscated and he kicked up such a fuss that everyone else was asked to hand their mobiles in as well."

"I'm glad you told me. I'd have been worried if I'd tried to contact anyone and not been able to get through. Do we know what's happening yet?"

"Elwood's getting the drones up in a few minutes. The moorland search and rescue teams are on standby. If we can secure the landing site and they consider a landing is possible, we'll be getting Terry out very soon."

"That would be a relief to everyone," Rina said.

"And reinforcements are coming within the hour. This should be all over soon, Rina."

CHAPTER 30

Mac was watching the split screen as the drones were launched, armed police guarding their operators. The sight of the island laid out below them seemed vertiginous and Mac, who still got travel sick when he wasn't driving and who even found watching George play computer games challenging, began to feel vaguely nauseous.

Rina, sitting behind him, seemed fascinated.

"What's that?" Sullivan asked just as the drone operator became aware of the object on the ground and adjusted to take a closer look.

"Looks like a body," Mac said. Like they needed another one.

Sullivan spoke to the operator, getting them to check the area again and a few minutes later Elwood and two of his people were crouching over the body, their body cams showing Mac and Sullivan — and Rina; they had practically forgotten about her, Mac realised belatedly — the body of a man lying on the ground. This, Mac thought, looked like the area from which the shot had been taken at Mia's window, though he couldn't be certain. He was no connoisseur of woodland and suspected that it all looked the same to him.

The man lay on his back, arms spread, a bullet wound in the centre of his forehead. A much larger exit wound in the back — it was possible to tell that even without turning him over.

Mac skimmed through images he had collected on his phone. "That's Ruari Brewster," he said, turning the phone to show Sullivan. "I found his picture on his film company's website."

"Certainly looks like him," Sullivan confirmed.

"He looks vaguely familiar," Mac said, frowning and trying to figure out where from.

"That's because you saw him at the wedding," Rina said. "He was ferrying things to and from the kitchen."

"He's not house staff," Mac said. "And he wasn't with the outside caterers. All their staff have been accounted for and interviewed. No one extra left with them."

"And most likely the house staff thought he was with the caterers and the caterers thought he worked for the hotel," Rina suggested. "He was in a dark jacket and light trousers, I think. Both the house staff and caterers were in black and white. You know how busy everyone was at the wedding. It wouldn't have been difficult to be invisible. The guests wouldn't have taken much notice of who was serving their drinks and the staff would all assume he was with the other group."

"It's possible," Sullivan agreed cautiously. "But Mia might have seen him."

"Possibly so," Rina agreed. "Perhaps that was the point. Charlie would possibly have seen him too. Though if I recall correctly, I only really remember seeing him just before the formal wedding breakfast. That was late afternoon, I can't say I recall spotting him earlier. In which case it's entirely possible he kept clear of both his siblings."

"So, he came across in the ferry, maybe changed when he'd got here, cut the lock in the cellar and then hid out until whenever he killed Charlie Brewster. That's assuming he did," Sullivan speculated.

Elwood was speaking to her, telling her that the helicopter was on its way, ETA less than five minutes.

Rina watched as Sullivan left to liaise with Elwood and the officers preparing Terry for departure. "Which begs the question," Rina continued as though there had been no interruption, "which of the siblings Ruari was working with?"

"If either of them," Mac said. "Rina, maybe he was working purely on his own account and, for the sake of argument, with Regis Crick. Better for him to cut both of them out of the game. There's no CCTV worth a damn here, no surveillance or security. Both of his half siblings here, vulnerable. And there's an air of showmanship about it all. A kind of 'look at me' ego at work that would certainly please Regis Crick, from what I know about him, and presumably appeal to someone like Ruari whose whole working life is about performance."

Rina nodded. It makes sense. "And then Crick decided he didn't really need a partner," she said.

* * *

Once more she was standing in the doorway watching others leave. Rina felt a pang, wondering if they'd have found a space on the helicopter for her had she asked.

It was practically a touch and go landing on the twilit lawn. The pilot set down long enough for Terry, carried by two of his colleagues, to be snatched up and the door closed. Then the helicopter lifted again, everyone else rushing back for the shelter of the house. Rina half expected to hear shots ring out; half expected there to be nothing. Her feeling was that the second gunman must have long since fled the scene. He would have made a wet, cold and difficult crossing but the lake was not the ocean, there would be no waves crashing over the bow of the boat. He could have made it across. Her attention was attracted to the ferry, the engines firing up as it started across.

She had been so intent on watching the helicopter that she'd not been aware of the other vehicles arriving on the other side of the lake. The promised reinforcements had arrived.

CHAPTER 31

It was a little after nine o'clock when Rina bade Mac good-bye. She could hardly believe that it was only twelve hours since Charlie Brewster's body had been found. Mac had been given the option of leaving with her and Miriam but had decided to remain. He had been first on scene, it was customary for the FOA to liaise with the team taking charge of the investigation and he would have felt that he was reneging on his duties had he gone.

The CSI team was standing down. All were exhausted and it was felt that the scene should be secured by the police teams before the civilian investigators were potentially put at more risk. None of them, Rina noted, had argued and she couldn't blame them.

They would make two crossings; Rina and Miriam in the second along with Mia's body. Sullivan had been curious when Rina had made the request that this be so. Rina had tried to explain that she felt she owed it to the young woman; she had at least known her briefly, had interacted with the difficult, diffident girl and there being no friends or family present to accompany her, it felt only right that Rina and Miriam should do so.

It was clear to Rina that DI Sullivan didn't understand her reasoning, but she made no objection. Someone had to travel with the body, which the CSIs had bagged and prepared for transport. It was no skin off her nose if Rina chose to be in the second boat.

Rina felt that Mac understood.

"I'll be with you soon," Mac said as he hugged Rina and then kissed Miriam. "In the morning at the latest."

Rina settled herself in the stern alongside one of the armed officers who had accompanied all of the crossings. They must all be weary by now, she thought, though they seemed no less alert. The second boarded after Miriam and the ferry cast off. Minutes later they were on the other shore and being ushered into a police four-by-four. Mia's body was loaded into a mortuary ambulance.

It was almost dark and Rina was aware of the flashes from the media cameras illuminating the churned-up grass, ploughed by tyres and feet and treacherously slippery under foot. She felt suddenly that she wanted to cry.

In the back of the Land Rover Miriam took her hand and as the vehicle started to move away, at the head of a convoy with a second police vehicle and the mortuary ambulance, Rina glanced over at her young friend and saw the tears coursing down her face. A sudden flash illuminated Miriam as one of the journalists ran alongside the vehicle, snatching a photograph. Rina was subjected to a moment of almost murderous rage.

* * *

Powerful light illuminated their path as Mac followed the newly arrived officers through the darkened gardens and towards the cottages. He was kitted out in fully body armour, a helmet, though he was still wearing plastic bags over his socks, his shoes sodden and cold. He had explained to Elwood how he gained access to the cottage and the sense he'd had of being watched. He realised uncomfortably that he'd probably been correct. Another bad dream in the making, Mac thought.

Across the water, the police helicopter quartered the terrain, the grid pattern search moving away from the island and onto the fields beyond once the infrared had disclosed nothing larger than a fox on the peninsula. The second gunman had fled, Mac had been certain of it before and now, unless the man was hiding underground, a distinct possibility in this terrain, then he was no longer present. The possibility that he'd gone into the tunnels had been taken account of and the exit was now locked and two officers were on watch from the tent that had been erected on the lawn above, infrared cameras pointed at the tunnel exit would warn them should a killer armed with a gun and a pair of bolt croppers try and get out.

Everything felt a little surreal, Mac thought. The darkness driven back by light so powerful that everything beyond their beams seemed impossibly black. The tiredness that he felt in his whole body; he ached as though he had the flu. The fact that he and his friends had come up here to celebrate a wedding and just a few hours later had five bodies to deal with, the three Brewster siblings and the Clarks, who so far as Mac could make out, had nothing to do with any of it but were still well and truly dead.

"It's the middle cottage," Mac told Elwood as they halted. Elwood motioned him forward and they went together through the back gate and into the kitchen. The white torchlight illuminated mud left by Mac's feet on his earlier visit. Mrs Clark was still lying in the hall. He'd almost expected her to be gone. Perhaps he had wished her gone; wished himself delusional, having imagined the bodies on the cottage floor.

Mac waited as two officers went up the stairs and announced all was clear. He could hear the doors to the next-door cottages forcibly opened and booted feet, heavy on the stairs. The quiet that followed told Mac there was nothing to be found. No gunman hiding out in one of the upstairs rooms.

"You say you didn't check out the houses at the end," Elwood confirmed.

Mac sighed, he'd already told him several times that there'd been no time, that he'd been alone, that once he'd found the Clarks his one concern had been getting the other couples to the relative safety of the house. He followed Elwood out of the house, was instructed to wait as a group of officers went forward to check the other residences. Wearily, Mac leaned against the wall and stared into the darkness of the wood beyond the light. He just wanted to go home.

He felt in his pocket for his phone and checked for messages. Was unsurprised to find none. He hoped Rina and Miriam would let him know once they'd arrived at the B&B or wherever they were to be taken. They'd have to give up their phones once there, but he would be with them for morning, Mac was determined about that.

* * *

A few miles away, Rina could see the helicopter moving back and forth, it's searchlight illuminating sodden ground. They had driven slowly down the driveway and across the twin bridges, one across the canal and one across the river, though the river seemed to have forgotten it was supposed to flow beneath the bridge. It had broken its banks and taken to the road and, though the driver told them the water level was lower than it had been, they still took it slowly through the inundation and waited on the far side of what was now an uncomfortably deep ford for the second Land Rover and the mortuary ambulance to catch up with them. No one liked the idea of the lower slung vehicle, with its sad cargo, getting stuck in the too deep water.

Then on again on the steadily rising road, clear of the floodwaters and making better time. A roadblock slowed them momentarily before officers waved them through. Who were they hoping to stop? Rina wondered. The roads were deserted and it was unlikely that Regis Crick, if that was truly the man being hunted, would walk down the road and into the roadblock.

She chided herself for being so tetchy. What else were they supposed to do?

She could see the helicopter again now the road curved, apparently finding nothing of interest, still intent on the slow, methodical grid search. She knew the helicopters were equipped with infrared that would disclose anything warm-blooded against the chill of waterlogged ground but she supposed the big search light was capable of covering a greater area more quickly.

There was another police roadblock ahead and this time their driver paused as it was moved aside. "Anything?" he asked.

"No one's been down this road in the past hour," he was told. "Only one car in the hour before that."

They drove on. A dip in the road ahead had filled with water. They slowed to get through and then drove on. In the rearview mirror Rina could see the other vehicles behind, the second Landy again slowing to make sure the ambulance got safely through. She lost sight of them as the road curved and then curved again.

"How far are we going?" Miriam asked.

"About another half hour. Are you warm enough?"

Warm enough to be getting sleepy, Rina thought. She'd welcome her bed tonight.

And then, as Rina was nodding, it happened. The figure stepping out into the road ahead and firing a shot directly through the windscreen.

Rina yelped. Miriam screamed and then swore. The vehicle was careening wildly and Rina thought for a moment that the driver had been hit. He yelled at them to hold on and accelerated hard, trying, Rina thought, to get past that figure in the road. A figure that fired again.

Rina released her seat belt and Miriam's, she ducked down behind the seat, pulling Miriam down beside her. The vehicle was accelerating still, and Rina, head tucked low, sensed that the driver was no longer in control. She raised her head and peered between the seats. If the driver was still alive, he was certainly unconscious, slumped forward and kept in place only by the seat belt. She caught a confused glimpse of the man in the road. Tall and thickset and the gun raised but pitching sideways, almost as though he'd been drinking heavily. In that moment, Rina could make no sense of that. He must have seen them in the rear seats, Rina thought. What did he want — them dead or the pair of them as hostages? Neither scenario appealed.

She heard the sound of the other vehicles coming up behind and was suddenly fearful that the man would fire again. That there would be more deaths. The vehicle they were in was still in motion, swerving drunkenly across the road and heading, Rina realised, towards the gunman. He moved suddenly, broke into a stumbling run and through a gate into the adjoining field. Perhaps, she thought, he hadn't realised they were travelling in convoy. Perhaps he was suddenly afraid there would be armed officers in the vehicle behind. A bloody pity there wasn't, Rina thought.

She was dimly aware of Miriam clinging to her and that she was clinging back, that they had come to a sudden rest, trapped in the thick branches of the hedge at the side of the road. They had tilted as a wheel wedged into a ditch or into soft mud but were still upright.

Then the blessed sound of the other vehicles pulling up beside them and shouts and running feet.

She raised her head as a door opened and the engine was silenced.

"You two all right?"

"I think we're fine," Rina said. Cautiously she lifted herself back onto the seat, urging Miriam to do the same.

"The driver. Is he dead?" Miriam asked. "Oh God."

They were helped from the car and taken away from the now silent vehicle. The helicopter had veered, Rina saw and was now tracking the gunman across the field. She heard the crackle of the Airwave radios, and the sound of someone speaking on a mobile phone and then Miriam's voice assuring Mac that they were both unhurt.

Rina found herself rerunning the events in her head. The first shot, the sudden swerve, the Land Rover spinning across the road. The feeling of impact . . . had she imagined that? He had been limping, she realised as he had tried to run away.

"I think we hit him," Rina said. "I think the driver clipped him as he swerved. I think that was when the gunman fired again."

From what she could gather from the fast exchanges between officers and helicopter, it seemed that she was right. The man was making his way across the half-flooded field, heavy going even for a fit and uninjured man, but he was definitely struggling. Definitely slowing down. And with no cover in the field or anywhere close by, unable to escape the surveillance of the bright light in the sky.

* * *

"He made it across the field," Mac told her later as he sat in the B&B, his arms tightly around Miriam. "But by the time he got to the road the Armed Response Unit was there. There was a bit of a standoff, but even Regis Crick isn't that stupid."

Wearily, Rina rubbed her hands across her face. She had seen George and Ursula and Tim and Joy and the other Peverill Lodge inhabitants and knew they were all safe and sound and wanted nothing now except for sleep. "He must have assumed that the driver would just pull over, if he pointed a gun at him," Rina said. "And I do think he tried, but the road is covered in mud, and he swerved and then Crick must have thought he wasn't going to stop and so he fired again. And we hit him. Or maybe we hit him first. Mac, I can't be sure."

"And you don't need to be. Police vehicles are equipped with dash cams. It will have been recorded."

Of course it would, Rina thought. She had forgotten that.

"I've spoken to Bridie," Mac added. "She'd seen the news. They want to come home. I told them to stay put.

There's no reason for them to come back to this mess, best to wait until some of the fuss dies down."

"It won't though, will it?" Rina fretted. "Six people are dead, Mac. Six!"

He nodded. "I know. I do know." And Rina could see he had nothing else to say. What was there to say?

EPILOGUE

A few days after they had all returned to Frantham, Mac got a call from DI Sullivan.

"Rumour has it that the Brewster empire has been absorbed by the Caprisi and the Donovans," she said. "With smaller bequests elsewhere, presumably to keep everyone happy."

"Not surprising," Mac said.

"No, I don't suppose it is."

Later that day Mac spoke to Fitch, just returned from a honeymoon cut short, even though Joy and Brian had reassured their mother and her new husband that the crisis was well and truly over. Mac told Fitch what Sullivan had said.

"I believe that to be the case," Fitch said. "I don't have the details, but Brian tells me that Simon Caprisi gave him a call and a bit of a heads up."

"That all happened fast," Mac said.

"Mac, these things do. A vacuum is not good for business. Not good for peace either. Look what was happening between the Brewsters just because their old man didn't lay things out the way they were meant to be. I'm told that when Ben Caprisi left the hotel he could see how things were likely to be played out. He called Donovan, they made contingency plans. That's all I know."

"Or all you're going to tell me."

"That too. Mac, better to have the Caprisis and the Donovans sort it and for everyone else to go away feeling they've got a piece of the action they don't have to fight for. There's less killing that way. I'd have thought you'd have had enough dead bodies."

It was hard to argue with that one.

"Think of it like what Joy called it. Realpolitik." He sounded proud of the phrase, Mac thought.

"She called it what?"

"Yeah, I know, our little Joy coming out with stuff like that. It means it maybe ain't what you'd like it to be, but it's what's actually happening, so you'd better deal with it."

Mac knew what it meant but Fitch sounded so impressed he didn't have the heart to say so. "I think that's the excuse governments use," he said.

"Yeah, but when they cock up, a lot of people die anyway, even when they tell us it's in a good cause." Fitch paused, then added, "I had a brother."

"I didn't know that."

"No. Straight as a die he was. Joined the army."

Mac waited but it seemed that was all he was going to get. "Oh," he said.

A little later Terry called him. "According to Crick, Ruari Brewster got into the house on the day of the wedding, there were people milling about all over so it wouldn't have been that hard to pass unnoticed. So long as neither Charlie nor Mia saw him, he would have been pretty safe, I suppose. He knew what uniform the outside caterers used and he got something that looked similar. He cut the padlocks off and opened the bolt inside the cellar. All pretty much what we suspected.

"Unfortunately, when Mrs Clark came looking for her necklace it seems she ran into Ruari Brewster or spotted him going into the house at the end of the peninsula. Crick isn't very consistent on that point. Anyway, unfortunately he mentioned this to Crick. He wanted to let it lie, but Crick became convinced she might have seen Brewster coming out of the cellar and thought she might be a risk if she remembered him later."

"So Crick killed her and her husband."

"Yeah. Bashed the pair of them with the bolt croppers. They were found close to the cottage, the blood and hair on them matches the Clarks."

"Do we know any more about the Clarks?" Mac asked.

"Not a lot, but they had debts and an insurance claim on a lost or stolen ruby necklace would doubtless have helped. Neither had a record so it's likely any attempt at scamming the insurance company was a spur of the moment thing. That's if she didn't just lose it. Or someone didn't take it, thinking it was the real thing and frankly that seems more likely, given that Mia was able to lay hands on it pretty sharpish. Whatever the truth of the matter, the Clarks are dead and Crick killed them. Wrong place, wrong time and it cost them everything."

"And how are you?" Mac asked.

"As well as can be expected, I suppose. The hospital patched me up, kept me for observation, sent me home. I'm due to see various kinds of shrink." He paused. "And I think I'll be looking for another job."

"Ah."

"Yes. Ah. You know, Mac, this feels like a wake-up call. Feels like something's telling me that life is too short and that if I was a cat I'd be on final notice. I've got family. I've got a sister with little kids I'd like to see more of. I've got a mother I'm pretty fond of and who's daft enough to be fond of me. I think it's time."

"What will you do?"

"Who knows? Just not this anymore."

That evening Mac and Miriam made their way to Rina's. It was Sunday evening and high tea had become something of a tradition.

"Have you ever thought of quitting?" Miriam asked him as they walked along the promenade. "Recently, I mean." They both knew that Mac had come very close and that probably only what he'd seen as lack of options had kept him from going.

"Not recently, no."

"I'm glad. You've got a place here. Friends, good colleagues, me." She grinned at him and he pulled her close.

"You," he agreed.

"But I'm telling you, don't you dare propose, at least not for a good six months or so. I don't think I could deal with another wedding."

Me either, Mac thought, as they knocked on Rina's door and were welcomed inside. Peverill Lodge, safe haven in a crazy world, where love was doled out in china cups or in the guise of cake or warm pudding. Miriam was right, Mac thought. When you'd found your place in the world, you'd have to be very stupid to want to leave.

THE END

THE JOFFE BOOKS STORY

We began in 2014 when Jasper agreed to publish his mum's much-rejected romance novel and it became a bestseller.

Since then we've grown into the largest independent publisher in the UK. We're extremely proud to publish some of the very best writers in the world, including Joy Ellis, Faith Martin, Caro Ramsay, Helen Forrester, Simon Brett and Robert Goddard. Everyone at Joffe Books loves reading and we never forget that it all begins with the magic of an author telling a story.

We are proud to publish talented first-time authors, as well as established writers whose books we love introducing to a new generation of readers.

We have been shortlisted for Independent Publisher of the Year at the British Book Awards three times, in 2020, 2021 and 2022, and for the Diversity and Inclusivity Award at the Independent Publishing Awards in 2022.

We built this company with your help, and we love to hear from you, so please email us about absolutely anything bookish at feedback@joffebooks.com

If you want to receive free books every Friday and hear about all our new releases, join our mailing list: www.joffebooks.com/contact

And when you tell your friends about us, just remember: it's pronounced Joffe as in coffee or toffee!

ALSO BY JANE ADAMS